Estelle's Ardent Admirer

THE BOOKSHOP BELLES
BOOK ONE

CATHERINE BILSON

EBONY OATEN

SHENANIGANS PRESS

Content Advisory

- Antagonism and emotional abuse from relatives
- Death of parents
- Rampant unfairness and sexism because women were considered second-class citizens
- Cats breeding uncontrollably as desexing pets had not been invented

We also advise people not to take any of the herbal remedies mentioned in these books. While some might work, they are not always reliable and indeed the quantities and efficacies would vary from person to person. Please do not constitute anything in these books as medical advice.

CHAPTER 1

The First Crate

Baxter's Fine Books, Hatfield, England,
Late June, 1814

Estelle Baxter, the eldest and definitely the most responsible of the four Baxter daughters of Baxter's Fine Books in Hatfield, Hertfordshire, nailed a rough piece of hessian sacking to the base of the newel post. Next, she crushed fresh stalks of catmint in her hands and rubbed them against the surface, smearing the coarse fabric with a brownish-green hue.

A black shadow dropped from a bookshop with a soft thud. Crafty, the family cat, descended from high above and immediately rubbed her cheek against her refurbished toy, purring happily. The white heart-shaped locket of fur on the black cat's chest revealed itself as Crafty rolled over to her back. The cat then grabbed onto the hessian with her front claws and kicked at it with her hind paws, as if possessed by ancestors taking down big game.

"Good girl, Crafty, we scratch the post, not the books."

She rewarded the mostly-domesticated cat with a gentle 'boop' on the head, then washed her hands and set about her morning routine before the rest of her sisters joined her after breaking their fast.

Estelle enjoyed the calm of the mornings, where she could get things done before customers arrived.

The sounds of horses and people passing on the High Street outside seeped through the bookshop's walls. The busy hotel and coaching inn next door ensured a steady stream of noise, day and night. When the stagecoach arrived from London, Baxter's Books would provide a welcome distraction to travellers while the horses were changed. It was a chance for them to stretch their cramped legs after hours of sitting inside a coach.

The bookshop interior was naturally dark, as they'd long since blocked the ground floor windows with book-shelves. The enormous bookcases solved two book-specific problems; they created extra storage as well as protecting the valuable and rare books from sunlight damage.

It did make visibility rather dim, though. This was another of Estelle's early-morning tasks, lighting the lamps behind their protective glass casings, so that customers could find their way about the shop. As so could Estelle. That visibility was something she could have used rather more of as she moved behind the shop counter and stepped on something wet and crunchy, that slipped sideways under her weight.

"Crafty!" she yelled, trying to see what she'd stepped in. Hobbling on one foot, she reached the shop entrance, unbolted and opened the door. The shop's welcoming bell tinkled. Sunlight revealed the revolting truth; the eviscerated remains of a quarter of a mouse on the bottom of her slipper.

"Oh Crafty, can you not?" Estelle said despairingly.

She peeked up and down the length of the street. People bustled about in front of the Red Lion, waiting for the next coach to arrive. Between Baxter's Fine Books and the Red Lion was the archway through to the stables at the back. Conveniently, there was a boot scraper by the steps of the nearest door. Estelle hobbled over and scraped the mouse remnants off the bottom of her shoe, making a disgusted face as she did so.

Just as she'd finished cleaning her shoe, the stagecoach from London arrived, laden with all manner of trunks and travelling cases strapped to the top, and several people crammed inside.

She darted back to the bookshop and tucked the small curtain on the door window to one side. It let light in a shaft of light that illuminated the floor, but did not fall upon any books.

The light revealed a trail of mouse debris leading to the back of the counter. Estelle sighed and reached for a cleaning rag and the ashpan beneath the counter, both placed in readiness for dealing with this regular chore.

Once she'd cleaned up the mess, Estelle made a

mental note to check behind the counter in the mornings as her first task from now on. Crafty was an excellent mouser, but lately she had developed the most disgraceful personal habits.

As much as Crafty - full name Wollstonecraft - caused problems, the bookshop did need a good mouser. Before the cat came along, they tried keeping mice away with copious sprigs of lavender and rosemary. It made the shop smell wonderful, but the desperately hungry mice still caused damage to several books a week. Crafty had taken to her designated role with fervour, and book damage had become a thing of the past.

The bell above the door tinkled. A tall man wearing a rakish travelling cape walked in, removing his high hat as he entered. Light shone on his golden curls as if announcing a visit from a celestial cherub.

At the advanced age of twenty-five, Estelle might have long given up the idea of matrimony, but that didn't mean she couldn't appreciate a fine specimen when he walked into her family's shop. She looked the gentleman up and down, taking him in from his well-tailored coat to his polished Hessian boots. *Rich*, she thought. Surely, he hadn't arrived on the stagecoach? A man who dressed like that would have his own carriage, or a fine horse to ride.

"Good morning," she greeted the customer.

He leapt in fright, then steadied himself and turned towards her voice, pressing a hand to his chest. "Heavens, there you are! Can't see a thing in here, it's so dark."

"It's to protect the books," she said. She really must

get more of the lamps lit. Her eyes had adjusted, but someone coming in from the street clearly took longer.

"I see! Well, there's a crate of them just arrived next door, they asked if I'd make myself useful and let you know."

Estelle stepped out from behind the counter. "Thank you. I'll return presently. You're welcome to look about the shop in the meantime."

"I'm happy to help," he said, offering a too-charming smile.

Odd, someone as well dressed as him didn't seem the type to perform manual labour like carting things too and fro. *He knows how handsome he is*, Estelle thought cynically as the gentleman laid his hat on the counter. He'd begun to take his gloves off as well, revealing hands that had done little in the way of physical work.

He might sound helpful, but Estelle figured he'd most likely get in the way. "You can make sure Crafty doesn't run out onto the street and upset the horses," she said.

He delivered an expression of confusion. "Crafty is...?"

"The cat. An excellent mouser, which is essential for protecting the books. Alas, she thinks horses are enormous mice and tries to catch them."

"My word!" he laughed, blue eyes crinkling at the corners in a way which told her he laughed easily, and often. She smiled back, a little charmed despite her cynical thoughts about him. He did seem a jovial fellow, and if he was as rich as his clothes made him appear, he might purchase several books.

"It was funny the first few times, but I do feel badly for the horses. Back soon." She headed out to the inn yard where a couple of burly men were pulling down a wooden crate from the luggage rack.

"Morning, Miss Baxter," Mr Thomas said. He was the muscle for the owner of the Red Lion, and used to carrying heavy trunks and cases up and down stairs.

"Good morning Mr Thomas. That does look exceedingly heavy," she noted.

He replied with a grunt, "That's because it's full of books."

"We could take some out to lighten the -"

The crate toppled down from the coach and landed on the ground, splintering and shattering to pieces.

"- load." Estelle finished with a pained wince.

What a mess! With a deep sigh, she stepped forward to grab from the top of the book pile, careful not to catch her skin on the splinters. She held faint hope none of the books would be too badly damaged. After all, they were known as *Baxter's Fine Books*, not *Baxter's Damaged and Scuffed Books*.

The noise brought people crowding around to see what was happening.

Mr Thomas shouted down, "Sorry about that, Miss Baxter."

He climbed down and offered to help her pick up the mess. The man used brute strength, and some of these books looked old. And delicate.

"I'll stack them into your arms if you like, that way I can sort as I go," Estelle said, thinking it would be best if

Mr Thomas didn't pick them up in his none-too-clean hands. He obligingly held out his forearms and she gingerly loaded a few books up onto them.

The golden-haired gentleman came out of the bookshop, obviously summoned by the sound of the crashing crate, and said, "I say, anybody hurt?"

"All fine," Estelle called back.

"Can I help?" he asked again.

He might not look very strong, but surely he'd be able to pick up a few books and bring them in. "Thank you," Estelle agreed to take him up on his offer, as she nodded to Mr Thomas to take his armfuls of books in.

She handed two thick books to the well-dressed man. In the light of day, she could see his sun-kissed complexion and stunning blue eyes. My goodness, he could make a woman swoon! He had the kind of glowing skin achieved by being somewhere warm. He made the softest grunt as he took hold of the books. Then he opened the cover of one and his eyes rounded in surprise. "How wonderful! I've been looking for this one for ages!"

Five books loaded into her arms, Estelle peered over at the one he was marvelling over.

Drat. The moment she saw the title page a heavy sigh poured forth. "I'm ever so sorry, that one's a special order we've been waiting months for, it's already spoken for." How was it they struggled to sell a vast array of books, but when one particular volume came in, two people claimed it?

"But I must have it," he said.

"We can talk once we've brought the rest of the books

in," she prevaricated, having no intention of selling him that particular book. That was another thing about this man she began to assume - if he had money, he was probably used to getting his own way.

Well, this book was already spoken for, and that was a fact.

Estelle looked at the sun in the sky and wanted to get the books inside. At least there appeared to be no chance of rain. It didn't take long to get the rest of the books safely inside, stacked in piles on the counter.

Her sisters arrived down the stairs and got straight to work. Marie opened the ledger to record each title and price. Louise carefully checked the binding of each one to see which would need repairs, while Bernadette placed bouquets of chrysanthemums and chopped lemon rind into cotton envelopes to deal with unwanted arrivals like silverfish and moths. Estelle delighted in the way the four of them worked together in harmony. They'd told their father everything would be under control while he was gone, and they were true to their word.

Meanwhile, their well-dressed customer had helped himself to a chair and was sitting by the door using the light from the window. He was absorbed in the book he wanted, but could not have.

"If you promise to take extra care of it, you may read it here in the shop?" Estelle offered by way of compromise. He was treating it carefully, which was pleasing to see.

The man shook his head. "Alas, this is not for me, but a gift for another."

She felt badly for him, but the situation was beyond

her control. "Again, I'm dreadfully sorry, but that book is already promised, and paid for b…"

"I'll give you double. No. Triple!"

Estelle sent up a prayer about not giving in to temptation, then patiently explained the situation to the man again. "I simply can't. He is one of our oldest and most valued customers."

"Tell me his name, I shall make him see sense."

That sounded quite ominous! And seriously bad for business if they handed out personal details to strangers. "No, sir, I could not. I must insist you return the book."

As she'd suspected, he was clearly used to getting his own way, as his jaw jutted stubbornly. Hoping he'd be sensible, Estelle held her hand out for the man to return the book.

With a groan, he said, "Very well," and gave it over.

He did not, however, let go of it straight away.

Estelle looked at the man, with his fine clothes and straw-coloured curls and leather gloves so new they were as smooth as silk. He wasn't used to people saying no to him. At all.

"Thank you," she said, as he finally let the volume leave his hands. "Is there anything else I might interest you in? As you can see, we have a wide selection…"

"No. Thank you." With a polite nod, the gentleman picked up his hat and departed, leaving Estelle staring at his back.

There goes a rich potential customer. What a pity I couldn't sell him this book!

Later that day, Estelle wrapped the precious book the handsome and rich stranger had wanted in an oilskin, then tucked it into her travelling satchel. Louise, Bernadette and Marie continued with their tasks as she bid them farewell. Crafty waited by the shop door to get out, but deft footwork made sure Estelle made it out while the cat stayed in.

A couple of crows had set up by the boot scraper, treating it as a buffet. Estelle walked through the archway to the livery yards, where she hired a horse for the day.

Serenity beckoned as she and the borrowed horse soon left the noise, bustle and smells of Hatfield behind.

Everything felt easier out here amongst the fields, as if leaving her worries behind her in town. The sun shone weakly from behind clouds. Swallows swooped above the grasses while sheep grazed nearby. The wind might be cool, but the freshness of it invigorated her.

A pang caught behind her ribs as she compared the bright outdoors with the shadows of the bookshop. *I love the bookshop*, she told herself, as if she needed a little extra convincing. Books were her livelihood and not just her future, but the family's.

But gosh, it was lovely to be out in the fresh air, riding side-saddle with the wind in her hair. Even if it was on a borrowed horse called Somerset Valley Four. At least the horse seemed quiet and didn't object to bearing a lady riding side-saddle. His balance was good, and she didn't have to focus too much on her horsemanship.

Travelling and delivering books was the most pleasant part of her life. In some cases it was a shame to part with them, but the prices collectors paid was far too good to pass up.

With time to think and simply be, her thoughts drifted to her father, who had recently travelled to the continent to hunt for rare books. She missed him, as they all did, but knew he was having an incredible adventure. Now that Napoleon was safely exiled to Elba, an Englishman like her father, must be having a wonderful time in France. He spoke fluent French, as they all did, thanks to their late mother, so he would be easily understood. Now that the fighting was over, he'd be making his way about unhindered. The thought of spending her days travelling the countryside and purchasing books filled Estelle with wistful longing. If only she could have gone with her father, as she had on so many of his local buying expeditions! Matthew would not hear of her going with him to France, however, saying it would be far too dangerous. Dangerous? Napoleon was locked up, things were safe again.

The real reason he didn't want to take her was because she needed her to look after her sisters and the bookshop in his absence, but he'd played the threat of danger for all it was worth.

A raindrop splattered her eyelid. Looking up, the clouds had grown ominously darker. Would the rain hold off?

Another drop hit her cheek.

Summer afternoon aromas no longer surrounded her

as the wind turned cooler. Being indoors so much, Estelle had not developed an ability to read the weather. Her father and Louise had the knack, but she and their late mother had never quite developed that skill.

Which would have come in handy about ten minutes ago, when she and Somerset Valley Four could have sheltered in a barn beside the road.

No point going back, she would push on and reach her customer. The book was in an oilskin, so even if the heavens opened, the treasure would be safe.

A few moments later, the heavens did in fact open.

The air soon smelled of mud and damp.

She urged Somerset Valley Four to canter, or at least trot, and the horse set off willingly enough. In mere moments, the beast stumbled badly. With a jerk, Estelle tilted in the saddle, clutching at the horse's mane to maintain her balance. Another excellent reason she should have ridden astride; how she wished she dared! But even though she never expected to marry, she needed to maintain some respectability in Hatfield for the sake of the business.

The horse stopped.

The rain, however, did not.

"What's the matter?" Estelle tried to urge the horse forward, but two steps and it was clear he was lame. With an exasperated sniff, she lifted her leg over the pommel and slid down to the ground. She checked the poor beastie, holding his near fore off the ground. Had he thrown a shoe?

The rain was really hammering them now, making

muddy puddles in the road. The two of them were drenched through.

"Let me look at your hoof, Sweetie," she urged, tagging gently at the horse's fetlock.

The animal obliged and she found his shoe was intact, but a walnut-sized stone had become wedged between the rim of the shoe and the tender frog. Smooth, and now slippery and wet, the stone resisted her efforts to grab it with her fingertips and pull it out. Estelle wrinkled her nose, wishing she had a hoof-pick or even a pocket-knife on her. A hairpin would merely bend. Looking about, she found a few short sticks; the first two snapped, but the third proved sturdy enough to wedge under the stone and flick it out. The horse made a soft huff of relief through his nostrils.

"Good boy." Relief spread through Estelle too as she set the hoof down and straightened up. "Can you walk?"

Somerset Valley Four walked forward at her urging. Glancing up at the stirrup near her shoulder, she realised it would be difficult to climb back into that side saddle. Estelle looked hopefully about for anything she might use to stand on to help her mount. There was nothing. Maybe it would be for the best to keep her weight off his back anyway, as his hoof might be quite bruised after that stone. Although he didn't appear lame now, it might be a different matter with her on his back. Plus, now that she was soaked through, she'd be far heavier than when they set out.

Taking the reins in her hand, she walked beside him. After all, she couldn't get any wetter.

After an hour of increasingly sodden walking, Lord Ferndale's estate came into view. Ferndale Hall was a delightful classical stone building surrounded by wooded parklands and fields full of well-tended sheep. From the smoke rising from many of the chimneys, Estelle knew she would soon be warm and dry. As well as being a reliable customer who paid on time, Lord Ferndale was an old friend of her father's who had a soft spot for Estelle and her sisters. His staff would probably furnish her with fresh clothes and a sturdy carriage and horse to return her home.

As she neared, a groom approached and offered to take the horse to the stables.

"Thank you, and please see to his near front hoof. I took a stone out but it could be bruised."

"Yes, Miss," he said, giving the horse's nose a rub.

The elderly butler, Mr. Thorne, gave no sign there was anything amiss as he opened the door and took in Estelle's bedraggled appearance. He did ask her to wait momentarily in the foyer, where she dripped onto the parquet floor.

He returned with dry sheets. Miss Yates, Lord Ferndale's elderly sister who acted as mistress of Ferndale Hall, soon arrived.

"Thorne said you'd need a change of clothes."

Miss Yates was such a dear to offer. "Thank you, I shall return them freshly laundered."

Miss Yates smiled, "Tish tosh, no need for that. Come with me and I'll sort you out."

Estelle always felt amongst friends with the Ferndales.

It also helped that Lord Ferndale was one of their best customers.

Miss Yates had never married but had made herself invaluable in Hatfield life, being on many of the ladies' committees and doing a great many good works for the poor of the parish. Despite being very wealthy and the daughter and sister of a baron, Miss Yates never gave herself airs or thought herself too good to associate with anyone. She was, in Estelle's opinion, a true lady, far more so than many who had actual titles to their name.

Estelle dried herself and put on one of the skirts Miss Yates' maid brought in. It was an older style with long belts of linen that slipped through eyelets, allowing it to be tightened or loosened depending on whether a woman was increasing or not. The jacket which matched it was of a similar style, with a waist far lower than was fashionable today. They were made of beautiful material and even more importantly, were dry and comfortable.

They might have been made decades ago, possibly around the time Miss Yates might have been expected to marry. They smelled of cedar and long storage.

Then it hit her. "Miss Yates, these are from your trousseau! I can't wear such fine clothes."

"I'd rather they be worn than be dinner for moths!" Miss Yates said.

Well, when she put it that way. Estelle smiled, smoothing her hand over the skirt's fabric.

"Do you or your sisters need dresses for the assembly?" Miss Yates asked.

The question stilled Estelle for a moment. She'd

momentarily forgotten about the Midsummer assembly, which was in a few nights' time. Everyone of importance in Hatfield would attend, while many more would attend similar public dances held for all the farm workers.

Until now, Estelle had assumed any of her older dresses would do. They would not be buying any new fabric until their father was home and he'd repaid the enormous loan he'd taken out to fund his trip to France.

"I'm not one to stand out," she demurred.

"I'll have some sent over in any case. Miss Marie might want something new. Or old, really. They are quite old, but you're welcome to alter them if need be. I've been busy sorting out the attics of late; so many things have been put up there for years and I don't want them to go to waste!" Miss Yates held up her hands as Estelle began to protest. " No, I won't hear of any objections. Who else would I give them to? You know Arthur and I have scarcely any family left, only Arthur's grandson, who has no wife and apparently has no inclination to take one. I should like you and your sisters to have them."

There was no gainsaying the stubborn older lady, who had a positively martial glint in her eye. Estelle acquiesced graciously, and gratefully. It would be so lovely to have a new dress, even if she had to remake the style entirely.

A few extra hair pins to set her tresses neatly, and Estelle and Miss Yates were in a fit state to head to the sitting room.

Lord Ferndale was waiting for them beside a roaring fire.

"Miss Baxter, my dear," he held his arms out for an embrace.

They truly were more like family than customers, Estelle thought, as she wrapped her arms around her dear friend and kissed his wrinkled cheek.

"I come bearing good news, I have the book you wanted!" She beamed as she opened her satchel and handed over the parcel.

Lord Ferndale unwrapped the oilskin and gasped as he revealed the precious tome within. Quickly, he stepped over to the window to get a better look at it, depositing the empty wrap on an occasional table. Horrified at the damp oilskin being so casually placed on the expensive rosewood, Estelle quickly grabbed it up and refolded it.

"Oh yes," Lord Ferndale said, opening the cover and reading the title page. "*The Collected Works of Philo Judæus*, and most gloriously bound! Oh my goodness," he gasped as he turned the first few pages, admiring the beautifully coloured, hand-drawn illustrations. "I cannot believe I am holding this in my very own hands."

"I am delighted that it's in your hands," Estelle said, smiling happily as she observed the joy on the old gentleman's face.

There was something so magical about matching a customer to the book of their soul. And such an old soul as Lord Ferndale needed a great many of them.

"You are a wonder," he said, carefully turning the pages and scanning the text. "How ever did you get hold of this?"

"You have my father to thank for that. A crate arrived

from France this morning, and that was in it. I came as soon as I could, because I knew you've been wanting it for some time."

"This calls for celebration, you must stay for tea."

Lord Ferndale was incredibly sweet to offer, and Estelle really was quite tempted, especially knowing how good his cook was. "I really should be getting back," she said thinking that perhaps she *could* be persuaded to just one cup of tea, and maybe a cake or two. "You and Miss Yates have done enough already, I have dry clothes and the rain shall ease."

As if to make a mockery of her words, the sky darkened and more rain began to fall.

A man walked past the sitting room's open doors. He was almost out of sight when he stopped and walked backwards.

He stared into the room.

Directly at Estelle.

"You?" he said.

Estelle's manners deserted her. "Oh no. Not you!"

CHAPTER 2

Dinner For Four

The words, "How do you know each other?" were on Estelle's lips when she also heard them spoken out loud, concurrently by both Lord Ferndale and the golden-haired gentleman who'd been in Baxter's Fine Books only this morning.

The annoyingly happy and handsome man who'd nevertheless driven her almost to despair.

Meanwhile, Miss Yates made a funny noise and said, "How entertaining."

As it was his house, Estelle turned to Lord Ferndale, her nerves jangling. She felt thoroughly set off-balance by this unexpected encounter.

The well-dressed man with the golden hair and tanned skin to match walked into the sitting room, blue gaze fixed curiously on Estelle.

Her body warmed in the most unwarranted way.

Lord Ferndale said, "I'd best make introductions. Miss Estelle Baxter, my grandson, the Honourable Felix Yates."

"Oh!" Estelle said, making a short curtsey to the man she now realised she'd been rather terse with this morning. "Pleased to make your acquaintance, Mister Yates."

Well, she'd been right about the rich part, at least. She'd met so many people, running the bookstore. The ones who placed orders would gladly give their names. If this man had placed an order with them this morning, she might have had the wherewithal to put the surnames together and realised he was a Ferndale. But as he hadn't, she didn't.

They both looked at each other and said, "The book!"

Estelle hid a giggle behind her hand, then turned to Lord Ferndale.

Lord Ferndale was perplexed.

Estelle explained, "This young man was in the bookshop only this morning, he arrived at the same time as my father's crate from the continent!"

"Grandfather, I must confess, I made rather a nuisance of myself in Miss Baxter's shop just this very morning. It is a delightful place, and there was one book I simply had to have."

"Let me guess," Lord Ferndale held up his new prize. "This one?"

"The very same!"

Miss Yates sidled up to Estelle and whispered, "I do love a little intrigue!"

"She would not sell it to me," the golden man she now knew to be Felix Yates said. "I offered to triple the price and she did not even blink!"

"You are too kind," Estelle said, knowing full well she

had paused at the offer, if only for a second. Money would solve a lot of problems at this moment.

Lord Ferndale looked imperiously at his grandson and said, "Were you aware of the base price before you offered to treble it?"

Now Estelle blushed and looked to the floor. It was rather déclassé to discuss the price of things in front of others, even if it was among Lord Ferndale's own family.

"I was not!" Mr. Yates said cheerfully.

"Then it's just as well she refused you, for you would have needed to come to me for a loan!"

Miss Yates whispered to Estelle, "Are they gambling?"

"Not yet," Estelle said quietly, so that only Miss Yates could hear.

It was a fascinating encounter, and she was rather enjoying herself.

The young Mr. Yates then said, "What a close-run thing!"

The two gentlemen shared a chuckle at this point, before Lord Ferndale asked his grandson, "Tell me, would you be buying such a book?"

"To give to you, of course!" he said, then gave a hearty laugh. "I knew you would love it. And I was right!"

He had a sense of humour at least, Estelle thought, and was able to laugh at himself, a skill she had found most gentlemen of her acquaintance singularly lacked.

"All's well that ends well," Lord Ferndale said then. "Although, if Miss Baxter here had accepted your price, she would have had thrice the money and I would have had the book all the same. So, I believe you owe Miss Baxter a great deal of money."

Estelle gasped at the direction the conversation was taking. How could Lord Ferndale possibly know how much debt they were in?

"Steady on," Mr. Yates said, suddenly looking horrified.

Estelle felt a little sorry for him now. Surely the family patriarch was jesting? She had already agreed an adequate price for the book.

But three times as much would have helped a great deal.

"I must be getting back," she said again, hoping Ferndale would offer her his coach and horses for the return journey. Even if Somerset Valley Four was sound enough to carry her, she would get drenched again if she rode outside.

"Alas, the weather is against you, as is my estate," Lord Ferndale said, looking between Estelle and Mr. Yates. "My carriage is at the wheelwright for repair and it's teeming out there. At least join us for a meal while you wait out the rain?"

"Yes, stay for dinner, do," Miss Yates urged.

Estelle hesitated, but it was the middle of summer and would be light until after nine. She'd have plenty of time to get home afterwards. She knew the Ferndale household kept country hours and would dine early. Another reason to accept: if she ate dinner here, there would be more food for her sisters at home.

That thought decided her, and she offered a gracious

smile. "That is very generous of you, Lord Ferndale, Miss Yates. I should be delighted to have dinner with you."

"Capital!" Lord Ferndale smiled warmly at her. "Now, do come through to the library. I've acquired a few books where the binding is looking rather shoddy; do you think your sister would have the time to rebind them for me?"

"I'm sure Louise could find the time," Estelle said, following Lord Ferndale to the library, thinking that even if Louise was busy, she would definitely make the time, considering Lord Ferndale's deep pockets.

"Your sister binds books?" a voice said behind her, and Estelle found to her surprise and slight annoyance that Felix Yates had followed them. A little like a happy puppy.

"We all have our talents," Estelle said dismissively.

"What's yours?"

What an intrusive question! Startled, she turned to look at him.

"Managing troublesome customers," Lord Ferndale answered for her, and Estelle swallowed a laugh. "A very managing female, Miss Baxter, and I say that as a high compliment." The he turned to his grandson and declared, "You should marry her, Felix."

Estelle choked, not sure who to look at or where to put herself as Lord Ferndale apparently decided to appoint himself matchmaker for herself and his grandson.

Of all the ridiculous ideas!

Ordinarily, libraries calmed Estelle, but her nerves were on high alert as Lord Ferndale continued to push his home advantage. "Young Felix here is my only heir. I've called him home because he must settle down," he said. "Whoever he marries will inherit this magnificent library, and one day be Baroness Ferndale. How does that sound to you, Miss Baxter?"

Heat roared up Estelle's neck at Lord Ferndale being so blunt with his decisions about their futures. They'd only just met, and although he was rather handsome, she knew nothing of him. She made a polite cough into her closed hand, declining to answer.

"Ignore him," Mr. Yates parried, apparently finding the idea just as insane as she did.

She could add 'sensible' to the things she knew of Mr Yates, as that was a sensible way to react to a grandfather making insensible comments.

Miss Yates joined in, nudging Estelle gently. "You have mentioned before that the library is your favourite room."

Oh no, now Miss Yates was joining in? The sweet woman could not truly be serious, this had to be a jest. A wicked thought crossed Estelle's mind, as she took in the dawning horror on handsome Mr Yates' face. The young sprig could do with being taken down a peg or three. "Well, I would dearly enjoy inheriting a library," she said, deliberately not saying anything about becoming a baroness.

<hr>

Felix could not recall the last time he'd felt this painfully uncomfortable. Usually he batted off his grandfather's entreaties, but all his witty comebacks deserted him in the face of Miss Baxter's very clear horror at the mere idea of being married to him.

Even with the temptation of Ferndale's library before her. She made a teasing remark, but he hadn't missed the instant denial that crossed her expression when his grandfather made the suggestion.

Why wouldn't she want to marry him? Did she have a better offer waiting in the wings? He tilted his head, considering the conundrum. She appeared ladylike, certainly, with the educated speech of the upper classes, but she worked in a bookshop! She was a far cry from the daughters of the aristocracy his grandfather was usually urging in his direction, most of whom were only too eager to throw themselves at his feet.

It intrigued him that Miss Baxter would show such evident horror at the mere idea of a match which would clearly be a vast elevation in her station.

He'd thought he was well-turned out and eligible. But perhaps he was unpalatable as a prospective husband?

That truly confused him, and he felt the cut deeply. He stepped back, so that he wasn't in the line of his grandfather's sight and the potential target of more barbs. He was … what had they called it? A fine specimen? Something like that. Ladies swooned in his presence, or at least pretended to. 'Pon rep, this woman certainly knew how to dent a man's ego.

His grandfather presented several books to Miss Baxter that required repair. Some mild, others close to falling apart. At least the conversation had safely returned to books instead of matchmaking, allowing Felix to muse silently on the interesting young lady before him.

She was pretty and her voice was pleasing, and she had to be clever to know as much about books as his grandfather. The woman was running a business, which was a rare thing indeed. The more he observed, the more he started to wonder why her face had expressed such displeasure at the thought of being married to him.

No sooner had he thought himself safe from interference, however, than his pesky grandfather brought the topic right back to marriage again.

"You'd be the perfect hostess of this estate, what with your knowledge and respect for books. The legacy in this room stretches back generations."

Felix wished himself back in Greece, far from duties and responsibilities and being shoved into Parson's Mousetrap. Not that he wasn't interested at all in marrying! He was. But not quite yet. Alas, any time he'd tried to get to know anybody, his grandfather had jumped the gun and declared they were already a great match.

Part of the reason he'd gone to Greece in the first place was to get away from the constant, swirling noise of family duty. Some of his friends said he was being ridiculous, that with such a small family he had things easy, but they didn't understand the pressure that came with being literally the last hope of a family's line remaining extant.

He had to have children or his line would die out. It made perfect sense, and he understood the ramifications of that.

But, he'd really like to get to know a woman first

before having her pronounced as suitable to be the mother of his children. He would at least like to like her, and, he rather hoped, she might like him in return.

The opposite of what he'd witnessed with his parents, who spent most of their lives making each other miserable.

Without his grandfather's pressure and interference, he would have truly enjoyed getting to know Miss Baxter some more. He already liked her sense of honour. He'd offered her more money for a book that was promised to another, and she'd refused. Yes, it had irritated the tripe out of him at the time, but now he understood why she'd done it. She was a woman of her word. She'd promised a book to somebody, and she delivered on that promise. Plus, she hadn't divulged who the book was promised to when he'd demanded to know, which meant she did not divulge personal information even for a decent price.

He also couldn't deny Miss Baxter was rather easy to look upon, with her dark hair, eyes somewhere between green and golden, and a neat trim figure. She had a healthy glow about her. And his grandfather and great-aunt clearly adored her, which spoke volumes for her character.

As much as he tried, he couldn't stay cross with Grandpapa. The old man had shown nothing but kindness to him after his father passed, and had continued to fund his education and even a Grand Tour.

Felix owed him a great deal, but did that extend to unquestioning obedience to marry the first woman his grandfather thrust in his direction? Surely not. He was his own man, and he would be the one to choose his own bride, not his grandfather.

When it was time to leave the library and walk to the dining room, he slowed his steps to allow the elders to enter the room first. Keeping his voice as low as he could, he muttered to Miss Baxter, "You are obviously good friends with my Grandfather, and he clearly adores you."

"Thank you," she said, with a sweet smile. "He has been a great patron of our bookshop."

"It's good to see him in a lively mood. I believe we are in for some japes."

She slowed her steps even more, creating a wider gap between themselves and the elders. "Japes?"

This would help him get to know her, and know whether she could join in with frivolous games or take life far too seriously. "We could play along, if that would be agreeable to you?"

Lord Ferndale said to his sister, loudly enough for all to hear, "You see, Florence? They are getting along, just as I predicted."

***

Grandpapa Ferndale may be a baron, but his informality in so many things extended to meal times. The table they sat down to only had room for six at most. Ferndale at the head, Miss Yates at the other end. It meant Felix and Miss Baxter sat in the middle, facing each other, with only a candelabra to block their view.

He was happy with the arrangement, as it meant he

could spend more time gazing upon her face and deciding which parts were the prettiest.

She wore different clothes now to the dress she'd had on this morning, he suddenly noticed. To his untrained eye, they looked out of date. The sort of clothing his grandmother, God rest her soul, wore in the family portraits on the walls.

Miss Baxter accepted the bowl of potatoes and served herself, then moved the candelabra to the middle of the table to create some room to put the bowl down. It blocked Felix's view of her. He took the potatoes and helped himself, then moved the candelabra out of the way and placed the bowl between them.

"Miss Yates, would you like some potatoes?" Miss Baxter asked.

His great aunt agreed and the bowls and pieces moved again.

That candelabra ended up blocking his view of Miss Baxter once again as various plates and bowls moved about the table like chess pieces.

It did not take Felix long to suspect she was moving the candelabra deliberately. There were certainly moments when it would have been more convenient or simpler to move something other than the heavy, multi-branched brass object, with the risk of hot wax dripping on her arm every time she lifted it.

"Stephens, this is a menace." Felix caught the attention of the footman carrying dishes in and out. "Would you move it to the sideboard, and light a few more around the room so we have sufficient light without risking wax in the syllabub? Thank you."

Yes, Miss Baxter had definitely been using the candelabra as a shield. Her mouth turned down at the corners as Stephens removed it, and Felix felt a small twinge of triumph at having outwitted her. He suspected her to be rather clever and that she might be used to having the upper hand in any battle of wits.

He rather fancied himself his equal in that regard, and sallied forth. "So, when would suit you for our wedding, Miss Baxter?" Felix said loudly.

All conversation stopped. Miss Baxter, who had been talking about the assembly with his aunt, froze in place before slowly turning her head to pin him with an icy glare.

"I do beg your pardon, Mr Yates; I must not have heard you correctly."

Japes, he mouthed at her. She glared right back at him.

"Having observed your gracious manners and charm this evening," he began, "I find myself in agreement with my grandfather that you would make an excellent Baroness Ferndale," Felix said cheerfully. "So. Shall I visit the vicar and ask him to read the banns?"

"Felix," his grandfather said despairingly. "This is not what I meant."

"Is this how ladies are courted in Greece?" his great-aunt asked. "It's rather direct. What fun."

Miss Baxter was clearly wishing him far away, and just as obviously mentally rehearsing and discarding insulting put-downs, from the sideways glances she was giving Lord Ferndale and Miss Yates. He could tell she was warring between insulting him and not wanting to insult her host and hostess.

She grasped instead at a convenient change of topic. "You have been to Greece, Mr Yates?"

"Indeed! Spent last winter there. Highly recommend Athens as a lovely place in the winter." He caught a wistful expression on Miss Baxter's face. "Where have you visited on your travels?" he asked, humouring her by extending the topic.

"Oh," she said, seeming more bruised than buoyed by the direction of the conversation. "Well, certainly not as far as Greece, but it sounds lovely in the many books I've read on Grecian history. One day I hope to be lucky enough to visit."

Felix cursed his silly jape. Unwed women did not have the same luxury as he, nor could Miss Baxter possibly have the same funds.

"We should go together," Miss Yates suggested. "You could be my companion."

Her face brightened at his great aunt's suggestion, before dimming again as she obviously realised Miss Yates was far too old and frail to embark on any such adventure. She smiled kindly at Miss Yates, though, and jealousy hit Felix hard. He'd do quite a number of reprehensible things to be on the receiving end of a smile like that from Miss Baxter.

"Well then," his grandfather declared, "You *shall* visit Greece. How about on your honeymoon with young Felix here?"

Her cheeks pinked and she gave the old man a wry smile. "Lord Ferndale, if you were anyone else I'd accuse them of making a jest at my expense. But you are such a dear friend I couldn't *possibly* be cross at you for wishing the best for me." She then changed the subject so artfully Felix could only wish he had a quill and paper with which to take notes. Clever, deft woman! She should have been a diplomat. "These potatoes are delicious. I believe your cook has seasoned them with rosemary to perfection. Is it from the cuttings Bernadette gave you last year?"

Grandpapa winked at their guest. "It is at that. Eight of the nine cuttings took, which is a marvellous strike rate."

Her expression eased as she appeared on sturdier ground with his grandfather..

"In fact," the old man continued, "Rosemary grows everywhere in Greece, does it not?"

A twinge of surrender marred her rather lovely brows at that. "I … believe it grows all around the Mediterranean region. It does well in the warmth. That's why it is best planted against a stone wall facing the sun, here in England."

Grandfather snaffled a bite of lamb and grinned, his eyes full of mischief. "You'll have to bring some plants back from Greece when you travel there. Perhaps on your honeymoon?"

Felix could almost feel sorry for Miss Baxter. Almost. He'd spent far too many painful evenings being the target of Grandfather's machinations; it was something of a relief to see the old man's attention focussed on someone else for a change. And Miss Baxter gave as good as she got, diverting the conversation with wit and humour every time it became too uncomfortable for her liking.

His great aunt then apparently took pity on Miss Baxter and changed the subject. "We were discussing the assembly."

"What's that?" Grandfather asked.

She raised her voice a little more, "The Midsummer Assembly on the twenty-fourth."

"That's come around quickly," the old man said, spearing another bite of lamb onto his fork. He then turned to Felix and said, "You'll be there, of course."

Felix tried not to audibly sigh at the thought. If only he'd delayed his visit by another week, it would have been over and he wouldn't have to be be paraded in front of every young woman within twenty miles.

"I haven't been to an assembly in Hatfield in years," he said. "Miss Baxter, do you always attend?" She would have been at least eighteen the last time he attended one of the assemblies, but he didn't recall meeting her. He would have remembered meeting someone as intriguing as she. He mentioned the year, and she shook her head.

"I was away that year, travelling with my father, purchasing books."

"Will you be attending this time?" he asked in hope. "You won't be off searching for books and avoiding the dance?" If she were there, the evening would be bearable.

"My father is in France at present, so my sisters and I shall attend."

"Well then," Grandfather announced. "You have a few days to get to know each other. It would be delightful if we could announce your betrothal at the assembly."

He watched Miss Baxter close her eyes and breathe deeply, as if sending up a prayer for strength.

Felix tried not to laugh, but he was rather enjoying the evening. *I could do so much worse for a wife.*

Morning arrived with the uncomfortable realisation for Felix that last night he'd made fun *of* Estelle Baxter, rather than made fun *with* her. He'd gone too far, and he felt badly now.

He had to remedy that.

He'd talk to her at breakfast. They would have a friendly chat and he'd find a way to apologise.

Miss Baxter might be a good friend to his grandfather and great-aunt, but he should not have mistaken that friendliness with too much familiarity, as he had at the meal last night. He barely knew her, and in the light of day, he couldn't help thinking he'd been unconscionably rude.

A mistake he needed to rectify if he was going to seriously court her. He was beginning to think that was actually an excellent notion. He could so easily see himself in Greece with Estelle, watching the sunset over the water from a villa in Patros, after yet another glorious day. She'd look at him and smile, and say something deliciously witty, and he'd have to lean over and kiss her and…

His stomach rumbled as he descended the stairs, distracting him from his thoughts of how Estelle's green-golden eyes would glow in the afternoon light, and informing him that he needed a hot cup of coffee and some eggs, bacon and toast immediately.

His grandfather was nearly finished with his kippers and kedgeree, and two more empty plates showed the women had already eaten and moved on with their day.

"You're too late," Grandpapa said in an annoyed tone. "That's what comes from sleeping the day away."

The old man waved his hand toward the window. Felix looked out to see a horse and rider in the distance, growing smaller by the second.

Last night's rain had moved on and the sun shone gloriously.

"There goes the best woman you'll ever meet," the old man said. "If you don't go after her right now, you're a prize fool."

Felix stood there, open mouthed in shock.

"Well?" his grandfather clattered his knife and fork together over the crumbs on his plate. "Don't stand there looking like a caught fish. Go and get her!"

CHAPTER 3

The Trouble With Relatives

The familiar bustle of Hatfield greeted Estelle as she and Somerset Valley Four returned to town. Thankfully, the horse seemed quite sound this morning, and had happily trotted and cantered when urged, so she had made excellent time on her journey home. She mentioned yesterday's incident to the stablehand all the same, so they could keep an eye on him. The stablehand patted the horse on the neck as he eagerly plunged his nose into a waiting bucket of oats.

If only her troubles were limited to a wounded horse. The bookshop door was wide open as she walked towards it. That did not bode well; it was too early to be open for customers.

Her cousin Joshua's ominous voice carried out to the street.

This was not a good sign at all. Joshua only ever visited them to make demands.

By a miracle, Crafty was up high on a bookshelf rather

than down on the ground, ready to escape. This was a cat that chased horses for fun. The only reason she might be hiding high above them was to keep out of reach of Benjamin, Joshua's eldest.

The way that boy looked at cats sent a shiver down Estelle's spine.

She caught movement between some shelves and knew he must be in the shop somewhere. Estelle quickly closed the door to prevent the cat's escape. The last time Crafty had run out the open door, she'd come home a week and a half later, half starved and pregnant.

On top of their pile of troubles, the last thing the Baxters needed was another litter of kittens.

Her sisters were by the counter. Joshua Baxter and his wife Phoebe were standing in such a way that they seemed to consume all the space in the shop.

Hoping her voice sounded pleasant and not at all cross, Estelle said, "Cousin Joshua, good morning! To what do we owe the pleasure of this visit?" One thing was certain; Joshua and Phoebe were not here to buy books. Joshua read nothing but his account ledgers, and Phoebe only looked at fashion periodicals, which she ordered sent direct from London. Estelle had offered to order them in for a better price, but Phoebe had snubbed her.

Joshua turned to Estelle, his scowling, belligerent expression souring her stomach. "I came to measure the windows for drapes, but I see they're all blocked. Please re-open the door. Can't see my hand in front of my face."

Phoebe added, "Have a maid light some candles at least. Somebody could fall and break their neck."

They did not have candles to spare, nor a maid to light them, but she wasn't about to tell her cousin that. Estelle pulled the little curtain aside from the window at the door. It provided a thin shaft of light. It was enough for her to see little Barnaby, Joshua and Phoebe's youngest child, reaching for a book.

"My darling," she said, scooping up the boy for a cuddle. It had the extra action of preventing him from touching any of the valuable books with his jam-covered hands. The little one was a dear, and loved having stories read to him. But he always seemed to have such dirty hands! Louise called him Little Sticky, and though Estelle should probably have discouraged the nickname, all of the sisters had ended up using it. So much so, she had actually called Barnaby Little Sticky out loud one day by accident, and had to hastily cover her slip-up. "I have a lovely story for you, Barnaby," she said as she took a handkerchief out of her pocket and wiped his pudgy and very sticky hands.

The middle son would be in the bookshop some-where. Something of a forgotten child, he was quiet and unassuming, saddled with the name Brutus. If his parents and older brother weren't quite so dreadful, Estelle wouldn't have minded having Brutus around more often.

Her mind jangled on something Joshua had just said about windows.

Thankfully, her sister Marie piped up with a well-timed question: "Why do you wish to measure the windows for drapes? The bookshelves block the sunlight to protect the books."

Joshua took out a piece of string from his pocket and made a rough estimate of the width of one of the bookshelves, which had a window behind it. "Because," he said, stretching it out, "I have it on excellent authority," another pause for dramatic effect, "That your father is dead."

Momentarily dumbstruck, Estelle stopped wiping Barnaby's hands. Her sisters at the counter gasped in unison. They looked across to Estelle, who looked back at them and wondered what on earth was going on.

Marie spoke for all of them, "He's not dead. He's in France."

"Same thing," Benjamin said with a sneer from behind a bookshelf. The child had a mean streak as long as the Great North Road.

"He is very much alive," Bernadette corrected stubbornly. "A crate of books arrived only yesterday morning."

Unperturbed, Joshua declared, "That means nothing. It could have been sent months ago. I hear he came to a bad end. Probably gambling."

Worries churned through Estelle at the thought their father might have perished somewhere on the continent.

If their father died, they would suffer emotionally, but even more than that, the shop would go to Joshua. He wasn't the slightest bit interested in the books within, but he did covet the building. If their father was dead, she, her sisters, their one maid, the cat and all their books would be out on the street.

Silence hung in the air as Phoebe looked about with a smug expression.

"When was he supposed to have died?" Marie asked.

Excellent question, Marie.

"Barely four weeks ago," Joshua said, without any hesitation as he kept right on measuring.

"Thank God," Marie cried.

Not the reaction Estelle had expected. "What do you mean?"

Marie's voice was full of joy. "He can't have died a month ago. There was a letter in yesterday's crate dated," she paused a little and unfolded a letter, "Not sixteen days ago. It must be a case of mistaken identity, dear Cousin."

Estelle could breathe again!

When she'd left yesterday to deliver the previous book to Lord Ferndale, she hadn't been aware there was a letter in the crate at all. Thank goodness he'd sent one, and that her sisters had found it.

One of the boys snorted with laughter from behind the shelves. Probably Benjamin.

She cuddled Barnaby in relief. He was no longer dangerously sticky, so she plucked a book of herbs from the shelf. It had detailed illustrations that would absorb his attention for a short while and opened it to show him, setting it on a footstool.

"Show me the letter," Joshua demanded.

"We may read it together," Marie said. "By the

window. You will see it is clearly his hand, and his signature at the bottom. He was alive at least 16 days ago, when he sent the crate of books."

Bernadette and Louise approached Estelle as Barnaby settled down with the book. She hugged her sisters tightly with relief, resting her head on Louise's broad shoulder for a moment. The tallest of the sisters and strongly built, not to say Junoesque, Louise's sturdy form was exceptionally huggable.

"I am so glad there was a letter in the crate," Estelle said softly, not wanting Joshua and Phoebe to hear.

"We only found it late yesterday, checking through the books," Louise said. "I thought some pages had come loose from the binding but it was Father's note to us slipping out. He really should take more care, we could have easily missed it."

That was nothing unusual for their father. He would probably have been so excited at finding the books, writing a note to them at all would have been an afterthought.

"We're lucky he sent one at all," Estelle said.

"True that," Louise agreed.

"Hey, that's an expensive book," Bernadette said, reaching down to the floor to take the book of herbs from Barnaby. "Don't let Little Sticky at it."

"Shh!" Louise said, at the mention of Barnaby's pet name.

There was more movement over by the door as Joshua called out for his family. "Right then, come along, we're leaving!"

Benjamin Baxter marched out of the shop without a farewell. Brutus, the middle child, looked shyly around the bookshelf at his cousins and gave a small wave. Such a sweet-natured boy with such an ill-fitting name. Estelle waved back at him.

Phoebe stomped over to Barnaby and scooped him up, holding him slightly away from her body as if she already knew his fingers would be covered in jam.

A horrible thought crossed Estelle's mind: *Phoebe probably spread jam over his hands before bringing him into the shop, just to annoy us.*

Joshua stood at the open door until his wife and sons had exited. He made a curt bow to Marie and simply said, "I shall see you anon."

Then he walked out, leaving the door wide open.

Marie rushed to the door and gently closed it. For a long moment there was silence as they all stood still, hoping desperately that Joshua would not take it into his head to return and browbeat them once more.

"They're gone," Marie said at last, peering out of the little window.

"Thank the good Lord!"

The four sisters rushed into a huddle to hold each other with relief and joy. With their father out of the country and debts piling up, Cousin Joshua and his plans for the building were an extra complication they did not need.

Estelle said, "Next crate that arrives, we must check for letters first."

"Yes," Marie said. "Thank goodness you found it, Louise."

Estelle gave Louise an extra hug of gratitude before saying; "I should have come back last night, I'm sorry you had to deal with Joshua on your own."

"We weren't on our own," Lousie said. "The three of us managed well enough, although Marie did step in dead mouse first thing this morning."

"Urgh, Crafty!" Estelle complained.

Marie added, "Exactly!"

As if responding to her name, the cat leapt down from the bookshelves and moved to her scratching post to sink her claws in to the hessian there.

Estelle sighed. "One more item to add to the morning checklist: Crafty's post, dead mice, then the day's correspondence. I have the payment from Lord Ferndale, so that should cover the correspondence fees for a good while."

Marie said, "It will also pay for the advertisements in The Times and the next insurance instalment, so we can breathe again for a little while at least."

They could have covered so much more if she'd accepted Mr Yates' better offer, but Estelle did not allow herself to dwell on that dishonourable thought. In fact, she didn't even mention him, or his higher offer.

Instead, she accepted the letter from their father that Marie held out to her.

"Thank you. I shall read this upstairs; I need to go and change. My clothes got soaked in the rain yesterday and I had to borrow some from Miss Yates, and though I'm sure the staff did their best, my riding habit wasn't quite dry when I put it back on this morning."

"Have you had breakfast?" Louise asked practically.

"Indeed I have, and a lovely dinner last night, you would have been quite envious. Though the conversation left much to be desired!"

Her sisters looked at her strangely.

"It was all very silly. Lord Ferndale was in a teasing mood and said I should marry his grandson."

"He what?" Marie gasped.

"I know. It was preposterous, but I humoured him all the same." Laughing, Estelle set off upstairs to change. She wouldn't be long, and then she'd come back down to help her sisters once the shop opened.

"Do you need some breakfast, Estelle?" Their house-keeper, Mrs Poole, looked up from peeling potatoes as she passed through the kitchen.

"Thank you, no; I had a lovely breakfast at Ferndale Hall," Estelle said cheerfully. Though it had been a good hour ago now, and the buttered scones on the table looked delicious… she swiped one to eat as she made her way to her bedroom.

The letter from her father was sparse, Estelle thought, taking a few moments to scan down it as she laced her shoes after changing her gown. Addressed from Orléans with a note that he was headed for Tours, and then either for Angers or Poitiers. Making a mental note to find a map of France once she returned downstairs, she laid the letter on her dresser for now and checked her hair in her small hand-mirror before making her way back downstairs. Correspondence from the continent could often be delayed, but as long as his letters and the crates of books kept arriving, they would know their father still lived. Joshua had given them a horrible scare, but that's all it had been. He couldn't harm them so long as their father lived.

The shop bell rang above the front door as she reached the bottom of the stairs. A well-dressed man walked up to the counter. Estelle stopped in her tracks as he removed his hat to reveal suspiciously familiar, tousled golden curls.

"Good morning!" Mr Yates said cheerfully to Marie, who was behind the counter, offering up her best serving-a-customer smile.

"And a good morning to you, sir, how may we assist you?"

"I was about to ask the same thing of you," he said, placing his hat on the counter. "Are you in need of anything? How can I help?"

"I beg your pardon?" Marie blinked in confusion.

Estelle blurted out, "Not you again! What are you doing here?"

Mr Yates turned to face her, his smile broadening. "Why, Miss Baxter, I've come to marry you, of course."

This time, she actually was going to kill him.

CHAPTER 4

Letting The Cat Out Of The Bag

Perhaps it had been a mistake to begin jesting with Miss Baxter again the moment he saw her, Felix recognised as soon as the unfortunate sentence left his lips and her pretty face darkened to a scowl.

He'd gone too far.

He'd come to Hatfield to smooth things over, and he'd made it worse.

The Miss Baxter behind the counter - so alike they could only be sisters, though the one behind the counter was wearing glasses - coughed, and then said in incredulous tones; "I beg your pardon - did you say to *marry* her? Estelle, who is this?"

"Please just go away, Mr Yates," his Miss Baxter said wearily.

"Yates?" one of the Baxter sisters said. "This is Lord Ferndale's grandson?"

"Estelle, do not chase away paying customers!" This

was a third Miss Baxter, emerging from among the book-shelves. Taller and sturdier than the other two, still the facial shape, the dark hair and intriguing green-gold eyes marked her inevitably as one of the sisters. Felix tried to remember how many of them his grandfather had said there were. He bowed politely to the newcomer.

"Good morning, Miss Baxter. Ah, but you are all Miss Baxters, are you not? Miss Baxter, will you not introduce me to your charming sisters before I get impossibly confused as to which Miss Baxter I am addressing? Or are you even Miss Baxter - which of you is the eldest?"

The tall Miss Baxter stifled a laugh behind her hand, and Felix grinned at her.

"Very well, Mr Yates," his Miss Baxter said ungraciously. "I am indeed Miss Baxter. This is my sister Miss Marie -" indicating the glasses-wearer "- and this is my sister Miss Louise. Over there is our youngest sister Miss Bernadette."

Felix blinked, and then looked again. He hadn't even seen the fourth sister, but there she was, sitting behind the counter in a dark corner, folding something up into small paper packets. She glanced up at him with a polite little nod before returning her attention to what she was doing.

"Ah, you are the sister who binds books!" he said to Miss Louise. "My grandfather speaks highly of your skill, and indeed, I admire the quality of your work. I quite covet his beautifully bound set of Daniel Defoe's works."

Miss Louise smiled at him in quite a friendly way and said, "How kind of you, Mr. Yates! I have enjoyed reading

Defoe's scandalous tale of Moll Flanders, although there were no chapters in the entire book where one could take a rest."

"That's possibly the least objectionable part of that tale," he said with a laugh. "There were parts of it that quite made me blush!"

Miss Louise continued, "Estelle brought back with her several books Lord Ferndale has commissioned me to rebind. I shall take care of them in a timely manner, I assure you. I will need a couple of weeks to get the materials I need, but the repairs themselves should not take long."

"I appreciate your dedication," he said, smiling her way.

They were all lovely in their own way, but there was something indefinable about *his* Miss Baxter that continued to intrigue him. "Honoured to meet you all," he added gallantly.

"How charming," Miss Baxter said in a mocking tone. "Now please either buy some books or go away."

"*Estelle!*" Marie and Louise exclaimed in unison, obviously quite shocked. "That's no way to speak to Lord Ferndale's grandson," Marie added.

A naughty thought popped into his head. "Now, is that any way to speak to your fiancé, Miss Baxter?" He shouldn't tease her, really he shouldn't, but goodness she was pretty when she was cross, her eyes flashing and pink colour flushing her pale cheeks.

"You are impossible!" Obviously furious, she stomped past him and behind the counter, snatching up a pile of correspondence from the desk and turning her back on him as she pretended to read it.

Felix grinned. Well, at least she wasn't trying to throw him out. He looked about the bookshop. Perhaps he should actually buy some books - he needed something to read, and his grandfather behaved about his library rather as a dragon might with a hoard of gold. Humming a cheerful little tune under his breath, he stepped along the aisle to examine a shelf of travelogues as the four sisters gathered together behind the counter.

Snippets of low-voiced conversation reached his ears as he browsed the books.

"Fiancé?" The single-word question was Miss Louise, he thought.

"Absolutely not. It's all a little silly. This is a jape between us, really. Yes, Mr Yates is Lord Ferndale's grandson, returned from a tour of Greece. He was at dinner last night, and Lord Ferndale thought it would be funny to say we should marry."

Dear me, Estelle sounded positively disgusted. Once again, Felix had to wonder what exactly it was about the thought of him as a potential husband that so repulsed her. It was certainly a novel reaction from a lady to the idea, in his experience.

"He's very handsome." That quiet voice, he thought, might be Bernadette.

"And quite obviously rich, from the look of his clothes. Not to mention he's Lord Ferndale's grandson! Why don't you marry him?" That *was* Louise, and Felix grinned at the Italian travel guide he was leafing through. He rather thought Louise might be an ally.

Estelle's reply was too quiet for him to hear, unfortunately. He leaned towards the counter, took a small step in that direction, and was distracted by a soft yowl underfoot.

"Hullo, puss." The black cat whose tail he had barely missed standing on looked up at him from unblinking green eyes. "Aren't you a handsome specimen?"

Felix liked cats, and this one was a beauty; large and healthy-looking with glossy black fur. He bent to scratch behind the cat's ears and was rewarded with a throaty purr.

The purring grew louder as he continued tickling the cat under her chin and rubbing her soft ears. The louder her satisfied purrs grew, the harder it became to eavesdrop on the conversation. He overheard something about their father in France, and snatches about marriage. He would have to stop patting the cat in order to hear more clearly.

As he straightened up again, his stomach rumbled, making even more noise than the cat.

"Mister Yates, have you found anything interesting?" the tallest one, Miss Louise, asked him.

He stood upright. The cat began rubbing herself against his shins, leaving thick tufts of fur behind on his boot tassels.

"Er, yes, these travelogues are intriguing," he said. His stomach rumbled again. Heat roared up his neck with embarrassment.

He should buy these books. Then at least the other three Baxters would welcome him in the shop. He also needed breakfast. He was having a hard time thinking clearly because he hadn't eaten anything this morning before racing off after Miss Baxter - his grandfather's expression of disgust had been such that Felix had turned on his heel in the very door of the breakfast-room and made haste for the stables.

He collected three books and approached the women at the counter. "I shall return soon and purchase these and most likely more. Could you recommend a respectable place to break my fast?"

Miss Baxter delivered the most delightful smile; he wondered if she might be warming to him at last.

His family had offered her a fine meal last night. She might return the favour this morning in her home. He assumed they lived nearby, perhaps in a house behind the shop?

Miss Baxter said, "The Red Lion on the corner is excellent at providing food for travellers at all times of day."

Oh, so she wasn't inviting him to sup with them. While she'd eaten breakfast before leaving the Hall, he wondered if her sisters had done so too. Perhaps they were all early risers and ate at dawn? Goodness, what a frightful thought to awake so early. Still, perhaps it might be time for morning tea and cake, in that case? But all of them were looking at him in silence, not one of them suggesting that a pot of tea and cake would be just the thing. Felix sighed.

His stomach rumbled again, and unless he wanted to

eat the books themselves, he needed to take up their suggestion of eating at the coaching inn.

"In that case, I shall bid you adieu for now," he said, delivering a respectable bow and walking to the door. As he pulled the door open and the bell rang, inspiration struck. "Perhaps I should write my memoirs of my recent travels. I saw little on the subject of Greece on your shelves. My recent experiences could prove enlightening. Are you expecting to receive any books about Greece in the near future?"

Miss Baxter leaned toward him, her hand stretched out, waving. "No."

She obviously wanted to wave him off, but he would not be distracted. He would ask the book binder of the family. She seemed to like him. "Miss Louise, you bind books. Do you think you could bind a book that I might get printed? After you've finished repairing some of my grandfather's books first, of course?"

"Of course, Mr. Yates," Miss Louise said. "The printer we use is on Market Street, Black and Sons, I can recommend…"

Miss Baxter rushed toward him, "Shut the…"

A black ball of fur streaked past his boots.

"… door!"

Oh hells. The cat had run out of the shop and vanished down the street.

Because he'd stood there delivering an extended farewell instead of simply leaving.

Miss Baxter grunted in frustration.

"Oh dear," Felix had wanted to help, not create distress.

"You want to help?" A look of determination came over Miss Baxter's face. "If you want to make yourself useful, go out and find that cat. Otherwise, in nine weeks you'll be helping us find new homes for yet another batch of Crafty's kittens!"

CHAPTER 5

Estelle Baxter Is Not Having It

That cat would be the end of them, Estelle thought as she closed the shop door. The back garden was safe and full of things to distract Crafty, including pots filled with herbs, and a high wall she could not easily get over. The attics connecting the houses were some of her favourite places to play and catch mice. Even the fulling mill farther back was an acceptable place for Crafty to be catty and enjoy the company of the people who worked there. But the front door out to the High Street was where she always found trouble. She terrorised the horses and caused no end of drama.

There were always horses in the high street, and a scared horse could cause terrible problems. People could get hurt. Carriages could break. And the horses themselves could get injured as well.

Not to mention the fact that Crafty was, once again, in heat. They all worked very hard to keep Crafty indoors during those times, but nevertheless at least once a year she would make an escape, find a suitor, and nine weeks later there would be a fresh litter of kittens they'd have to find homes for.

But, instead of seeing three faces of concern, she was met with disdain from her sisters.

They must be upset about the cat, too?

"Why are you so rude to Lord Ferndale's grandson?" Louise asked, looking dreadfully disappointed.

Wait, they were upset with *her*? "He let the cat out!" Estelle answered indignantly. Was it not obvious?

"If you'd been nicer to him," Louise said, "he'd still be in the store and Crafty would still be safely inside."

They were making this her fault? "I wasn't rude to him." She folded her arms across her chest defensively, ignoring the tiny voice of her conscience which pointed out that she'd hardly been polite to him either. "He's the one making fun of me for sport!"

"You were rude," Marie disagreed. "His family gave you a fine dinner last eve and breakfast before you left this morning. He was clearly seeing if you'd return the favour and offer him some tea and cake."

Estelle shook her head. "And we have cake to spare?"

"Well, no. But that's not the point," Marie said. "I can't work you out. He's very charming, clearly he has plenty of blunt, he's going to buy some books, yet you chase him out like he's some street urchin."

Bernadette piped up, "How did he ask you to marry him?"

Estelle made a deep sigh. "That's the problem. He didn't. It was a joke between Lord Fernadale and he. It went on a little too long, that's all. But it was only ever spoken in jest. Of that I'm sure. Lord Ferndale said that Mr Yates should marry me because he - Lord Ferndale, that is - thinks I would treasure his library as it deserves if I were to inherit it, which is the most nonsensical reason to get married I've ever heard, frankly."

She gulped in a huge amount of air to make up for that long, bizarre explanation. Because that's what it was. Bizarre. And nonsensical. "Why Mr Yates went along with it for even a moment, I can't imagine. But to get to the heart of the matter, Mr. Yates never directly asked me. He just asked when we should set the wedding date and started talking about going on a honeymoon to Greece!"

"Oh! Greece would be wonderful for a honeymoon!" Louise exclaimed.

Estelle glared at her. *That* was what Louise chose to fixate on, out of the whole ridiculous situation?

Bernadette said, "He might ask you directly, if you showed a little interest."

Louise and Marie began muttering their agreement that Estelle should show Mr Yates some interest.

Bernadette took this as encouragement. "I think you're mad to turn him down without at least getting to know him a little more. He seems nice, he's obviously rich, he's very handsome, and he clearly likes you. I don't see the problem."

That was the frustrating thing with having such a gap between the eldest and the youngest. Bernadette had such romantic notions, but not much reality to base those notions upon at only eighteen years of age. It wasn't her fault and Estelle didn't want to sound patronising by correcting her.

Louise said, "She makes a good point."

Marie nodded.

Bernadette beamed.

This was so unhelpful. Why were they even having this conversation when there were far more pressing matters to concern themselves with. Like the mountain of debt their father had dumped on them, and their cousin interfering in their lives and threatening to throw them out so he could have the building. "He's unaccustomed to being told 'no'. I could tell that about him yesterday. And he's spoilt."

"So what?" all three replied at once.

Estelle gritted her teeth and decided to ignore them, since they all appeared to have collectively lost their wits when she left them to their own devices for a single night. Pulling up a chair, she reached for the correspondence that had arrived that morning. "There's a great deal here, is this yesterday morning's post as well?"

"No, and don't change the subject," Louise said. "You should get married, before you're too old."

"Ha!" Estelle said, "I'm already far too old, so if anyone is going to get married to get us out of our financial troubles, it will have to be Marie or you, Louise."

"Why can't it be me?" Bernadette asked.

"Because you're the youngest," Estelle replied by reflex. "You're only eighteen. Getting married at eighteen is…"

"Something a lot of people do?" Bernadette stared at her. "Mama was eighteen when she married Pa, Estelle."

"Times were different then," Estelle said, reaching for the correspondence, aware even as she did so that her sisters were not going to let this subject drop.

After all, no serious suitor had ever presented himself to any of them before. And she didn't think any of them had ever dreamed that such a suitor might be as handsome and wealthy as Mr. Felix Yates.

He's not a serious suitor, Estelle reminded herself sternly. For some reason, he'd decided to take his grandfather's silly matchmaking idea and make a great jest of it, which would be all very well if *she* were not the butt of the jest.

The papers in her hands reminded her of serious things. "Father left us in charge of the bookshop, we have our instructions. Running off to marry was not amongst those instructions, were they?"

"If I recall correctly," Louise said, "he told us to use our initiative."

"That's as may be," Estelle said. "Which is why I am calling on all of us to use our initiative and find better ways of helping produce income. The advertisements in The Times are working very well at delivering more customers. We have a great deal of new books and we must let our customers know which titles have recently arrived. Marie, I take it you've completed the inventory of the books that arrived yesterday morning?"

"Nice try," Marie said. "But you know the best way out of our many troubles is if you marry Mr Yates."

The heat searing through Estelle could have set the books in the shop aflame. She loved her sisters dearly, but at this moment they were trying her very last nerve. "Father would be most upset to discover we spent his absence in argument instead of amity."

That had them making soft mutters of agreement. Finally, something was going Estelle's way.

"Speaking of Father," Louise said, "I hope he writes more regularly, so we can keep Cousin Joshua at bay. That was a very unpleasant confrontation."

That brought another round of agreement as well.

"He has left us in a delicate situation," Estelle agreed.

At least there was peace again in France, which gave them one less thing to worry about.

The doorbell rang as new customers arrived. They looked about and smiled as they entered. One lady had a copy of their last advertisement from The Times and enquired about an almanack. Estelle was only too happy to assist them and not have to answer any more questions about marriage and Mr Yates from her inquisitive sisters. She was soon learning about this lovely couple, a Mr and Mrs Craddock, who were journeying north and had made a point of visiting their shop on the way through.

They soon had several titles they wanted to purchase, and promised to visit on their return south after the summer. Estelle wrote their details in their ledger and made a note of the topics they enjoyed.

When she waved them off, Estelle turned around and beamed. "Let's get the next advertisement sent into The

Times this very afternoon, it is definitely worth the expense."

With the front door open, the noise from the street filled their ears. Estelle turned to see Marie with her hands over her ears.

"Sorry Marie. I forget how noisy it gets when the post carriage heads off." She closed the door quickly, wincing in sympathy with her sister. Marie was sensitive to loud noises and would often find a megrim coming on if she was exposed to them for long.

Soon Estelle and her sisters were working through the rest of the correspondence, sorting out orders and requests. The expenses were stacked into another pile, arranged by due-dates. It would be a close run thing to keep ahead of them. Estelle chewed on her lips as she mentally totted up the total owed; a truly terrifying sum. She re-sorted the pile by creditors who could be put off and those who could not.

Marie fulfilled several orders and wrapped them safely, ready to send out with the next mail-coach to London.

"So long as the crates of books keep arriving, we will be fine," Estelle said, more with hope than evidence. "Father's letter said he was heading to Tours next. I can only imagine what might arrive!"

"I just hope he sends a better letter next time," Marie said.

A young lady came into the shop, opening the door so carefully the bell didn't ring. Bernadette put down her stitching and walked over to her. The other three carried on talking as if nothing was happening. This was what they did, they gave Bernadette and her customers privacy.

Louise asked, "Wasn't our mother's family from the Loire region? Isn't Tours close to there? Or am I confusing it with somewhere else?"

"Yes, it was the Loire," Marie said. "Perhaps he might take a detour in book hunting and look up Mama's family?"

Estelle shook her head, "He would have to literally fall over them to notice, he'd be so blinded by the vast array of books."

They shared a giggle at that. Their father had had two great loves in his life, their mother and books. They sometimes suspected he loved books just that little bit more.

"I can't really blame him for going," Estelle said. "I'm still a little cross he didn't take me along. We used to travel all over England on our book hunts."

Louise shrugged. "He said France wasn't safe."

"Yes but Napoleon is in exile, the Terrors are over!" Estelle complained. "I would have been safe by his side. And anyway, our mother was French, Mama taught the language to me as well. I think I could probably even pass as French, if I had to! Certainly better than Father can."

The others shrugged. Estelle continued. "Anyway, Mother was French, and she was fine."

"No she wasn't," Marie said. "She had to flee France, and almost all of her family are dead. I'd hardly call that safe."

"I'm glad she did," Louise added. "If she hadn't, she

would not have met Father and none of us would be here."

They heard the rear door open and close, as Bernadette quietly took their customer to the courtyard to pick herbs.

Marie said, "Perhaps if he finds one of Mama's cousins he might gain local knowledge to help him negotiate good prices. I can only imagine how much extra the French are demanding when an English accent does the asking."

The front doorbell rang and it was a delivery for Louise. She excitedly accepted the small bundle and thanked the man. Then she took herself upstairs to the kitchen. In a short while, acrid smells assailed Estelle and Marie.

Estelle stood up and called out, "Louise! You must shut the door when you make glue, it stinks out the whole shop!"

"Sorry!" Louise called back, "I forgot, and I can't step away as I have to keep stirring."

Estelle ran upstairs and opened the window at the landing, hoping the stairs would act a little like a chimney and draw the smells upwards and out of the building.

From there, she spotted Bernadette and the young woman collecting herbs. The young woman looked miserable and was retching. Poor lass.

"Sorry about the smell," Estelle said, "Louise is making glue again."

Returning downstairs, Estelle firmly closed the door at the bottom of the stairs and held her nose to cover the smell. It was hideous. The only thing for it was to wedge open the shop door to the high street.

Well, the cat had already escaped, so the damage was done.

It only served to remind Estelle of how cross she was with Felix Yates for pretending they were getting married, and for letting the cat out.

It was a close run thing which of the two topics annoyed her the most.

CHAPTER 6

Felix and The Cat

As Miss Baxter closed the bookshop door behind him - almost slammed it on his heel - Felix let out a great sigh.

"I'm making an almighty mull of this," he said to nobody in particular, before turning to look up and down the street, in vain hopes of spotting a large black cat. He had rather thought he'd made a friend in the cat. She'd certainly purred loudly enough, and left her fur on his leg! Glancing back at the door, he met Estelle's eyes briefly through the window before she scowled and turned her back.

"So pretty, even when she's angry," Felix murmured wistfully.

He should not be having so much fun teasing her. It wasn't the right thing to do, obviously. His grandfather had started the whole thing and now he didn't seem able to stop himself.

Well, he really should.

He should be kind. He should help. Properly help, and not just ask if he could.

He *would* help, Felix decided. Starting with getting the cat back.

Where should he even start looking? He sniffed the air, nodding thoughtfully as the scent of cooking beef reached him. What discerning cat wouldn't want to investigate that delicious scent? His stomach rumbled again, and Felix's mind was made up. He'd kill two birds with one stone, hopefully; find that damned cat and find something to fill his stomach!

The tantalising scent turned out to be coming from the Red Lion, where he was regretfully informed that the noonday meal wasn't ready yet, but he could have a slice of cold game pie and a tankard of small beer, if that suited.

By that time Felix would have eaten stale bread and drunk swamp water, so he thanked the innkeeper politely and broke his fast, hoping he did not appear too uncouth as he sat in a corner of the dining-room and stuffed pie into his face as fast as he could get it down.

"I don't suppose a large black cat has been in here this morning?" he asked the maid who brought his beer over.

The maid stared at him, then shook her head. "Mr Haye don't hold with no cats in the Red Lion, sir. They makes him sneeze. We gots to chase them out if we sees them."

"Hm." Felix handed the girl a sixpence and sat back to drink his beer. The bookshop cat - Crafty, he thought Estelle had called her - was presumably smart enough to know where she wasn't wanted. He'd best go looking somewhere else. With a regretful glance at the scant crumbs of pie crust left on his plate, he drained his tankard and left it on the table.

The sooner he found the cat, the sooner he could go back to Estelle and start being actually useful.

Five hours later, Felix was hot, tired, hungry again, and exceedingly frustrated. There were plenty of cats in Hatfield, and a goodly number of them were black, but none of them were the large, sleek animal he'd petted in the bookshop. The locals he spoke to were all quite helpful, pointing him in the direction of whichever black cat they'd happened to see last, but it did mean he did quite a lot of walking, criss-crossing the town in search of the elusive feline.

Hatfield was so much larger than he'd remembered, but it had been a few years since he'd last been in town. Bisected by the Great North Road, it was positively bustling with activity, and not just when the post-coaches came through. In a square to the west of the road he found a busy market well-patronised by the locals. He saw a striped ginger cat sitting on a man's shoulder. Farther down where someone was selling chickens, he saw a dark shape and got his hopes up, but it turned out to be only a shadow. He paused to buy some apples from a grocer, thinking he might take those to Estelle as a peace offering. Ambling along the street munching on one of the apples, he stopped in his tracks as a pair of bright green eyes in a round dark face turned up to him.

The cat let out a querying, "Meow?"

"You!" Felix dropped the apple core and pounced; the cat slid away from his clutching fingers and fled. Felix gave chase, apples toppling from his coat pockets as he ran. "Oh, no you don't!"

He finally cornered the cat in an alley with walls too high for the beast to leap; apparently realising the game was up, the blasted creature sat down and began to wash its tail insouciantly.

"You horrible animal." Grabbing the cat up, Felix tucked it under one arm and strode towards the book-shop. "What a chase you've led me."

The cat purred, entirely unconcerned with Felix's annoyance. Felix smiled at the cat and gave it a chin scratch. It purred, although the purring sounded a little different. Ahhh, that's because he was outside, not in a bookshop where sounds were more muffled.

"And I dropped the apples!" Ah, but there was still one in his pocket, Felix realised, as it bounced against his hip on the opposite side to the cat. He could give that to Estelle, at least. A poor peace offering, but he had to start somewhere.

The door to the bookshop was wide open, perhaps to encourage Crafty to return without hindrance? Being mindful of not letting the cat out again, he kicked the wedge holding the door open and the bell above the door jingled cheerfully as it closed.

He had the cat, and he'd closed the door. He

approached the counter with a broad smile. To his delight, Estelle was the only Baxter sister at the counter at that moment. She looked up at him expectantly, her delightful eyes flashing. It warmed him all the way through, and he rather liked the idea of making her smile more.

All too soon her brows began to crease into a frown.

She should be smiling, he'd returned triumphant!

"I have the cat!" Felix said hastily, depositing it on the counter before Estelle could begin to reproach him again. "And an apple. It's a peace offering. I had more, but I dropped them chasing the cat," he apologised regretfully.

Fine, the apples as a peace offering wasn't going so well, but he had the cat!

Estelle looked from the shiny red apple he had placed beside the cat, to the cat, to Felix, and back to the cat again.

This was not the grateful welcome he'd expected. Perhaps she'd had a troubling day with querulous customers. If that was the case, he'd cheer her up by purchasing a great many more books. Anything to see her smile again.

She puffed out her cheeks and appeared to be trying to think of something to say.

"We have got off on the wrong foot rather," Felix started to say, "And I would like to apologise for making fun at your expense. It was badly done of m..."

Estelle interrupted him, "I'm afraid that's not our cat, Mr Yates."

"I... what?" Felix looked down at the cat, which

looked up at him from those bright green eyes and miaowed again. Exactly the same sound it had made when he almost stood on its tail earlier, he'd have sworn it!

"If I'm not mistaken," Estelle reached out, picked the cat up and turned it around, looking under its tail, before nodding as though satisfied. "Yes. As I thought. This is Charles, one of Crafty's sons. A *male* cat, Mr Yates. And Crafty is a female cat, which I think should have been obvious to you when I noted that if you did not find her, you would need to help us find homes for her kittens."

"Oh."

He hadn't even thought to look under the damned cat's tail.

Utterly deflated, Felix sagged against the counter. "How did you know it wasn't the same cat, even before looking? They are both large, glossy and black, and make the same noises."

How many black cats *were* there in Hatfield?

Estelle sighed and said, "Crafty has a shorter tail than this one. A horse stepped on it, and she lost a couple of inches from the end. And this fellow has a small piece missing from his ear, see?"

Estelle gave Charles a scratch under the chin all the same and this time he made a very different noise to Crafty.

"I can hear it now. He sounds like a phlegmatic old man! Crafty's purr is much more melodic."

Then Estelle did the most extraordinary thing. She delivered a beautiful smile in his direction. It filled him with enough vigour to slay a dragon. In reality, all he had to do was find the right cat.

"I think you'd better return Charles to whence you found him, Mr Yates. And find Crafty. The real one this time." Estelle picked up the apple off the counter, polished it against her skirt for a moment, and held it up. "Thank you for the apple, though," she said. "I was a little peckish." She took a ladylike little bite.

He'd been dismissed. And no surprise, because he'd failed. He'd brought her the wrong cat. At least she was smiling, even if it was to make fun of him. He'd rather like to see her smile again, and he'd like to be the reason for the smiling. He only hoped it was not at his expense next time. But then again, even if it was, he deserved it. Bringing her a male cat! What a chump he was!

With a sigh, Felix scooped the obliging Charles up under his arm again and departed the bookshop with his head hanging low. The door bell tinkled as he opened and closed it.

It seemed he could do absolutely nothing right when it came to helping Miss Baxter.

Hopefully, he would at least be able to return Charles to the spot where he found him without being accused of cat-napping. In broad daylight, no less. A few people were looking at him askance, and he supposed he did look rather foolish parading down the street in his great-coat and top hat with a noisily purring black cat tucked under his arm. This cat left fur strands all over his coat. A good thing the animals did not make him sneeze like the innkeeper!

At least Charles was being quite decent about the whole business and wasn't carrying on and trying to slash holes in his clothing. Felix found the spot where he'd first spotted Charles, set the cat down and gave him a few scratches behind the ears, which the cat accepted with more friendly purrs before slinking off down an alleyway.

"Back to square one," Felix muttered dismally, looking about him and wondering where to look for Crafty now. Or how he would even identify the cat if he did find her, beyond having the sense to look under her tail. Oh yes, her tail was a little shorter than normal. But how long was a normal cat's tail at any rate?

He was outside an apothecary shop, and as he looked about in some despair the door opened and Miss Bernadette Baxter stepped out, a basket over her arm. She smiled when she saw him.

"Good afternoon, Mr Yates."

"Miss Bernadette!" He doffed his hat and made her a polite bow. She closed the shop door and stepped down to the street, and as she did so Felix could not help but notice that she was listing a little to one side, obviously compensating for the weight of her basket. "I say, Miss Bernadette, that basket looks jolly heavy. Would you allow me to carry it for you?"

She hesitated only a moment before saying "That would be very kind of you, Mr Yates. Thank you."

He relieved her of the basket and offered his free arm. To his delight, she tucked her hand into the crook of it with a smile.

"Are you returning to the bookshop, or do you have more stops to make in your shopping? I'm happy to be of assistance," Felix offered, thinking that if he couldn't find their cat, at least he might be of some small use to one of the Baxter sisters.

"I am indeed returning home. You're very kind to offer." She glanced sideways up at him as they walked, chewing on her lower lip a moment before asking gently, "How goes your search for Crafty, Mr Yates?"

"Very ill," he admitted sorrowfully. "I thought I had her and triumphantly presented her to your sister… only to learn that I had instead found Charles. I did not even think to look under the tail!"

Bernadette burst out laughing. She put her free hand to her mouth to genteely suppress the laughter, but giggles bubbled up still and Felix found himself grinning too, amused by his own foolishness.

"I'm afraid Miss Baxter must think me the veriest twit," he confessed, "and I do so want her to think well of me."

Bernadette ceased laughing, though her eyes were still bright with mirth. "Why, Mr Yates?"

"I beg your pardon?"

"Why is it so important to you that Estelle think well of you? We teased her about you a little, I confess, just to see her blush, but the truth is that she is not your equal in consequence. Our father is away and our cousin Joshua would not protect us from so much as a flea, so we must look out for each other. If your intention is to trifle with my sister's affections, I must ask you to cease and go far, far away."

What a serious little thing she was! Giving her the courtesy of taking her seriously, Felix stopped walking and looked Bernadette full in the face.

"While Miss Baxter may have thought my grandfather was jesting when he proposed her as a suitable wife for me, Lord Ferndale says nothing he does not truly mean. If he believes Miss Baxter to be a suitable prospect for my marriage, that is endorsement enough for me… and in truth, it is high time I settled down. My intentions are not trifling, I do assure you."

Bernadette looked at him oddly, and Felix wondered if she had expected him to say something different. She didn't say anything else, though, merely resumed walking, and he had perforce to proceed too or else drag her to a stop.

"Have you bought plenty of books from the shop to at least appear interested in her most favourite thing in the world?" Bernadette asked.

The books! "Oh dear, I keep forgetting. I had her put some aside but we were so distracted with me presenting the wrong cat, and having to return said cat, I did not complete the purchase."

Oh dear, Felix, you are rather making a mess of things.

Bernadette shook her head. "When you come back with the right cat, make sure you buy some books. Then you'll have something more to talk about."

"Thank you, I shall." Her advice was a boon.

Then she delivered even more good information.

"Crafty has a white patch on her chest in the exact shape of a love-heart," Bernadette said finally as they came to a stop at the bookshop door. "Though she has had quite a few kittens who strongly resemble her - as you discovered with Charles - so far as I know, she is the only black cat in Hatfield with that exact marking."

Of course! Only now did he realise he'd seen that very marking when scratching the cat under her chin that morning! What a dolt he was to not remember.

Bernadette said, "And her tail is a little shorter because…"

"… A horse trod on it," he finished.

"Ahhh, so you know about that? Well, good luck finding the real one this time. And when you come back, make sure the door's closed behind you."

Handing Miss Bernadette her basket, Felix once again doffed his hat and bowed to her.

"Thank you, Miss Bernadette, I very much appreciate your guidance."

"Thank you for carrying my basket," she said in response, before nodding and opening the bookshop door. "Good day, Mr Yates," she said over her shoulder.

Aside from his dispiriting task and no luck finding Crafty, it was an otherwise glorious day. Felix had paid much more attention to Hatfield than he had before, and found himself growing fond of the buildings and the ambience. One building in particular.

Alas, he could not return to it until he found the right cat.

His stomach rumbled, reminding him of how late it

was. The sun was low, but it was also high summer, and it would not set for another hour yet. A slice of game pie and an apple had been poor fare compared to what he would usually consume during the day.

"If I were a cat, where would I be?" he asked himself as he walked down another laneway, peering up and down.

He made a heavy sigh of defeat and kicked the ground. A stone flew up and hit an old door lying sideways.

Three cats ran out from behind the door. They were partially black, but had large white patches in various places. Even he could tell at this distance they were the wrong ones.

Harsh shadows stretched across the lane from the setting sun. The day had defeated him. He walked back to the Red Lion with a purpose: he'd eat a quick meal then get a room for the night, so he could rise early and hunt for Crafty.

When he walked in to the Red Lion, he was met with a wall of humanity. The stagecoach had lately arrived and the place was packed with travellers. The aromas of travel-weary humans and cooking smells assailed his senses. He caught sight of the maid he'd spoken with earlier in the day. "Any chance of a room for the night?" he asked.

"'Fraid not. We're all up to the rafters tonight."

He really wasn't having any luck today at all. "Is there anywhere nearby you can recommend?"

"The only one near is The Swan. Ya takes a left at

Salisbury Street. Can't miss it." Then she bustled over to a table and removed people's empty beer tankards, then turned and slapped a man on the arm who pinched her bottom. "We keeps our 'ands to ourselves 'ere, matey. It's not that kind of 'stablishment!"

In another fifteen minutes, thirsty and with swollen feet from walking around most of the day, he found The Swan and rented a room. It was hardly busy, and he really thought his luck had finally turned the corner. Alas, the reason for the inn's lack of clientele soon presented itself. He sat at a long table with many other diners eating the most unpalatable food he'd ever had; a greasy stew of potatoes and a meat he had the terrible suspicion wasn't beef despite the landlord's description, and bread which was stale and hard without even butter to soften it. Even the tiniest villages in Greece offered better sustenance than this. Nobody else appeared to be complaining, but perhaps they were heavier into their cups than he. The ale wasn't as bad as the food, though that wasn't saying much. He should probably have tried for a meal at the Red Lion, even if they didn't have a room for him. Ah well. He knew better now. Tomorrow was another day.

He drank heavily from his tankard, and was at least happy that it was having the effect of softening his tired muscles.

His bed awaited. He only hoped it was of a higher standard than the fare.

It wasn't, of course, but he was too tired to care.

CHAPTER 7

The Bills Mount Up

"Was that Mr Yates with you?" Estelle asked inquisitively as Bernadette came back into the shop, hefting her basket up onto the counter with a gasp of effort. "Has he found Crafty yet?"

"I think you already know that if he had, he would be back in here presenting her to you rather like a dog with a ball he wants you to throw," Bernadette said.

The image her words invoked was so funny Estelle couldn't help but laugh. Mr Yates really was rather like a large amiable hound, eagerly goofy but liable to cause havoc if let off the leash.

"What was he doing with you?" she asked, once she managed to control her giggles.

"He carried my basket, very kindly." Bernadette hesitated briefly before admitting, "I asked him about his intentions towards you."

"You did what!" Estelle clutched at her throat.

This was getting beyond a silly jest if her sisters were getting involved.

"Someone had to!" Bernadette said. "And while he's obviously courting you to please his grandfather, I don't think he's doing so in jest, Estelle. I think you should take him seriously and give him a chance." Hefting the basket up again, Bernadette nodded as though she'd had the last word and set off to the back of the shop.

Drat it, she did have the last word, because Estelle couldn't think of a single thing to say. She sighed, picking up the pile of books Mr Yates had left and said he would come back to pay for. If only he had! Chastellux's *Travels in North America* in two volumes was priced at one pound and five shillings, and there was a Lalande *Voyage en Italie* for sixteen shillings as well as several cheaper volumes. Over three pounds in total, if he did come back to pay for it.

The church bells pealed the hour and Estelle sighed. Four o'clock was when they closed the shop. Getting up from the stool behind the counter, she made her way to the door and opened it to peer up and down the street. No sign of Mr Yates, nor of any other potential customers. Closing the door again, she bolted it and began to reshelve the pile of books, pushing each one back into place on the shelf with perhaps just a little more force than really necessary.

The front of the shop tidy, Estelle extinguished the lamps and made her way upstairs, nose wrinkling as the faint traces of the glue Louise had made earlier assaulted her nose. Louise's bookbinding was very necessary to the shop's continued profitability, but it was a messy, smelly craft.

"Dinner's almost ready, Miss Estelle." Mrs Poole, their housekeeper-companion, looked up from where she was slicing bread at the kitchen table with a kindly smile. "Why don't you go and wash up."

Someone had filled the water jug in her room again, Estelle discovered gratefully when she made her way there, and she poured fresh water into the bowl, damp-ened a cloth and wiped her face and hands. For a moment she thought of skipping dinner and falling into bed. The servings would be small. One less mouth to feed would give the others a little more. She was about to remove her shoes when Mrs Poole called her down.

It would be rude not to attend. She would serve herself last and make sure the others had enough first. Perhaps she could get Felix to take her to lunch tomor-row, to make up for the little they had in the house.

"You're not eating much, Estelle." Mrs Poole noticed.

"I must be too tired," she said, feeling worn down from the last day. "I did have a large meal last night with Lord Ferndale, and I'm probably still full from breakfast this morning." It wasn't entirely a lie, she had eaten very well.

Louise piped up, "Speaking of Ferndale, I will have a couple of his books ready by tomorrow. They are in the vice now and the glue will be set nicely by the morning."

Estelle smiled at her sister. "Maybe it's the glue smell that's stolen my appetite. It truly does stink."

Louise shrugged and said, "I'm used to it."

Bernadette then said, "When Mr Yates comes back, he can take Lord Ferndale's books with him, and pay the account at the same time."

"And he can purchase the ones he took from the shelves," Marie noted.

"Oh! I put them back," Estelle said.

Cries of "why?" and "whatever for?" filled the small room.

"There seemed little point in having them remain on the counter. He had ample opportunity to purchase them throughout the day, and he did not. I assumed he didn't want them."

Bernadette rolled her eyes. "You're a terrible saleswoman."

"Worse than me," Marie said.

Ouch! Marie was great with numbers and music, but not with people.

"I don't mean to add to the family's woes," Mrs Poole said diffidently, "but the butcher's account is due."

That must be why there was no meat on the table this evening. With a deep sigh, Estelle nodded to her sisters and realised she'd need to put her politeness aside and push Mr Yates to purchase more books. Her sisters' stomachs depended on it.

"By the way, has anyone seen Crafty? She wasn't yowling at me while I prepared the meal tonight," Mrs Poole said.

"Mr Yates let her out onto the High Street," Estelle said.

"Oh dear," Mrs Poole said. "In that case, I'd be adding

several more books to his pile and demanding immediate payment. Sure as night follows day, that cat will deliver more kittens in due course."

Louise said, "I'm surprised you haven't found a treatment for that, Bernadette."

The youngest Baxter sister shook her head and said, "Have you tried getting herbs into a cat? It's like Hercules wrestling the Nemean lion!"

The room filled with much-needed laughter.

The day dawned brightly through the open window next to Estelle's bed. The daily bustle from outside was her alarm clock. Estelle rose early and dressed for work. At the foot of the stairs she checked the hessian and realised it hadn't been shredded because Crafty was still missing. Just in case the cat had returned, she checked for eviscerated mice behind the counter.

No bodies, which was a good thing because it was one less mess to clean up. Alas, it did provide yet more evidence that Crafty had spent the entire night at liberty and had not come home through Estelle's bedroom window.

She pulled open the front door and scanned the length of the street. Horses were being walked by grooms, and a stagecoach pulled in, loaded with people and packages. There was no cat taunting them. Mixed blessings, Estelle sighed to herself.

"There you are," Louise said from behind. "Any sign of the cat?"

"Alas," Estelle said with another sigh.

"Hope she comes back soon. I heard mice in the ceiling last night."

They both shuddered in unison.

It was as if the mice had their own gossip network and spread the word whenever Crafty took one of her unauthorised leaves of absence.

"I'm off to the tanners for new leather for the books Lord Ferndale needs repaired," Louise said, "I don't suppose I'll be able to pay them at the same time?"

"There might be enough," Estelle said, leading her sister back into the shop and closing the door behind them. She searched the small tins behind the counter and counted various coins. "How much do you think it will be?" It was starting to look scant already. She'd come home with Lord Ferndale's payment for his rare book, but she hadn't taken an advance on the books he wanted repaired. Well, she hadn't needed to, he reliably paid upon delivery.

But lately, it felt as if money had wings and flew out the door faster than it came in. She sighed, beginning to stack coins to make up the total Louise had named.

"The tanner is generous with terms, I can ask if we could pay him once Mr Yates pays for those books," Louise suggested.

Yet another reason to ask for Felix to buy more books. Being pushy with sales was something that never sat comfortably with her. Her father had never had those kinds of qualms. Why should he? He was a man running a business. The sisters had always been in the shop, of course, but it was their father who'd mostly handled the money.

"No, you need more leather. No leather, no bound books, no money coming in. Here you are."

"Estelle?" Louise looked thoughtful as she picked up the coins and put them into her pocket.

"Yes?"

"Why are you running a shop when you hate asking people for money?"

"Do I really?" she asked back.

"Yes. You do. Bernadette has no trouble at all, by the way. She asks for money or payment in kind up front with the herbs."

"She does?" Goodness, how daring!

"And they pay her, those who can. Not much, mind, but they do pay. Maybe ask her for money for any other due accounts. She might have some put by."

Louise headed upstairs and Estelle stood there in the shop giving herself a stern talking to. She had to be more forthright asking for money, no matter how uncomfortable it made her. The rest of the family relied upon her! And Bernadette was rarely paid in coin, no matter what Louise said. Estelle was well aware that at least half the produce on their table had been provided to Bernadette from folks who hadn't cash to spare, but could give a few potatoes or a fish they'd caught in the river.

Well, Estelle would start with Mr Yates. Yes, he'd be her first triumph. She retrieved the books she'd put back last night, and selected a couple more along the same vein. Then she added up the total, made a small note and wrapped them all in some string, ready to hand over when he should return.

"Post for you, Miss Baxter." Mr Thomas, the head porter from the Red Lion, poked his head in the door.

"Parcels?"

"No, just some letters." Mr Thomas put them on the counter and looked about. "Is Mrs Poole about this morning?" he asked in a too-casual voice.

Estelle hid a smile behind the letters as she picked them up. Mr Thomas' unrequited adoration for Mrs Poole was something of a standing joke for the Baxters. The housekeeper bore their gentle teasing in good part, though Estelle sometimes wondered if Mrs Poole had the freedom to do as she pleased, whether she would have encouraged the ostler's suit. Mr Thomas made more money than one might have expected, tips from well-heeled travellers lining his pockets to the extent that he owned a little cottage a few streets away.

"I'm sorry, Mr Thomas, she went out early. Perhaps you'll see her walking back a little later."

"Per'aps," Mr Thomas said, drooping a little. "Well. You 'ave a good day now, Miss Baxter. If

any rich gentry come along, I'll be sure to tell them to come and buy books!"

"I appreciate that, Mr Thomas." A thought struck Estelle. "You can tell Mr Yates to come in and pay for the ones he chose!"

"Mr Yates?"

"The tall blond gentleman who helped carry the books in when that crate broke the other morning."

"Oh, 'im. Ain't seen 'im."

"He didn't stay at the Red Lion last night?"

"No, Miss Baxter." Thomas shook his head, before touching his cap and taking himself off.

"Well. Mr Yates must have ridden back to Ferndale Hall in the dark." Estelle shook her head. "Silly man." She hadn't seen much of a moon last night. It would be one thing to travel that road after dark in a carriage well hung-about with lamps, but quite another for a man alone on a horse! "I hope he didn't break his fool neck," she murmured, finding her letter-opener and beginning to open the letters. All three were from regular clients, asking that she look out for particular books for them; Estelle made a face as she read down the lists. Very rare and expensive books, which would be helpful for their business. Unfortunately none of them were in stock.

They kept a ledger of the books to keep an eye out for, and the clients who were looking for them. Dipping a quill, Estelle carefully transcribed the details from the letters, sanding the ink to dry before setting her quill down.

The shop bell tinkled, and she glanced up, smiling as she saw a familiar face. Young Ruth Millings, the vicar's daughter, a sweet girl who loved to read and often stopped by the bookshop. Her father was very strict and gave her no pin money whatsoever, so the Baxters had long since begun allowing Ruth to read whatever she wished in the shop in exchange for her helping out with some small tasks.

"Good morning, Miss Baxter," Ruth said in a cheerful but quiet voice, taking off her bonnet. "What can I do?"

"Some dusting, perhaps, and the floor needs sweeping," Estelle said, thinking that wouldn't take too long and then Ruth would be able to find a quiet corner and sit down with whatever book she wished to read.

"I passed by the printer's shop on my way here and Mr Black asked me if I'd give you this." Ruth handed over a piece of paper, folded over and a drop of wax added on the fold to seal it.

Estelle winced on the inside as she took the paper, but she kept her expression unconcerned as she nodded to Ruth. "Thank you so much."

Ruth collected a duster from under the counter and disappeared back among the shelves, humming softly to herself. Estelle waited until she was out of sight before cracking the seal on the note from the printer.

"Eek," she muttered as she stared down at the kindly-worded note and the distressingly large sum written at the bottom of the paper; the total amount Baxter's owed to the printer.

A large proportion of Baxter's daily income came from the sale of periodicals and pamphlets printed locally. The printer had to be paid, or the bookshop simply wouldn't have the goods to sell. Goods that people wanted.

"You look worried." A voice startled her, and Estelle gasped and dropped the note. Marie stood in front of the counter, brows raised. "I'm sorry, I didn't mean to scare you."

"Quite all right." Estelle picked up the note and held it out to her sister.

Marie pushed her glasses up her nose and read the note, pursing her lips. "Gosh. Twenty-two pounds. That's a lot of money."

"And I just gave most of what we had to Louise to pay the tanner," Estelle said glumly. "Even if she gets all those books Lord Ferndale wants bound up and we deliver them straight away, the payment still won't cover the whole bill."

Marie hummed thoughtfully, coming around the counter and pulling the accounts ledger from the stack. "How much did you give Louise?"

"Four pounds and eight shillings," Estelle said, watching as Marie took the quill and wrote in the amount.

"If only Father hadn't borrowed quite so much money to take to France with him," Marie murmured, and Estelle nodded in agreement. Matthew Baxter had good reason for doing so, of course; they quite understood that the current instability in France meant cash upfront was the only payment many people would accept. Purchasing rare books, not to mention his travel costs, would not be cheap. But the loan had left his daughters in a precarious position, needing to generate constant income to pay not only the bookshop's regular bills but also keep up payments on the bank loans.

"I think we can find about half of it now," Marie said

at last, lifting her head from the ledger. "If they'd accept a partial payment, with the promise to pay in full once Lord Ferndale pays for his order."

"I'm sure they would," Estelle said in relief. "They are always very obliging, and we do put so much business their way."

"Without us, I'm not sure they'd *have* a business," Marie said dryly. "I'll gather up the money and get Bernadette to take it around. The printer's son is quite sweet on her."

"He's fifteen!" Estelle said, amused.

"Doesn't stop his eyes from being out on stalks whenever Bernadette smiles in his direction." Marie shut the ledger with a snap. The bell tinkled and two ladies came in, coming straight to the counter to ask if the latest fashion magazines had arrived from London. Estelle tried not to leap out of her seat to assist them.

"Certainly, Mrs Pharell, Miss Johnson! Right this way."

The day passed much as days usually did in the bookshop, with a steady trickle of customers spending small amounts. Bernadette went out to drop off the payment to the printer and came back with the good news that the printer was happy to wait until the end of the month for the rest.

"It's the twenty-second," Estelle said, counting rapidly

on her fingers. "And there are only thirty days in June, so that's… eight days."

"By which time Mr Yates will have paid for that lovely pile of books and Louise will have finished her commission for Lord Ferndale," Bernadette said cheerfully. "So we'll have the money!"

"For *that* bill," Estelle muttered gloomily as Bernadette took herself off again. She mustered a thin smile as the door opened and a well-dressed lady and gentleman entered. Taking a short break while their horses were changed, Estelle guessed, assessing the value of their clothes with a single comprehensive glance. She smiled more welcomingly.

"Good afternoon sir, madam! Welcome to Baxter's Fine Books. Is there anything I may assist you with today?"

It transpired that the couple were commencing a long journey to Scotland to visit family, and both had left London without adequate reading material. Estelle was delighted to help the lady to a selection of Minerva Press novels, and the gentleman to an expensively bound copy of Warner's *History of the Rebellion and Civil Wars in Ireland*, though from the amount of input the gentleman had into his wife's selection of novels, she rather thought the history might remain untouched during their travels. The couple paid a little over four pounds for their haul of books without quibbling or asking for a discount, and Estelle wrapped the parcel for them with a happy smile and many well-wishes for their travels.

"Well, that makes the day rather better," she

murmured, re-counting the coins and banknotes before noting the sale in the ledger. She cast an annoyed look at the large pile of books still sitting on the counter, awaiting the return of Mr Yates.

"He's probably not coming back at all," Estelle said loudly.

"Who, Miss Baxter!"

Estelle nearly jumped out of her skin, she'd forgotten Ruth was in the shop. "Good grief, you startled me! I didn't realise you were still here." Hand over her wildly thumping heart, Estelle studied the younger girl. Ruth Millings was only fourteen, but she was quite the prettiest creature Estelle had ever seen, with wheat-gold curls, wide blue eyes and a heart-shaped face.

"I do beg your pardon, Miss Baxter. I was reading." A light flush rose on Ruth's lovely face. "I just heard the clock chime four o'clock, though, I had best be off home."

"Indeed. Thank you for your help," Estelle said, though she didn't think Ruth had done much. Probably sequestered herself in a quiet corner with one of the novels from the circulating shelf. Poor girl. Ruth's father was so strict he wouldn't even allow her a subscription to their small circulating library, and allowed only the occasional purchase of a book he considered to be "sufficiently improving" to his daughter's mind. These were usually some deadly dull sermons or treatises on why women were born to be subservient to men.

Estelle locked the bookshop door after Ruth left, extinguished the lamp and made her way up the stairs to join her sisters. Dinner tonight was vegetable soup, from the smell of it, probably mostly potatoes and carrots from their own garden with an onion or two and a handful of herbs to at least make it a little less bland. Estelle fingered the money in her pocket, the money the well-heeled couple had paid for their books, and figured that they could at least pay the butcher and get some meat for tomorrow night's dinner.

She opened her mouth to tell the others about the sale, but Mrs Poole spoke first. "At least we'll dine better tomorrow night, my dears."

Estelle blinked in confusion as her sisters all nodded in sage agreement.

"I beg your pardon?" she said.

"The Assembly!" Bernadette paused with her spoon halfway to her mouth, staring at Estelle. "The Midsummer Assembly? It's tomorrow night?"

"Midsummer's Day was yesterday," Marie noted pedantically, "but they decided to hold the Assembly on Friday night."

The Midsummer Assembly was a Hatfield tradition. Estelle had missed the last two years, away with her father on book-buying expeditions, and hadn't thought much of the ones before that which she'd attended. They were jolly occasions, and there was dancing, but her chances of forming any attachments had always been slim. Hatfield simply didn't have that many people. Looking around at the excited anticipation on her sisters' faces, she hated to dampen their joy, but... "We don't have suitable dresses," she said.

"Of course we do!" Bernadette actually laughed.

"Miss Yates sent over some of hers weeks and weeks ago. You've been too busy, but we altered one for you."

The sneaky old dear! Estelle had thought Miss Yates was being overly generous, and hadn't mentioned the clothes again at breakfast, hoping they would be forgotten. All this time, she'd already sent them!

It wouldn't be difficult to make a dress for her, as she and Marie were almost identical in height and form. It was so kind of her sisters to make an extra dress.

She thought of another objection. "There's a cost. Two shillings a head, isn't it? We really can't afford it!"

"My dear, it's not a choice." To her surprise, Mrs Poole interrupted the conversation. "The funds go to benefit the Hatfield Poor Society, and I'm on the committee. I must go, and it will look very odd if I don't bring you girls along with me. I'll pay, if you are so tight for funds…"

"Absolutely not." Estelle could not possibly allow Mrs Poole to pay for them. They paid *her*, not the other way about. Oh, if only her father hadn't borrowed quite so much money!

And if only he was able to send crates of books home more regularly!

Reluctantly, she put her hand into her pocket, drew it out and placed the little pile of coins and banknotes on the table. "A couple came into the bookshop today, and bought several books. I suppose we could use a little bit of the money to attend…"

"Will your Mr Yates be there?" Bernadette asked.

Heat stole through Estelle's face. Mr Yates was not 'hers' at all, but if she pointed that out it would only bring on another round of teasing. She managed an, "I am not sure," and hoped the matter would quickly die.

Mrs Poole spoke up, "Miss Yates will be there, of course. She started the committee. And Lord Ferndale is a patron, so he'll be there. I'm confident young Mr Yates will be in attendance."

Bernadette's eyes shone brightly as she turned to Estelle. "You must dance with him at least twice. It shall be a jolly scandal!"

Feeling cheeky, Estelle said, "I suppose if I danced with him four times, the town would never hear the end of it!"

CHAPTER 8

Felix Isn't A Quitter

Having spent a miserable night in an uncomfortably hard and lumpy bed with a draft blowing on him the whole night, Felix fled The Swan not long after dawn. He made his way back to the Red Lion and was able to obtain a decent breakfast, at least, though the dining room was deplorably packed with other guests. Finishing his eggs, sausage and bread, he paid his shot and debated what to do next. He suspected it was likely to be another fruitless day of looking for the darned cat. First, though, he really should go and get some fresh clothes - he'd only brought one change of linen in his saddlebags, and he would rather like a bath too. The bed at The Swan had been none too clean.

Mind made up, he pushed back from the table and stood up. He'd ride back to Ferndale Hall, bathe and change, pack some more clothes and be back in Hatfield within a few hours to resume searching for Estelle's cat.

His plans immediately fell to pieces when his grandfather discovered him dressing after completing his ablutions.

"There you are, Felix! I missed you last night at supper. Have you been entertaining yourself in Hatfield?"

Quite the opposite. Hatfield seemed to be entertaining itself at his expense. "Grandpapa, it's lovely to see you, but I cannot remain. I am on a mission!"

"Excellent!" the old man clapped his hands together with glee. "Has she accepted you?"

"Ah, not yet. You're getting ahead of yourself. First, I must retrieve a cat."

Silence hung in the air between them for a while, until his grandfather said, "Not sure I'm familiar with that phrase. Is it the new variation of 'slaying a dragon' to win the heart of a fair maiden?"

Felix made a wry chuckle. "It could well be. Their cat, Crafty, accidentally ran out onto the High Street and she got away. Miss Baxter has entrusted me to find her and bring her safely home."

The old man smirked. "Entrusted, demanded, same difference."

Felix's shoulders sagged. "Demanded is perhaps the more accurate description. However, I have omitted pertinent information. I was the one to let the cat out, so I must bring her home."

His grandfather laughed directly at him, and Felix deserved his derision.

"That seems fair. And I take it you accepted this task after you bought multiple books from the store, discovered how much you have in common with each other, dropped to bended knee and asked her to marry you?"

Felix pressed his lips together in frustration.

His grandfather needled him even more. "You gave up? That's not the Ferndale way!"

"I did not give up. Rome wasn't built in a day, and all that. I have not given up. I simply …" he didn't know what he'd done. He scratched his neck in thought. He still hadn't bought the books, which was a terrible oversight.

Well, he hadn't thought it would take so long to find that blasted cat!

Grandpapa said, "You didn't give up because you have barely started, is that what I'm hearing?"

The old man could be so infuriatingly accurate at times.

"All will be well once I find Crafty's whereabouts. Then I shall win the heart of the fair maiden." He made an exaggerated bow to his grandfather.

Instead of seeing a smile on the old man's face, he saw a frown. "Well? Don't just stand about pontificating! Pack your things and get to it!"

"That was the plan, Grandfather. If you'll excuse me."

"Is that Felix?" a female voice called from outside his door. "Don't you dare send him off again without a decent meal in his belly, brother! And I want to hear all about how your courtship of Miss Baxter is proceeding!"

"It would proceed a great deal better if I wasn't being pressed at every turn," Felix muttered under his breath, but aloud he called back; "Yes, Aunt Florence, I shall certainly stay for dinner!"

It would still be light enough after dinner for him to ride back to Hatfield tonight, he thought. Although… perhaps he should have reserved a room at the Red Lion before he left, it suddenly occurred to him. He shrank from the thought of another night at The Swan.

"I'll stay the night," he decided. "Go back in the morning. Take a room at the Red Lion for a few days, until I find the cat."

"Crafty might have made her way home on her own by then," his grandfather pointed out.

For a moment, Felix was cheered by the idea, but then his shoulders sank again. Yes, Estelle would have her cat back, but if Felix wasn't the one to deliver the elusive feline, it wouldn't make her look any more kindly upon him. He'd have to find some other way to win her favour. Well, he'd buy a trunkload of books, that would surely help?

Felix enjoyed an expansive breakfast the following morning and was packed and ready to head back to Hatfield. Grandpapa walked out to the stables with him. "Now that you're back, it would be good for you to familiarise yourself with the duties of the barony.

It was as if someone had tipped a bucket of cold water on Felix. "You're not ill, are you?" he asked in sudden terror.

"What?" his grandfather laughed with shock. "Not in

the slightest. But you need to learn about what's involved. May as well make a start."

"What aren't you telling me?" His grandfather had always been old, obviously, but was he looking tired? Felix saw no hints of frailty about him. But perhaps he hadn't been paying attention?

"I'm fine. But I do need some help. The town council meetings can be a trial, and I feel like I'm being boxed in. I think you should attend with me at the next one, and start taking on some of the duties that will one day be yours."

It started to make sense to Felix; this must be why the marriage chatter had started up so suddenly. His grandfather must be hiding his poor health. "I would be honoured to assist in any way you see fit," he said, suddenly feeling the weight of responsibility.

Felix mounted his horse and the groom attached the saddle bag. His grandfather's request replayed in his head as Hatfield came back into view. He would not let the family down.

That meant he would not let Miss Estelle Baxter down either.

From his position high up on horseback, he had a better view of things, and kept a keen eye out for any black cats with shorter tails and heart-shaped white patches on their chest.

His saddle was making him itchy this morning, and he wriggled uncomfortably, wondering if the groom who cleaned it yesterday had used some new type of leather oil or something. He was used to spending hours and even days in the saddle after spending so much time travelling, but today he could not wait to get down from his horse. What a strange sensation that was. Perhaps he was actually falling for Miss Baxter? Perhaps this unease was the result of forming romantic attachments. How fascinating!

He was glad to dismount at the stables behind the Red Lion, and leave his horse with the grooms to care for. He tried his luck again to see about a room for the night and was delighted that they had one!

"I'll take it for a week," he announced, and paid in advance.

It was a top floor room, so he had to climb several flights of stairs, but the thought of not having to return to The Swan any time soon filled him with lightness. This had to be *A Good Sign* that things were playing out in his favour, especially if he needed to remain in town to keep searching for Crafty.

The close proximity to Baxter's Fine Books also played its part. The dormer window looked out across the rooftops towards Miss Baxter and her sisters.

He gave the porter a coin for his troubles when the man brought up his bag, and set about washing his hands and face after his ride. A cool breeze flowed through from the two open windows, bringing the smells of the hotel into his room. Hops, roasted vegetables and pastries. There was also something freshly earthy and … yes, the smells of the street included fresh horse droppings. He closed the windows and turned to the bed, thinking he might have a short rest before resuming his search.

Were his eyes playing tricks? There on the dark brown cover was a round black lump. The black lump opened her green eyes and miaowed. Then she stretched her body and made a little squeak of effort.

Felix reached for her. "Crafty?"

The cat made a miaow, as if she recognised her name.

He gave her a scritch under her ears and she leaned into it, purring into the bargain. It certainly had the same tone as the cat from the shop. He rubbed the top of her head and then checked the front of her chest.

His heart leapt into his throat. There was an undeniable white patch right there. Was it shaped like a heart? It was hard to tell with the cat still in her prone position.

He patted her again down the length of her body. She flicked her tail. Was it shorter than usual? That still eluded him. How short was a shorter tail?

His own heart beating faster, Felix lifted her up and examined her by the light of the window. It was indeed a heart shaped patch on her chest.

"Crafty!" he cried out. He hugged the cat close and looked out the window, over the rooftops to the Baxters' abode.

He couldn't wait to see the expression on Estelle's face when he returned triumphant.

Crafty did not appear particularly pleased to be hugged, nor to be carried down the stairs and out of the inn under his arm. He recalled the serving maid who said the landlord was allergic to cats, so made sure to keep the cat well out of Mr Haye's sight.

"You are a good deal less obliging than your son,"

Felix told the cat, unhooking an exceedingly sharp claw from the back of his hand. "Still, your mistress will be pleased to see you, and I am her most devoted servant, though apparently I'm to shed blood for the privilege of serving her." He managed to get the bookshop door open and step inside with Crafty still secured under his arm, though she twisted about and tried to climb up his lapels, caterwauling loudly.

"Crafty!" Estelle cried out with delight, coming out from behind the counter.

Felix closed the door and leaned back firmly against it before releasing the cat, who left yet one more scratch down his hand before leaping down and streaking away among the bookshelves.

"Please tell me that actually was your cat," he begged Estelle, "and I did not kidnap yet another unfortunate creature?"

"That was definitely Crafty." Estelle actually smiled at him! Lord have mercy, she was so pretty when she smiled, Felix wanted to swoon at her feet. He might well swoon from the stinging in his hand where the cat had drawn blood.

"Well done, Mr Yates; where did you find her?"

Her voice was music to his soul. "She was asleep on my bed."

Estelle blinked and cocked her head at him, obviously bemused.

"I've taken a room at the Red Lion," Felix elaborated. "It was merely a lucky coincidence, I suppose, that Crafty had chosen that particular bed to lie on."

"Crafty's not permitted in the Red Lion; cats make Mr Haye sneeze. You're very fortunate indeed that nobody shooed her out before you could find her, Mr Yates. Unfortunately, since she was out for two nights and I highly doubt she was sleeping in that room this whole time, she has undoubtedly been, ah, *visiting* with her paramours."

"Oh." Felix realised what Estelle was getting at. "Kittens?"

"In about nine weeks. Yes. Kittens."

"Well." Felix straightened up and put on what he hoped was his most earnest and trustworthy expression. "I am an honourable man, Miss Baxter; I shall do the right thing by your cat, since I feel responsible for the situation. I shall endeavour to find good homes for her offspring."

"I appreciate your valour," she said, still beaming.

Her smile filled him with a warm inner glow. But the stinging sensation burned strongly on his hand where Crafty had ploughed a red line through his skin.

Miss Baxter looked at his injury and said, "It appears you have paid a heavy price. Let's have a look at that."

The words, "It is but a scratch," were on his lips but he shut them hard the moment she took his hand in hers.

The touch of her hands upon his tender skin sent his heart soaring. Her gentle caresses soothing his soul. He decided to say nothing at all lest he break the enchantment.

Miss Baxter tisked and slowly shook her head. "I'll get some balm so it doesn't get any worse. Wollstonecraft has cut deeply."

"Er, Wollstonecraft?"

"Yes." Miss Baxter looked directly into his eyes - still holding his hands - and blinked long lashes. "It's her full name, but we only call her that when she's been naughty. And she's been incredibly naughty doing this to you." Then Miss Baxter looked about the shop and caught sight of the creature on the top of a shelf. "It's straight to bed for you, Wollstonecraft, with no supper. You hear me?"

Heart hammering against his chest, Felix could only stand there and hope no customers would enter the store to interrupt them.

His good luck continued as Miss Baxter called out to Marie to mind the shop so they could move to the kitchen upstairs to tend his wounds. He followed her up the narrow stairs at the back of the shop and into a surprisingly large kitchen area, well-lit by sunlight pouring in through a tall window. After the dimly lamplit shop, he had to blink a few times for his eyes to adjust to the brightness.

"Sit, sit." Estelle urged him to take a seat at the table, and Felix sat down and let her wash his hand with a clean rag and some water, and then smear some eye-wateringly smelly yellow balm on the scratches.

Her hands were caressing him the whole time, and he nearly stopped breathing.

"Here." She dispensed a little of the balm into a small vial and stoppered it, handing it to him. "Rub a little of this in twice a day until the scratches are completely healed. Come back and see me again if you begin to feel feverish at all."

Felix looked at the dresser on the east wall of the kitchen when she put the pot back on a shelf. There were rows and rows of pots and bottles, bundles of dried herbs hanging up, and none of them looked as though they belonged in a kitchen.

"You're interested in herbs?" he asked curiously as Estelle placed the kettle on the stove.

Estelle paused for a moment, glanced over at him. "Somewhat," she said, a little evasively. "My mother taught me. It's Bernadette's passion really, but we all know the basics."

"Undoubtedly a very useful skill," he said honestly, intrigued by yet another facet to her. Miss Baxter was a woman with a great many talents.

"Tea?" Estelle offered.

"I should love a cup of tea. With honey, if you have any."

"Do you have a sweet tooth, Mr Yates? I did notice that you certainly did justice to the desserts served at Ferndale Hall."

He admitted that he did. It was lovely to be able to sit and merely watch her as she moved about the kitchen, her hands deft as she took down two cups and a teapot, spooned tea leaves and placed a pot of honey on the table. She also opened a biscuit jar and pushed it in front of him, with an apology that she had no cake to offer.

"But these smell delicious. Caraway seed?" Felix nibbled at the biscuit and found it excellent, spicy, buttery and crumbly. "Did you make them?"

"Not I. Mrs Poole, who is our housekeeper-companion

- she lives with us, to give us countenance while Papa is away." Estelle looked briefly conscious. "I probably shouldn't be alone with you, actually…"

"We might be forced to marry?" He grinned, to lighten the moment. "I certainly wouldn't mind."

"Has anyone ever told you that you are a menace, Mr Yates?" Her words might have been damning, but she delivered them so sweetly his heart swelled. She was smiling too, though, as she used a hook to swing the kettle off the hot stove and pour steaming water into the teapot.

"Oh, frequently," he said cheerfully. "But my charm wins most people over in the end."

She actually laughed before taking a seat at the table and reaching for a biscuit herself. They shared a cup of tea and a little inconsequential chatter before Estelle said that she should really be getting back to the shop.

He committed the scene to memory, as he watched her sip tea and nibble on her biscuit. He drank his tea deliberately slowly, to prolong their time together.

Eventually though, he ran out of tea and she did not offer a second cup.

Also, he was trying very hard to sit still, but his seat itched and he had not the faintest idea if it was the result of the chair or himself. Too afraid to look, he did his best to ignore it.

"Thank you, Miss Baxter, for both the sustenance and the medical attention." Felix rose politely and bowed to her. "And now that I have completed my mission and returned your cat, I can complete my purchase of books. I still need to look for a gift for Grandfather's birthday next month, too; perhaps you can make some suggestions?"

Estelle looked quite delighted at these remarks, and said that of course she could help him. "I put aside another few books I thought might interest you," she said as they descended the stairs back into the shop. "You're under no obligation to take them, of course…"

"One can never have too many books, Miss Baxter. Unless I already own them, I have no doubt I'll find them of interest."

Estelle showed him the rather large pile of books on the counter. Felix only saw one he already owned, which he removed regretfully from the stack. "That's an interesting choice," he murmured, picking up Shaw's *Travels Into Barbary*. "Do you have any other books on Barbary, or Egypt perhaps?"

"A very good copy of Norden's *Egypt and Nubia*, two volumes in one. On elephant paper!" Estelle took a ring of keys from her belt and unlocked a bookcase at one side of the counter. "One of the best books we have. It might make a suitable gift for your grandfather, if your budget stretches to it."

"Dare I even ask how much?" It was a large, stunningly beautiful book, bound in hand-tooled Russia calf leather.

"Thirteen pounds."

Felix let out a low whistle, but he set the book on the counter and opened it carefully, leafing through a few of the thick pages, admiring the beautifully printed plates. "Worth it, I dare say. This is a rare book, Miss Baxter, and in magnificent condition. I'm a little surprised my grand-father hasn't already bought it."

"He doesn't know about it yet." Estelle smirked a little. "It arrived in the crate of books my father shipped from France - the books you helped carry in a few days ago. The book I delivered to Lord Ferndale was one he'd been searching for, for a long while. We hadn't catalogued this one at that point. I was planning to show it to him next time he called into the shop."

"Well, it won't be here." Felix closed the book. "Wrap it well for me, would you? It'll be a marvellous surprise for his birthday." And he was making Estelle happy too by spending lots of money on books, he thought as she picked up the book with a wide smile. A winning situation all around.

In fact, now that he was here, he wanted to add more to the account, if it meant more beautiful smiles from Miss Baxter.

He returned to the shelf of travelogues to browse some more, bidding a polite good morning to Miss Bernadette as she entered the shop in company with another woman. Miss Bernadette nodded in return, but made no effort to introduce her companion to him, indeed hurrying the other woman past him to the back of the shop.

"Wait here. I'll have it for you in a moment," he heard Bernadette say, before the sound of feet pattered away up the stairs.

The woman stood at the foot of the stairs, head bowed, twisting her hands together anxiously. She looked like a farmwife, not really the sort of person he'd expect to see in a bookshop, and indeed she wasn't looking at the books at all, Felix couldn't help but notice.

Bernadette returned down the stairs and pressed a packet into the woman's hands, saying to her in a low voice, "There are five portions here. Brew a tea and take it morning and night. Now, you're sure you haven't quickened?"

"Oh yes, Miss Bernadette. Only missed my courses by a week." The woman clutched the packet to her. "I can't have another one. We've too many mouths to feed as it is."

Oh. Those sorts of herbs. Felix turned away discreetly as Bernadette reassured the woman she was doing the right thing and escorted her out of the shop.

"Bernadette!" His sharp ears picked up Estelle hissing at her sister. "You must be more careful!" She was speaking French, he registered in sudden surprise. Felix was fluent in French, having been tutored since he was small in the modern languages by his grandfather. Estelle's French might be even better than his though, he thought as she went on, rapid and colloquial, her accent perfect. Where did a young woman from Hertfordshire learn to speak French like that?

Curiosity piqued, he made his way back to the counter with two more books in hand. Bernadette fled with only a quick sideways glance at him; he offered what he hoped was a reassuring smile. Bernadette was engaged in women's business which was absolutely none of his, he judged.

"You speak excellent French," he noted as Estelle packed up his books, wrapping them carefully in brown paper. "Where did you learn it, and with such a good accent?"

"At my mother's knee." Estelle tied a coarse twine around one package, securing it with a firm knot. "She was French, from the Loire Valley. Papa met her there in 1785, before the Revolution began, and they married and came back to England. A good thing too. Her parents were aristocratic. We haven't heard from any of her family, save for one distant cousin, in a very long time."

"I'm so sorry. Is your mother still alive?"

Estelle shook her head, sorrow passing across her face. "She passed five years ago."

"You must miss her very much," Felix said gently. He felt responsible for the shadow of grief that crossed her pretty face.

"Always." She mustered a small smile. "What of your parents? I know Lord Ferndale said you are his heir… your father?"

"Passed when I was quite young. My mother still lives; she remarried when I was eleven and lives in Ireland now. Her new husband has an estate near Wexford, in the south."

The transaction neared completion as he handed the money her way. His hand rested on the books, but he found his feet did not want to remove him from Estelle's presence.

"Terrible business, what's happened in France," he

said, starting up a new conversation as an excuse to remain in the shop.

Estelle nodded and said, "It is a little safer now, at least, with the Corsican secured on Elba."

"You must be terribly worried about your father?"

Estelle let out a sigh. "I daresay we won't be truly at ease until he is safely home."

"I did want to head over there to fight," he said. "But Grandfather vetoed it, on account of me being the sole heir to Ferndale."

She delivered another smile that made his heart rally and asked, "Do you always do what your grandfather asks of you?"

He read the double meaning in that question and gave a polite laugh. "Most of the time, yes. I am, of course, fully capable of making my own decisions. And mistakes. But he is a sensible man and has an exceptional head on his shoulders."

This conversation was marvellous and he found himself enjoying Estelle's company a great deal. They should have more of these, he decided. They would get to know each other as they talked of books and travel and languages.

The bell rang and more customers entered the store.

"Please excuse me, Mr Yates," Estelle said. "Thank you for your generosity, it is well-timed."

Ahh, yes. Being a bookshop, there would often be other customers. He couldn't monopolise Miss Baxter the whole time. "Of course!" he nodded and lifted his hefty collection of books. Then he spoke a little louder for the benefit of the new customers. "Thank you for these marvellous books, which are in excellent condition."

He left the store - careful to make sure not to let the cat out again - and blinked into the light. The bell tinkled as the door closed behind him. He swiftly walked back to his room at the Red Lion and set the books down on the side table. Momentarily he scratched his arm in thought as he contemplated having a lie down to start reading one of them. The aroma of fresh baked goods wafted in through the window on the warm summer's breeze. Perhaps he would get some food first, then come back and luxuriate in bookish goodness.

In the public room, there were several people already enjoying a meal. He nodded to the maid that he would like a table. Within a few minutes, he was seated near a window, digging into a satisfying stew with freshly-baked bread and a small pot of dripping on the side. The seat of his pants itched, but he was in a public house and this was not the place to scratch. Perhaps he was allergic to cats, like the hotel landlord? But then, wouldn't his hand be itching more, if that were the case? He wasn't sure how allergies worked, as he'd thankfully never experienced that particular affliction yet.

The itching could be ignored, mostly, if he focused on the food. Yes, that would help enormously. And the beer. It tasted better at the Red Lion than The Swan. When the maid came to take his plate, Felix asked about reserving a table for that evening's meal. He'd had the splendid idea of treating the Baxter sisters and even their housekeeper if she wanted to, to a deliciously filling meal.

"Tonight?" The maid scoffed as she cleared his empty tankard. "The 'ssembly's tonight. Nobody will be eating down here. Half the town'll be in 'tendance upstairs. There'll be food there to eat."

"Is that this evening?" He must have lost count of the days. Hardly surprising with his focus on Estelle and searching for her cat. "Do I have time to return to Ferndale House so that I may dress for the occasion?"

"I'd not worry about that, sir. You'll be the best dressed one there as is!"

The whole town, did she say? Felix smiled at the thought that the Baxter sisters would be there. One of them in particular.

CHAPTER 9

Estelle Feels Pretty

Locking the door at the end of the day, Estelle sighed happily to herself. A steady stream of customers had come into Baxter's and she'd found books for nearly all of them. A broad smile crept over her face as she and Marie counted the day's generous takings. If only every day could be this good. Or even every second day. Estelle wasn't greedy.

"I'm glad you've taken my advice and become more assertive about asking for money," Marie said.

"I can't claim all the credit. Mr Yates paid for his books without prompting, and he bought several more, including an expensive one from the locked cabinet!" The moment she mentioned Mr Yates, she knew her sister would ask about him, so she kept talking about many of the other customers in an effort to distract her sister. "A few more days like today and we should clear all our bills. I wonder when the next crate of books will arrive?"

"Nice try," Marie said as they went up to the kitchen. "Is Mr Yates coming to the assembly tonight?"

The question implied they'd discussed the assembly, but the subject had not come up in their conversations since they'd spoken about it at Ferndale Hall. "It might be a little declassé for him?" Estelle said, not sure whether she wished he would be there or not. The man confounded her intensely; she would soon be mixing up her left and right at this rate!

"Why would you say that?" Marie handed over some money to Mrs Poole so she could pay the bills for the butcher and the grocer. "Miss Yates chairs the hospital committee, and Lord Ferndale would never let her attend without him. I'm sure Mr Yates will be there in support of them. And it's the perfect opportunity for Lord Ferdale to show the town his grandson is home."

In the kitchen, Bernadette was fixing Louise's hair, pinning up a mass of fine braids into a coronet.

"Your gowns look so lovely!" Estelle gasped. "Goodness me. And you made these from the gowns Miss Yates sent over?" She couldn't imagine Miss Yates wearing anything so fashionable.

"Some of those old gowns used yards and yards of fabric." Marie swished her narrow skirt around her ankles. "I could nearly have made two gowns out of it!"

"Wait until you see yours," Louise said.

"Stop moving your head, Lou," Bernadette commanded.

Louise kept talking. "You've had the world on your shoulders lately, Estelle, you deserve something nice."

"Oh!" Estelle shook her head. "But you needn't have bothered. I'm far too old for assemblies."

Marie smirked and said, "You'll change your mind when you see the dress."

Mrs Poole and Marie shared a conspiratorial laugh and retrieved something from a hanger behind the door.

Estelle's mouth dropped open as they revealed the gown to her; a shimmering length of green - was that *silk*? - stitched all over in fine silver thread. "It's incredible!"

Louise said, "You can thank Miss Yates in person when you see her tonight. She will be delighted to see us."

"Stop moving your head!" Bernadette demanded in exasperation. "Marie, you'd better get started on Estelle's hair, or we'll all be late!"

Soon the five of them were ready. Estelle took her mother's amethyst cross out of the small treasure box on her dresser and hung it on a mauve ribbon around her neck, marvelling at her reflection in the mirror. She did not look like the studious, hardworking Miss Baxter of Baxter's Fine Books; she looked like a young lady of fashion.

"Not a thought in my head but frivolity and dancing," she murmured, laughing at the nonsensical image. Frankly, it was highly unlikely anyone would even ask her to dance, but still she intended to enjoy the music and perhaps watch her sisters take a turn or two about the floor. Every eligible bachelor would no doubt want to dance with Bernadette.

They locked up the bookshop for the night and left

Crafty in the kitchen, chewing on a fish head that Bernadette had bought from the market.

They made their way up the stairs of the Red Lion to the large rooms on the first floor, regularly used to host wedding parties, assemblies, harvest feasts and any event in Hatfield where twenty or more people might all wish to gather in the one place. Music was already playing, a jaunty tune from fiddle and piano, though as yet there was no sound of dancing feet, just an ever-increasing volume of chatter as they neared the doors.

Marie winced and slowed, making a face.

"Are you going to be all right?" Estelle asked sympathetically, pausing beside her sister.

"It is quite loud," Marie said, but she put on a brave smile. "I'll manage, I get so few opportunities to dance, and I do enjoy it."

Estelle linked arms with Marie. "Come, let us go in together."

The room was a riot of bright colours, ladies in gowns every hue of the rainbow and some of the men in waistcoats just as bright. Estelle couldn't help but smile as she took in the dazzling spectacle. The sound of happy humanity enveloped them, as did the warm mixture of perfumes and pomades as people dressed for the occasion.

"Will you dance with Mr Yates, do you think?" Marie asked slyly. Estelle missed a step and stumbled, glad of her sister's arm helping to keep her from falling flat on her face.

"He won't be here," she said with a disbelieving laugh. "Goodness, an assembly such as this? Far too ordinary for the likes of him."

Why must they continue to mention that man? Just because he was handsome and rich and the grandson of one of their oldest family friends did not mean he was suitable marriage material. Not that Estelle had even entertained that topic. Too much.

"I think you just don't want him to be here," Marie pointed out. "Lord Ferndale and Miss Yates are already here," she added, giving them a wave.

Estelle wanted to tell her sister to be quiet, which might perhaps have started an argument, but they were interrupted by their cousin Joshua marching over and standing before them, eyeing them up and down with a sneer on his face.

Urgh, that man! Estelle steeled herself for another confrontation.

"Good evening, Cousin Joshua," Estelle said as politely as she could manage.

"Where did you get those gowns?" Joshua demanded, without so much as a greeting in return. "Ridiculous for Matthew to leave children in charge of a business, when you are spending all the profits…"

"We are not children, Cousin Joshua," Estelle said, an edge to her voice as she steadied her breathing. Her heart was already pounding faster, but she was determined not to let him cower her. "And I do believe the business's finances are none of your concern."

Marie gasped in shock. To be honest, Estelle shocked herself at how bold she sounded. Joshua's face turned puce, but Estelle held her ground and did not back down. She was sick and tired of Cousin Joshua criticising them and browbeating her and her sisters; his blatant lie a few days ago about their father's demise had been the last straw. She couldn't wait for the next crate of books to arrive. She'd triumphantly wave the next letter from her father in Joshua's face.

"The finances *are* my concern," Joshua countered. "The terms of the inheritance are that a business must be operating in that building, or it must be forfeit. It's hardly running a business if there is no profit."

The absolute weasel to bring that up! There was no way to keep this discussion going without it descending into scandal. That he would bring this up at a public assembly was simply outrageous. It was on the tip of her tongue to give him a set-down when they were interrupted with the most perfect timing imaginable.

"Miss Baxter!" a delighted voice exclaimed. Estelle gasped as Mr Yates came striding toward her through the crowd, gaze focused on her as though there wasn't a single other person in the room. "What a delight to see you here! Miss Marie." He offered Marie a quick bow, though his gaze returned quickly to Estelle's face. "Miss Baxter, say you have a dance free for me? I shall be quite devastated if all your dances are promised already!"

His appearance was indeed the most fortuitous timing, as Joshua Baxter stood there, not sure if he should say something or move away.

Was he awaiting an introduction? Estelle almost laughed at the comical thought of Felix thinking she would be so popular as to not have any spare dances on her card. She had barely arrived; how could all her dances be promised when she had not spoken to a soul yet?

"You are too kind, Mr Yates," she said, because he'd intervened at the perfect time. "I am quite at leisure to dance with you." It would have the pleasant side benefit of providing an escape from Cousin Joshua. It might also make him peeved to see her having a jolly time and enjoying herself.

"Excellent! And since I have no doubt that you are far too proper to dance more than one or two sets with me, Miss Baxter, it would be my pleasure to dance with your sisters as well - you'll save one for me, Miss Marie?"

"I should be delighted, Mr Yates." Marie looked highly amused as Mr Yates bowed to her again before seizing Estelle's hand, placing it on his arm, and marching her onto the dance floor to join the other couples forming up to dance the first set., leaving Cousin Joshua staring after them with an outraged expression on his face.

"You look absolutely beautiful," Mr Yates said in an admiring tone as they faced each other, waiting for the music to commence.

Estelle couldn't help but blush. "Thank you," she murmured.

"Not that you aren't exceptionally pretty at all times, but that colour is quite stunning on you. Brings out the green in your eyes. I am enchanted!"

He was ridiculous, but he sounded so earnest, Estelle found herself smiling genuinely at him. He smiled broadly back, and it was with a light heart that she skipped along the line of couples, spotting in passing Lord Ferndale and Miss Yates watching on with indulgent smiles.

The dance was a country dance which only brought them back together as a couple for a moment or two every now and then, but Estelle thoroughly enjoyed herself anyway. It had been too long since she'd joined in a dance, and the steps came back to her like a fond memory.

When the music came to an end, Mr Yates bowed gracefully to her, and she made a curtsy.

She turned to walk off the dance floor only to be confronted by a wall of sour, disapproving faces. Cousins Joshua and Phoebe, some of Phoebe's cronies who thought nothing should happen in Hatfield without their say-so, and Reverend Millings, the vicar of St John's.

Estelle never understood why the vicar came to assemblies and other events at all. He was one of those people who believed any kind of fun or frivolity was a shortcut to Hell, and never failed to say so in his Sunday sermons. He glared down at her with disapproval now, but as she was quite accustomed to such an expression from him, it didn't cut the way it used to. She could almost ignore him because this was his standard facial setting.

Cousin Phoebe, however, was a little more difficult to ignore, especially as she grabbed Estelle's elbow and pinched. Estelle suspected she might have a bruise there tomorrow, and pulled her arm away sharply.

"How do you know Lord Ferndale's grandson?" Phoebe hissed, and without waiting for Estelle to respond, immediately continued, "and how dare you not present him to us, you must introduce us immediately!"

Estelle was about to ask why Miss Yates hadn't introduced them already, considering Phoebe had been standing near the Ferndales already, and she knew who Felix was. The noise of the evening drowned out the ability to think of a reason to refuse, but Estelle took her sweet time in any case. She nodded slowly to Phoebe that she'd heard the request, then turned equally slowly to look about the room to find where Mr Yates had gone.

He was not with his grandfather or great-aunt, which surprised her. Ah, there he was, by the lemonade table.

Phoebe grabbed her forcibly by the elbow and pushed the two of them forward. "There he is, now come on!"

There was a hint of desperation in her cousin's voice warning Estelle that the evening could become a lot worse if she didn't comply. She wouldn't put it past Phoebe to have a very public conniption and make an enormous, ghastly scene where she'd make Estelle out to be the villain in the piece.

As they came closer to Mr Yates, Phoebe gave out a sudden, theatrical laugh and said, "Cousin Estelle, how you jest so!"

She hadn't said anything, because Phoebe was simply calling attention to herself. It had the desired effect of making Mr Yates turn around though. He saw Estelle and beamed a heart-melting smile in her direction. Then saw the woman standing beside her and a slight furrow crossed his brow.

He was so utterly marvellous in recognising Cousin Phoebe's tactics, as he delivered a wonderful set-down: "I don't believe we've met?"

Phoebe pretended it was a lively jest and made another overly-enthusiastic laugh.

Estelle spoke up, "Mr Yates, please allow me to introduce my cousin-by-marriage, Mrs Baxter."

Phoebe darted a look her way and Estelle couldn't truly explain why she'd added the clarifier.

"Mrs Baxter, I'm delighted to meet another of the estimable Baxter ladies of Hatfield. This town is truly blessed to have them."

Phoebe turned herself about in such a way that she managed to push Estelle out the way. Then she possessively placed her hand in the crook of his elbow. "I am Mrs Joshua Baxter; my husband is the most esteemed Magistrate of Hatfield."

As she spoke, she managed to guide Mr Yates away from the lemonade table and Estelle, which had been her purpose all along. Soon the two of them vanished into the crowd, leaving Estelle by herself. A slight pang of worry caught her, but she figured Mr Yates would cope with Phoebe.

A lemonade would be just the thing, so she picked up a glass. Then she saw Miss Yates nearby and retrieved one for her as well.

"Miss Baxter, you are a darling!" Miss Yates said,

accepting the glass of refreshment. "That colour suits you to a nicety!"

"I cannot thank you enough, Miss Yates, for your generosity. My sisters were so happy to have the material to make so many new dresses."

"I'm so pleased to see the clothes put to good use. And you look resplendent in the green, it's my favourite colour as well."

"Thank you again." Honestly, if Estelle spent the entire night thanking Miss Yates it would not be enough. The dear lady was so generous, almost to a fault.

"Tell me, dear, what is Mrs Baxter doing with our Felix?"

Estelle rolled the name Felix around in her head and found she rather liked it. Because, she had to admit, she was rather beginning to like him. Not simply for his looks, but the way in which he'd rescued her from Joshua earlier, and was wary but polite to Phoebe, had truly lifted him in her estimations.

"Mrs Baxter wanted to be introduced, and now she and cousin Joshua and Reverend Millings are trying to bend his ear. I would hazard a guess they're talking about how unsuitable assemblies are."

"Not so unsuitable they don't attend, mind," Miss Yates quipped.

Estelle giggled behind her hand. "I guess they need to be in attendance so they bear witness to so much depravity. We'll receive a stern lecture this Sunday, I'm sure."

Now it was Miss Yates' turn to giggle. "I do like your company, and your mind, Miss Baxter, you make me feel young. Now, how are you and Felix faring, this evening? I did see you dancing. I'm glad he took my advice. I trust he didn't crush your toes?"

Far from it, he danced like a dream, and she felt herself flush a little at the memory. "He is a fine dancer, Miss Yates, and he spared my toes."

Miss Yates put her empty glass down on a nearby side table.

From across the room, Felix turned back to Estelle's position and appeared to be mouthing the word 'help'.

Estelle said, "He appears to require extraction. Should we?"

"Pshaw, he has survived sailing the Mediterranean. He'll survive a few minutes with your cousin. I'm sure it's character building."

A swoop in her stomach told Estelle she really should offer assistance. He'd come to her rescue, she should return the favour. Perhaps one of her sisters might want to dance? He had mentioned he would be happy to entertain them. Marie should be next; she'd much prefer to have a dance before things turned too noisy, as they often did as the evening progressed.

But no. From their position across the room, it appeared Cousin Phoebe was introducing Felix to her bosom friend Mrs Grey, who had three daughters to fire off; the eldest Miss Grey was simpering up at Felix as he bowed politely over her hand. Phoebe and Mrs Grey were obviously hinting very hard that Felix should ask Miss Grey to dance. It would be exceedingly rude if he refused to comply with the request. A moment later Felix and

Miss Grey - Estelle sternly corrected herself and called him Mr Yates in her head - had joined the next forming set.

Estelle turned away, feeling faintly queasy. She simply couldn't look. It shouldn't matter that Mr Yates was dancing with the pretty, blonde, fashionably dressed Miss Grey. It really shouldn't.

But somehow it did matter, very much, and Estelle did not like the squirming, pinching sensation in her stomach, the hot anger that burned her throat.

I'm jealous, she recognised, and thoroughly disliked herself for it.

"Those look delicious, my dear," Miss Yates said, perhaps in an attempt to distract Estelle, as a maid put a platter of little pies and sandwiches down on the table behind them. "Why don't you have a bite to eat?"

Estelle mustered a smile. "They do look good. May I prepare a plate for you too, Miss Yates? We can sit down just here."

They sat down and nibbled delicately. Mrs Poole shortly joined them, chattering away happily to Miss Yates about the Hatfield Poor Society and how the donations from the assembly would be used. The two dear friends were on a few of the town committees, including the hospital committee. Hatfield didn't have a hospital as yet, which was why they needed a committee to make sure they did eventually get one. It was mildly diverting listening to Mrs Poole and Miss Yates exchange gossip, and there was a lovely gem that had Estelle grinning to herself. Mrs

Phoebe Baxter had been trying ever so hard to be included in those committees, but somehow, she missed their meeting times.

It didn't take a genius to work out Miss Yates and Mrs Poole were the ones who set those meeting times and were accidentally-on-purpose making them at the same time Mrs Baxter was otherwise engaged.

Estelle sat and watched the dancing, and found herself drawn to Felix. He had a jovial expression as he partnered with Miss Grey. Then her eyes moved to where Phoebe and Mrs Grey were watching events keenly.

There was something about Phoebe Baxter that had the power to extract all joy from the evening, and Estelle suddenly felt exceptionally tired.

"Don't worry, dear," Miss Yates leaned over, "Nothing will come of *that*," she said, indicating Miss Grey.

It shouldn't matter who else Felix - Mr Yates - danced with. After all, she'd begun the night half-hoping he wouldn't even be here. She'd had one dance, and any more than two with the same gentleman would set tongues wagging. Therefore Mr Yates had to dance with more ladies simply out of politeness and hospitality.

"Perhaps Marie would like to go home," she mused, but no; Marie was not where Estelle expected. Her sister was dancing, with a sturdy young man she distantly recognised as a tenant farmer from the Ferndale estates. Sighing, Estelle sipped on her lemonade, and allowed herself to be drawn into the conversation between Miss Yates and Mrs Poole. Their suggestions were quite interesting, especially about the need for a hospital in Hatfield, and where it might be located. Soon she forgot about the frustrating Mr Yates and Miss Grey and entered fully into the topic.

She'd become so distracted she didn't hear the music finish.

"You did promise me a second dance, did you not, Miss Baxter?" A deep voice speaking close to her ear startled her, and she looked around to see Mr Yates standing beside her, leaning down to speak with her.

He looked so happy with himself, she immediately became cross with him. "I thought you seemed to be enjoying yourself too much to do any such thing." Immediately she wanted to snatch back the catty comment as soon as it left her lips. What was wrong with her tonight?

He gulped a little, but then regained his composure swiftly and that endearing smile of his was back. "I could not possibly achieve more enjoyment than I would gain from dancing with you again. Your cousin Mrs Baxter seems determined to present every eligible young lady in Hatfield for my attentions, though, and I should prefer to claim another dance with you before all of mine are spoken for." He cast a slightly hunted look over his shoulder, then turned back to her and said, "Please?"

That one word melted her resolve and she knew he needed rescuing. "I should be very pleased to dance with you," Estelle admitted, "and of course you did indicate earlier that you wished to dance with my sisters. Though I would not hold you to it, you could use such a promise as an excuse not to offer a dance to every young lady my cousin presentes to you."

Mr Yates brightened as she made the suggestion. "You are as brilliant as you are beautiful, Miss Baxter," he praised.

The guilty and slightly sick feeling in Estelle's stomach eased. It was as if Mr Yates had discovered the secret to making everyone he met feel utterly charmed in his presence.

They had snatched conversations as they danced again, him complimenting her dress and she in turn praising his dancing proficiency. They kept as far from Phoebe as possible, but there were moments where the dance steps demanded they promenade near her clique. When that happened, he would say something complimentary about Estelle that made her blush, and always loud enough for everyone nearby to hear.

A few steps later, they were heading away from Phoebe's group. He appeared almost shy as he scratched at the back of his neck. He couldn't possibly be nervous, could he? Perhaps he was. Previously, when they'd held conversations, it had been in the quiet of the shop. Maybe he was a little like Marie in character, where loud music made it hard for him to concentrate. Even when she'd berated him for returning the wrong cat, he hadn't appeared so nervous or shy as to - he just did it again, rubbing the back of his neck before he took her hand to lead her in a twirl.

As he moved, she could have sworn she caught a reddish mark above his collar. It was right where he'd scratched. Perhaps he had applied waters from Cologne and had developed an allergy? She smiled his way, then turned her head to scan the room to see if she could find Bernadette. Her youngest sister might have a balm for such an affliction, but Estelle could not see her at the moment.

They continued dancing and talking when they came together for brief moments.

"I do appreciate how much you care for my great-aunt," he said. "She thinks a great deal of you, and your sisters."

That was an easy one to follow. "Miss Yates is a dear friend, and much-loved member of the community."

Again he seemed to nervously rub the inside of his arm against his neck, as if he was caught with nerves or had some kind of irritation. The next time they came together and held hands, she deftly slipped his sleeve further up his arm. Three raised dots in a line. Lightning fast, she pulled the sleeve back and held her breath. She was certain nobody had seen her, and kept dancing and chatting to appear as normal as possible. She talked of the weather, simply for something to say. "Yes, it is a lovely, mild night. We are lucky it is not too hot, nor is it raining."

At last the music finished and she carefully muttered that they should slip away without letting anyone see them.

Mr Yates beamed with delight, but she furrowed her brow. She had most definitely given him the wrong idea, and would need to set him down gently.

When there was nobody to overhear them, she delivered the blow. "Mr Yates, I do not wish to make a scene, but I fear you have signs of bedbugs. Meet me in the archway next to the bookshop in five minutes."

His face sobered and she felt immediately sorry for him. She was not attempting a moonlight assignment with him, she was attempting to protect him, and by extension the Ferndale family, from social ruin.

CHAPTER 10

Scratching the Itch

Two minutes later, Estelle was in the small courtyard behind the bookshop, picking herbs in the darkness. Gently rubbing the leaves released the aromas which told her she'd picked the correct lemon-scented geraniums. Another minute and she was back near the archway beside the Red Lion, where she found a Mr Yates-shaped shadow waiting for their assignation.

"This is all rather rum," he said, rubbing at his sleeve.

"Perhaps in time we may look back on this and laugh, but right now shove these herbs up your sleeves and … er … into your breeches." She was incredibly grateful for the darkness, so he wouldn't see her furious blushes. "Now, put this coat on and pull it tightly, you're going to follow me through the shop. Walk through quickly and smoothly so the bedbugs don't drop off into the shop and eat the books."

bedbugs in a bookshop would mean financial and social ruin. This was a disaster.

In half a minute, they were in the courtyard where she retrieved a small hurricane lamp. There was a large barrel that collected water from the roof. Bernadette used it to water the plants if it hadn't rained for a few days.

"In you get," she indicated the barrel.

Mr Yates took the coat off and looked about for the best place to hang it..

"Leave it on the ground. It will need to go in the barrel as well. If you give me your shoes, I can fill them with geranium and wrap them in oilskin."

Mr Yates lifted the hem of his shirt up a little and exposed his smooth stomach to the hurricane lamp. He had raised dots on his skin there too.

He groaned. "Not again!"

"You've had bedbugs before, Mr Yates?"

"On the boat back from Greece," he confirmed. "Awful things. Oh dash it all, I should have realised what this was earlier." He climbed into the barrel and yelped at the sudden coldness. Water splashed freely over the sides and Estelle had to step back. He tried his best to submerge, but it wasn't a particularly large barrel.

"Not sure what's worse," he said, "The cold water or the splinters I'll earn from the barrel."

In the light of the hurricane lamp, Estelle could see far too much detail of his torso through his wet shirt.

"I'll need to bring out a bucket of water and some lye," she said.

In the kitchen, Estelle had a cold drink of water for herself first, then took a soup ladle back out to the courtyard with her. She was starting to feel itchy now, but it could only be the *thought* of bedbugs, not the actual creatures. She hadn't danced that closely with Mr Yates.

Thank heavens it hadn't been a waltz, not that such a scandalous dance would ever be performed at the Hatfield Assembly!

She handed over the soup ladle and said, "You'll need to wet your head and start washing. Then when you're ready to get out, leave your wet clothes in the barrel so the bugs stay in them and drown."

She turned to leave him to it, but he called back, "You're not about to abandon me in a cold barrel of water, are you?"

"Er, I was, actually, er, about to put the kettle on the stove."

"To warm my bath?" He sounded hopeful.

"To make us some tea." She would need an extra spoonful of honey to soothe her nerves when all this was over.

Felix stood up, his drenched shirt clinging to him as he peeled it off his body.

Estelle could virtually set the bookshop on fire with the heat pouring through her face and neck. Not for the first time she was grateful for the darkness.

"Tell me about Greece," was all she could manage. Not bad considering her brain had turned to cold porridge.

"Greece is beautiful. And warm. And so very different in so many ways. It is a country with an old soul, yet a vibrant, young spirit."

Pangs of yearning shot through Estelle. Travelling

must be so delightful, but also out of reach for her she may as well hope to visit the moon.

"You would love it," he added.

"I'm sure I shall. I mean, would. I mean … I don't know quite what I mean. It sounds lovely." She bit her lip to stop herself blathering. Then a practical thought kicked in. "I must get you some dry clothes."

It gave her the excuse to slip away and allow her heart to stop racing so fast. Her face burned with embarrassment at the predicament they were both in. Thank heavens she'd removed him from the assembly when she had, although no doubt several people, including Phoebe, would notice their absence. She'd have to think of a suitable lie to tell when her cousins next came over and made demands.

As she sorted through some of her father's clothes, she thought back over the evening. Had anyone been close to Mr Yates at the assembly? Oh goodness, cousin Phoebe had wrapped her hand across his arm! She prayed the bugs had stayed on Mr Yates and not wandered into new territory. As much as she disliked her cousins, she did not wish them pestilence.

A few moments later, she had a fresh shirt and a pair of her father's trousers for Mr Yates.

"It's not the fine cloth you're used to," she said, walking back to the courtyard. He was standing in the tub, his wet skin gleaming golden in the glow of the hurricane lamp as he tipped a ladle of water over his head. It sluiced down his body and reminded her of classical sculpture.

He mustn't have heard her, for he didn't make the slightest move to turn in surprise or cover himself.

Estelle coughed loudly and said, "I'll leave these here for you, when you're ready. I'll get to making that tea."

Felix froze as he heard the last few words from Miss Baxter before she returned to the bookshop. How long had she been there? She must think him a libertine, but he'd thought he was quite alone at the time. How else was he to remove his infested clothing without standing up in the barrel? At least he still had his breeches on! He'd have to climb out and remove them. Before doing that, he blew out the hurricane lamp so the darkness provided modesty.

Dragging on the clean clothes over damp skin wasn't the most pleasant of experiences, but he was dressed soon enough. Leaving his bug-infested fine clothes to soak in the barrel, he fumbled his way barefoot back inside by the faint light of the moon.

"Ouch," Felix muttered as he stubbed his toe on the way up the stairs. "Oh, ow, ow!"

"Are you quite all right, Mr Yates?" Estelle appeared before him with a lantern in hand, concern written across her beautiful, expressive face.

"I think I have a splinter in my toe!" He half-hopped over to the table, sat down ungracefully and lifted his foot onto the opposite knee, trying to peer at the end of his toe.

"Let me."

He heard the laugh in Miss Baxter's voice, and closed his eyes in silent humiliation as she gracefully knelt down, placing the lantern on the table. *I am constantly humiliating myself in front of this admirable woman. She must think me the veriest dolt.*

"Just a moment." Estelle rose to her feet and went to the dresser which Felix was mentally calling 'the apothecary's dresser'. She opened a drawer and returned with a small brass instrument in hand.

"What is that?" Felix asked nervously. It looked quite sharp.

"Tweezers." She held the instrument out, and he saw that it was basically a thin shim of brass folded over in the centre, the two ends meeting at a sharp point. "The splinter is too small to grasp with my fingers, but I think I can get it with these. It is under your toenail, I fear withdrawing it is going to hurt somewhat."

His toe was already throbbing quite magnificently, so Felix shrugged. "Better out than in, I think!"

"Hold still, then." She probed gently at his toe.

She was touching his skin and sending bolts of something rather delightful into his veins.

Felix hissed as Estelle gently withdrew the splinter, but the throbbing decreased immediately and he let out a sigh of relief.

"Wait there." She returned to the dresser and brought over a pot of salve, carefully daubing a little onto the tip of his toe. "I will find you some stockings to put on; I need to put some herbs in your boots for the night, and I'm afraid my father's feet are rather smaller than yours, so his spare shoes will not fit you."

"It doesn't matter. I shall make my way back to my room at the Red Lion…"

"You certainly shall not! That room must be cleansed and… oh, Marie."

The second Miss Baxter had just entered the kitchen and was staring at Felix sitting at the table in only a damp shirt and trousers, her mouth agape.

Estelle hurried over to her sister and caught her by the elbow, drawing her back into the stairwell. Felix couldn't hear their conversation. Estelle came back into the kitchen at the end of it.

"I've sent Marie to go and fetch your things. Everything must be cleansed, all your clothes, and the linen at the Red Lion. If it spreads…" Estelle shook her head. "Mr Haye will be furious."

"I didn't even sleep there!" Felix protested.

"You spent two nights at The Swan?" Estelle asked, sounding incredulous.

"Well, no, I could only tolerate one, so I went home to Ferndale Hall…"

Estelle threw up her hands in horror. "You took bedbugs to Ferndale Hall! Oh, my. I will have to let Miss Yates know."

Felix hung his head miserably. "What a ghastly mull I'm making of things," he muttered.

"Oh, Mr Yates." He heard sympathy in Estelle's voice,

and a moment later she swished past him and went to the stove. "Let me make a cup of tea and find a bite to eat - did you even get to sample the food at the assembly?"

"Not a thing," he said sorrowfully, realising his stomach was beginning to grumble.

Estelle replied, a hint of laughter in her tone; "I already know yours is an appetite which requires regular satiation." She set half a loaf of bread on the table, and a jar of honey, followed by an apple and a dish of raspberries. "Here. The best I can do at this time of night."

"A feast!" Felix brightened, picking up the knife she offered and carving a thick hunk off the bread. "Some for you, Miss Baxter?"

"Perhaps a little." She put the teacups on the table and took a seat opposite him, accepting the slice of bread he cut for her and drizzling some honey on it.

"Bread and honey and fruit," Felix said reminiscently. "I could almost be back in Greece, though it would be figs and oranges rather than apples and raspberries."

"I should like to hear more about Greece," Estelle said, and he heard a wistful longing in her voice. "How long did you spend there? Did you see the Parthenon and the Acropolis?"

"I most certainly did!" This at least, he could do; he could entertain her with stories of his travels.

They were so deep in conversation he barely noticed Marie come in; she paused to tell Estelle that all of his clothes had been placed in the barrel, before excusing herself quietly and going to her room.

They were still talking an hour later when the music

next door quieted and Mrs Poole came in with the younger Baxters. All three stopped in the doorway to gape at him.

Estelle jumped hastily to her feet. "Did Lord Ferndale and Miss Yates leave?" she exclaimed.

"Yes, about half an hour ago," Mrs Poole said, obviously puzzled. "Mr Yates…"

"I didn't tell them about the bedbugs!"

The word *bedbugs* had comprehension dawning on all three of their faces, and Felix was relieved that they all seemed to take it as a matter of course that Estelle would have dropped everything to assist with his problem.

"Staying in Mr Baxter's room tonight then?" Mrs Poole asked with a wise nod. "I'll just turn the bed down for you, Mr Yates."

"Thank you so much, Mrs Poole."

"You seem quite familiar with Mrs Poole," Estelle asked curiously as Mrs Poole and the two youngest sisters left the kitchen.

"Mrs Poole has been on committees with my great-aunt for years and years. She always had a sweet in her pocket for a hungry young boy." He gave a fond smile. "Her circumstances diminished rather after she was widowed, I think? Is that when she came to live with you?"

"Mr Poole and my mother died during the same influenza outbreak," Estelle said with a nod.

"A tragic loss." Felix nodded sympathetically. "It's dreadful to lose a parent."

"How did your father pass, if you don't mind my asking? He must have been quite young."

"Not yet thirty." Felix ate the last raspberry and shook his head. "I was just a boy; I don't really remember much of him. He had little interest in me anyway." He should not speak of his miserable childhood, when really, he'd been raised with all the material comforts money could buy.

Estelle gaped. "Why in the world not?"

"My father had little interest in life in anything that was not solely for his own amusement and pleasure. He was, to put if frankly, a wastrel and a great disappointment to my grandfather. I do my very best to be as unlike him as possible."

<hr>

Estelle stared at Felix in shock. What a dreadful way to feel about one of your parents! "Is it your grandfather that has told you these things, about your father?"

"Not solely my grandfather. Everyone who ever knew him has said these things, Miss Baxter." Felix shook his head ruefully. "Do not think it is just my grandfather's disappointment talking. The only useful thing my father ever did was marry my mother - picked out for him by Grandfather, and an estimably sensible woman - and sire an heir on her. They did not get along, at all. He died falling off his horse blind drunk while returning home from a visit to his mistress."

"Oh, my word." Estelle covered her mouth with her hand. "How dreadful!"

"He was little lamented, certainly not by my mother. And though she was fond of Grandfather and Great-Aunt Florence, when she met an eligible gentleman who offered for her in London a few years later, they were happy to give their blessing for her to remarry."

"But she moved to Ireland and left you behind?" Estelle asked, feeling a great deal of pity for the young boy Felix must have been. Fatherless, and then virtually abandoned by his mother too!

"Well, I had to go to Eton, and it's too far to travel for holidays. And I am the heir to Ferndale."

Felix smiled fondly. "Grandfather has been teaching me about the estate since I was small. He's asked me to sit in on the next town council meeting, so I can learn how to run those. I am determined to be a worthy successor to him."

"I don't doubt that you will be," Estelle said sincerely.

"Really?" There was surprise in his blue eyes as he met her gaze. "You don't think I'm..."

"What?" she asked, puzzled.

"Well... a bit of a dolt. I do seem to be continuously making a fool of myself in front of you." He gestured helplessly down at himself, at the damp, ill-fitting shirt, as though to indicate the entire bedbug situation.

"Bedbugs can happen to any unfortunate soul, Mr Yates. And so can stubbing one's toe, or letting out a cat in heat who is determined to escape. What matters is that you are willing and able to remedy the situation, and to listen to the advice of those who are willing to help."

"You mean that," he said softly. "You don't think I'm a fool."

"No, I don't think you're a fool at all."

They stared at each other in silence, the pool of warm lamplight making it feel very close and intimate, as though it was just the two of them in the house, perhaps just the two of them in the whole of England.

Very slowly, as though giving her time to move away if she chose, Felix reached out and rested his hand atop Estelle's where it lay on the table.

His hand was very warm.

She didn't move.

"Estelle," he said quietly, and his use of her given name sent a shock up her spine. Her eyes opened wide.

"Felix," she almost whispered in return.

"I'm glad you don't think I'm a dolt. I may seem foolish at times, but I promise you, I am a serious man, I take my responsibilities seriously - and I mean it when I say you are the only woman I have ever truly considered courting."

"I believe you," she whispered into the fraught silence which fell after he stopped speaking.

"And since you are not dismissing me out of hand, may I take that as some small encouragement?" He smiled, and then he rose slowly to his feet and came around the table, never taking his eyes from hers.

Estelle sat very still.

"I'll go to your father's room now. Good night... Estelle."

"Good night," she said, and Felix leaned down and pressed his lips to hers.

The kiss was soft and tentative, a brush of warmth that sent sparks racing along her skin, igniting intoxicating, terrifying feelings. Estelle's heart raced as Felix's lips lingered against hers, sweet and gentle. She felt the world around her dissolve into nothingness; no worries of bedbugs or responsibilities - just the two of them in their own bubble of shared discovery.

His touch was cautious, as if he were afraid of breaking the moment, and her mind raced with thoughts she had never allowed herself to entertain fully.

Did she truly dare to embrace this burgeoning connection? But as he pulled away, a fleeting expression of uncertainty flickering across his features, she realised this was a doorway opening, and she didn't wish to let it close.

"Felix..." she started softly, unsure how to voice the whirlwind of emotions within her.

"Sorry, I shouldn't have..." he began, stepping back slightly. "I didn't mean to overstep..."

"No," she interrupted, her pulse quickening. "No, I wanted to say..." but her words fell into silence, the gravity of the moment bearing down on her. She didn't have the words to express herself.

A half-smile crossed his lips, and he touched her cheek gently before stepping back. "Good night," he said quietly. "Sleep well."

Estelle watched him cross the kitchen and go down the hallway to her father's room, and the warmth in her chest blossomed even brighter. Because he hadn't pressed her; he'd seen her hesitation and confusion, and he'd stepped back and given her the time and space she needed to figure out her own feelings.

Sleep well. She almost laughed over his last words. With so many thoughts chasing themselves around inside her head like a litter of Crafty's kittens with a ball of wool, she'd be lucky if she got any sleep at all!

CHAPTER 11

A Bubble of Happiness

As she had predicted, Estelle slept poorly. Her thoughts were filled with a blue eyed man with golden curls, his lips on hers. She rose from her bed gritty-eyed in the early hours of the morning and made her way downstairs. She had to finish the job from last night and make sure those bed bugs were destroyed. To her grim satisfaction, there were visible small insects floating on the top of the water. Pulling out Felix's clothes, she snapped them in the air to flick any remaining insects away. Then she wrung them out as best she could and hung them on the wall hooks near the lavender bushes to dry in the sun. Marie came out to help when she was halfway through the job. Together they tipped over the barrel, rinsed it with a fresh bucket of water from the pump, and left it to drain and dry.

"Phew." Estelle wiped perspiration from her brow. It was already a warm morning, perfect for drying clothes. "Thank you for that."

Marie nodded in acknowledgement, then hesitated before slowly drawing something out of her pocket. "This came yesterday. I didn't want to upset you before the assembly."

"Oh." Estelle looked at the folded paper her sister held out rather as though she might look at a venomous snake. Eventually, she removed her apron, drying her hands on it before taking the paper from Marie. "Thank you," she murmured, and Marie nodded before turning silently away.

It's bad, then.

With a sigh, Estelle took herself into the bookshop and sat down on the stool behind the counter, grateful at least that it was Saturday and she didn't have to open the shop.

Unfolding the paper, she sat staring at it for a few moments.

An extraordinary sum stared back at her on the paper.

"Eighty pounds," she murmured, before putting her head in her hands, her elbows on the counter on either side of the paper. "*Eighty pounds*. Dear God."

It was a letter from the bank where their father had taken out his loan before leaving for France, stating bluntly that reports had reached them that Matthew Baxter had passed away and they were therefore requesting earlier and larger repayments be made on the loan.

Cousin Joshua, Estelle thought bleakly. Her heart began pounding in her chest with unexpressed anger. This had Joshua's hallmark of nastiness all over it.

She thought they'd seen him off, but he was already a step ahead. While the sisters had been able to refute Cousin Joshua's lie with the fact of Matthew's letter, all it would have taken was a note to the bank about the possibility of his never returning and the conservative money men would have panicked.

Cousin Joshua probably notified the bank first, before he'd paid them a visit that day as he so casually measured the windows for drapes.

And now, Estelle somehow had to find a payment four times larger than she had expected. Even Felix's huge purchase the day before wouldn't cover it, not to mention the other debts she had already mentally earmarked that money for.

A floorboard squeaking made her look up. There was Felix coming from the stairs through the bookshop towards her. In the shop's dim light, she could not see the gleam in his eyes, but her memories fixed them in place anyway. He wore her father's clothes, the shirt too baggy but the sleeves too short. His stockinged feet were quiet, but the age of the building meant the bookshop's wooden floors did bend in a few places.

Felix stopped in his tracks on seeing her, and Estelle realised her panic and devastation from the bank's letter must be showing on her face. Her cheeks were wet, and she swiped hastily at the tears, trying to compose herself.

"I am glad we aren't open today," she said, trying to sound light-hearted, "because anyone coming into the bookshop at this moment would realise you had spent the night here. That would be quite the scandal."

"Estelle," he said quietly, eschewing the opportunity she had offered to jest with her. "Whatever is the matter? What has happened?"

She hesitated, looking at his handsome face, the concern written all over it. *He's a good man. Maybe I should just… marry him. To save the bookshop, save my sisters. The solution is right here in front of me, offered up on a plate.*

"Please let me help." He reached across the counter, placed a hand atop hers. "Whatever it is. Let me help."

She was so very close to giving in. Now she warred with herself and wondered why she was fighting it so much. What was she so afraid of giving in to? A life of leisure, a handsome husband and no debts for her sisters? She should grab at that with both hands. "Did you really mean it?" she asked. "About wanting to marry me?"

Felix didn't hesitate. "Yes. I meant it. I still mean it."

She was the one who hesitated, and he looked closely at her before taking his hand off hers. She felt the absence of his touch and wondered if he was pulling away. No, he was getting closer, making his way around the counter to stand beside her.

"I want to marry you, Estelle," he said quietly when she looked up at him. "But I want you to say yes because *you* want to marry *me*, not because I can solve a problem for you. I'll help you even if you don't want to marry me, because I admire you greatly and my grandfather and great-aunt are extremely fond of you and your sisters. You don't have to marry me in order to get my help."

Tears started running down her cheeks in earnest then, and Felix groaned as though in pain.

"Estelle, dearest, please don't cry! I can bear anything but that." He leaned forward, as though to kiss her, took another step in order to get close enough… Estelle closed her eyes, waiting for that delicious sensation of his warm lips on hers again.

There was a peculiar, squishy sort of crunching sound and Felix's lips did not make the distance to land on hers.

"Ugh," he said instead.

Estelle's eyes sprang open.

Felix was looking down at his feet, a strange queasy sort of expression on his face.

Estelle looked down too.

"Oh no. Crafty!"

"What *is* that?" Felix very gingerly backed away, looking with horror at the mess on his stockinged foot.

Estelle didn't know whether to laugh or cry at the mess. "I'm afraid it appears to be a disembowelled mouse. Please tell me you have a strong stomach?"

"Reasonably." He still looked a little queasy, though, for which Estelle could hardly blame him.

"Don't move," she cautioned, hoping to avoid the mess being spread over the floor. "I'll run upstairs and get some clean stockings."

"Thank you," Felix agreed, gingerly sitting down on the stool once she vacated it, and Estelle hurried for the stairs, mentally condemning Crafty to the fires of Hell for the untimely interruption. "You'd probably be quite happy there. Have Lucifer's minions at your beck and call," she muttered as she passed Crafty atop one of the bookcases, meticulously cleaning her paws.

Crafty did not deign even to notice her, and Estelle sighed. "I suppose it's for the best. I need a clear head to think, and his kisses are very confusing!"

Alone for a moment, she thought back to the bank's letter of demand. Perhaps they might agree to go back to the original payment schedule, if she showed them her father's letter that arrived with the last crate of books? That would at least calm their fears that he would be unable to repay the loan. But of course, they might not even entertain taking an interview with a woman unless she had a … oh dear, unless she had a husband with her to speak business.

The only way out of this mess was the path that led to marrying Felix Yates. Not an entirely terrible proposition, but she still couldn't quite make it all make sense yet. It didn't sit right with Estelle to marry for convenience. He was indeed a lovely man, but how well were they really suited to each other?

When she made her way back downstairs with a pair of clean stockings in hand, Bernadette had made it downstairs to the bookshop with Felix, and was using a rag to dispose of the remainder of Crafty's offering. Bernadette was obviously trying quite hard not to laugh at Felix's predicament, and Estelle gave her a stern glare. Poor Mr Yates did not need them laughing at him, on top of everything else! He'd been surprisingly helpful, even if he did seem to make something of a mess of things at first.

The best way to remove the mirth from Bernadette's face was to show her the demand letter from the bank. It had certainly swept away her own good mood in quick time.

"Oh dear," Bernadette said. "That makes me queasier than cleaning up mouse entrails."

Estelle handed over the stockings to Felix and he stepped away to dress his feet.

Turning to her youngest sister, Estelle said, "I was wondering if we should send them father's letter? To prove he's still with us?"

Bernadette shook her head and said, "I would keep that letter close. Do you think this is Cousin Joshua's doing?"

"The timing is far too suspicious to be coincidental," Estelle confirmed. "This disaster has our cousin's manipulative fingerprints all over it."

There was no other reason the bank would suddenly demand repayment at this point. Unless something had happened in France that had reached the bank's ears but not theirs, which was also a horrifying thought.

Bernadette worried at her bottom lip in thought. "As long as the crates and Father's letters keep coming, we know he's still alive. Marie's good with letters, she'll know the right things to say to the bank."

Felix said, "These are most comfortable. I thank you. I am sorry to listen to your private conversation, but might a letter from myself to the bank be of assistance in some way? Having a grandfather who's a baron does sometimes smooth things over."

Estelle's whole body felt on edge, as perhaps if Felix

did have the solution to their problems after all, without marriage.

Bernadette nudged Estelle and said, "See, accepting someone's help isn't the end of the world after all."

The words, "you'll keep" were on the tip of her tongue when Mrs Poole called down the stairs that breakfast was ready.

Felix's stomach gurgled audibly, which made all three of them giggle, despite their worries.

They made their way to the kitchen for breakfast. Mrs Poole had added another chair to the table and they were sat a little closer to each other than usual. Mrs Poole indicated the chair next to Estelle for Felix. He pulled out Estelle's chair for her and she accepted the assistance.

"I need to thank you, Miss Bernadette," Felix said. "You show a remarkable talent with herbs. Thanks to your balm, the scratch Crafty gave me has almost entirely healed already." He held up his hand and showed how small and thin the cut looked. It had healed over and wasn't at all red, much to Estelle's relief. If it had turned red and hot, it could become infected.

"Thank you, Mr. Yates. I learned all about herbs at my mother's knee," Bernadette said.

"What sort of ailments do you treat?" Felix asked.

Louise darted her eyes toward Estelle as if this could be some kind of a trap. Estelle looked at Bernadette and shook her head slightly. Her youngest sister rolled her eyes.

Of course she's not going to tell a man - almost a complete stranger - what she really does! Estelle offered a small smile of apology for doubting Bernadette's good sense.

"Lots of small things," Bernadette said. "Nothing to put the town doctor out of a position, of course. I find talking with people for a while puts them at ease. The herbs smell delicious and make people feel better when they add them to tea. Ginger, when I can get it, is very good for anyone with a sickly stomach. I would dearly love to grow it, but the plant itself is hard to find."

"Is that a suitable topic for the table?" Marie asked. "I'm trying to enjoy my breakfast, not hear about people's sickly stomachs."

That remark shut things down for a moment, until Felix said, "This bacon is delicious, Mrs Poole, thank you." Then he turned back to Bernadette and asked, "Lord Ferndale has a cough that comes on at night. It concerns me a little. Would you have anything to recommend?"

"Oh yes. A cough at night is common, as the sun goes down and the night air cools. I have a cucumber and mint tonic that can help."

"Thank you, and I'm sure Lord Ferndale will be most appreciative."

Louise piped up, "I'm nearly done with the rest of his book bindings. The glue should be dry on the last one by midday."

Felix delivered her a beautiful smile, and Estelle couldn't help but feel warmed by association. Last night, he'd smiled at another woman and jealousy had spiked inside her. But now he was smiling at her sister and it felt so natural, as if he were already a member of the family.

"Tell me, Miss Louise, how are you so proficient at book binding and repairs?" he asked, showing every appearance of genuine interest.

Louise attempted to brush his compliment away. "I suppose I've been doing it so long it's easy for me now."

"I've seen what you've already done for Lord Ferndale's favourite titles. I had some books repaired in London many years ago, and the quality was nowhere near as good."

Louise blushed and shrugged a little. "Thank you," she said, spreading some jam on her toast. "It's important to shave the edges of the leather at the correct angle, otherwise it gets too bulky when you fold it over."

"How clever," Felix encouraged. "I promise not to divulge your trade secrets."

"Well, my father showed me how, and I thought about some better ways, so I tried them, and they worked. The secret is in the stinky glue, which everyone hates. I'm not overly fond of it either, mind, but it works very well. It does take slightly longer to dry but it's worth it for the life of the book."

"I thank you for your diligence," Felix said. "Have you thought about promoting your services to readers in London? I'm sure you could charge London customers more."

Marie chimed in, "That's a good idea. Shall I add that to our next advertisement in The Times?"

Felix added, "As long as you're not suddenly over-whelmed."

Louise nodded. "I have two book vices to hold the books in position while the glue sets. That puts a limit on the number of books I can repair at any time."

Felix asked, "Is there room in your workshop for another vice or two?"

Louise stammered, "Er, well, there is room."

Estelle heard the unsaid part - *there is room, but there's no money to buy extra vices and clamps.*

Felix had brought up an excellent point. Louise was incredibly skilled at what she did, even with the hideous smell that came with glue-pot days. If they could expand, they might even take in an apprentice.

The chatter at the table between Felix and her sisters calmed Estelle. His questions proved he had been paying attention to their lives and their skills, and displayed genuine interest in their endeavours. She nibbled on her toast and watched him turn his attention to Marie, asking about her interests and hobbies, and listening as Marie shyly said that she liked to play the pianoforte, when she had time.

I thought him selfish and spoiled, interested in nothing but his own amusements, when first we met, but I was quite wrong. He's not just trying to impress me, either. He genuinely cares.

Everything Estelle learned about Felix Yates seemed to be another point in favour of her accepting his marriage proposal.

"Now." Felix clapped his hands together and looked around the table. "Since it seems I shall have to wait for my clothes and boots to dry, how can I make myself useful to you here today?" He smirked a little. "Since I have something of a height advantage over even Miss Louise, perhaps you might put me to work dusting the tops of the furniture and door frames?"

"Oh, no, sir, we couldn't possibly expect you to work," Mrs Poole said immediately, just as Estelle said; "That is a capital suggestion, Mr Yates."

"Estelle!" Mrs Poole gave her a warning look.

"What? He wants to help, and Saturday is our cleaning day!"

"He is a guest!" Mrs Poole shook her head reprovingly.

"Perhaps you would like to spend the day reading, Mr Yates?" Bernadette suggested diplomatically. "After all, if there is one thing we are not short of, it is reading material, and there is a very comfortable reading chair in Father's room…"

"Certainly not." He rose from the table and carried his plate over to the wash basin. "No gentleman would sit at his leisure and allow the ladies about him to do all the work. I shall begin by washing these plates, and then perhaps carry some more water up for you?"

Carrying heavy buckets of water up the narrow stairwell was a chore all of them hated, and even Mrs Poole could not find it in herself to decline such a generous offer. Indeed, Estelle was quite amused half an hour later, to discover that she was not the only one watching with appreciation as Felix made light work of hefting some heavy buckets of water up onto the kitchen table before pouring them into separate jugs to take to the bedrooms. Mrs Poole, busy kneading dough, had her eyes more on Mr Yates' broad shoulders moving under his thin linen shirt than on her bread mix.

Estelle herself gave up any pretence of dusting the herb-dresser and just stared.

He was, after all, rather worth staring at. Especially last night, as the water dripped off his torso in the lamp light. Though she should definitely not be thinking about that!

Mrs Poole fanned herself a little as Felix took the empty buckets and headed off down the stairs again. Catching Estelle's eyes on her, the older woman let out a rather self-conscious little laugh.

"Fine figure of a man, Mr Yates," Mrs Poole observed, her cheeks pink.

"He really is," Estelle agreed shamelessly. Whatever she might find objectionable about Mr Yates - and she was finding less and less to object to as she came to know him better - his looks had certainly never fallen into that category.

Although her distraction because of them was certainly a concern, as she paused to watch him carry in more water and accidentally knocked a large ceramic pot of lavender off the dresser, which promptly broke and scattered all over the floor.

"We're supposed to be cleaning up, not making more mess!" Bernadette chided as she came over to help Estelle clean up.

"Well, at least the house will smell nice," Estelle joked, tearing her gaze away from Felix with an effort.

Usually the time dragged on Clean-Up-Saturdays, but with Felix's able assistance, the time moved so much faster than usual.

The whole time they worked, Felix didn't once press Estelle about his suit, or about helping with the loan. Instead, he continued to engage her sisters in conversations that catered to their interests, and even coaxed an enthusiastic conversation with Mrs Poole about her cooking prowess.

True to his word, Felix used his height to reach the top of the bookshelves. Crafty tried to catch the ends of the feather duster as he swept it along the timber. Felix made a game of it, which lasted a solid fifteen minutes.

Understanding dawned on Estelle. She owed this decent man an apology. He wasn't as frivolous and wool-headed as she'd first thought. He was a realistic person who managed to find joy in daily life. He was the grandson of a baron, heir to a considerable fortune, but here he was performing manual labour. He'd offered to help and had followed through. But in helping, he'd also seized a moment to appreciate a little harmless fun when the opportunity arose. Watching Felix play with Crafty until the cat was nearly exhausted added another realisation. Somewhere along the line, Estelle had lost that ability to appreciate the happy moments that came along in life. Considering the last few years, that was hardly surprising. Their mother had died only a few years ago. Grief and sorrow had followed. Then their father had left them to manage the business while he was travelling in France, taking out an enormous loan that the bank now wanted repaying in much larger deposits. Add to that Cousin Joshua's attempts to see them out on the street, and it was hardly surprising she didn't have much joy in her life.

Marrying Mr Yates would lift an exceedingly large portion of their burden, and being around him would surely help her find more joy in the everyday?

With an extra pair of hands assisting them so ably, they finished the clean up earlier than usual. The warm southerly winds had dried Mr Yates' clothes and he was soon back to his regular elegant appearance.

Crafty had not merely fallen asleep after playing with Mr Yates, she'd plummeted. She was stretched out on the windowsill, legs in all directions like a furry black starfish, making snuffly noises.

Felix smiled at the cat and turned to face the sisters, all seated at the kitchen table enjoying a well-earned cup of tea. "Ladies, I thank you most humbly for taking such great care of me, and sparing the Red Lion from an infestation of bed bugs. Please allow me to take you all to dinner there tonight, as a small token of appreciation."

"Yes please," Bernadette said immediately.

Louise gave a broad smile as she prodded Marie, as if the two shared an unspoken understanding. Had they made some sort of wager?

Estelle said, "It is we who should be thanking you, Mr Yates, for all you've assisted us with today."

Mrs Poole wiped her hands on her apron and said,

"We can discuss who needs to thank whom over dinner. I for one would appreciate a fine meal that I don't have to cook."

"Excellently put, Mrs Poole," Felix said.

Estelle knew when she was outnumbered. But she also thought she should be on the lookout and appreciate good things when they presented themselves. Starting now. "Thank you, Mr Yates, that would be most generous of you."

The Red Lion was full of warmth and cheer. Travellers leaving and returning to London, several friends from Hatfield at other tables, and the aromas of fine cooking. There was a fire in the hearth, but at this time of year it was more for ambience than necessity.

Their table of six dined on the finest roasted vegetables crisped to perfection in tallow. Felix ordered so much roast beef, there was enough for two slices each. He drank small beer while they had ratafia. Estelle watched in appreciation as Felix held court, holding conversations with her sisters about their various projects. He animatedly joined in sharing their interests. There was laughter and lightness, and full bellies. The crease between Mrs Poole's brows softened as the pressures of the past few months faded away.

Estelle committed the evening to memory as she became even more determined to enjoy herself when such moments presented themselves. Accounts and bank loans and even thoughts of Cousin Joshua could not penetrate her happiness at this moment.

It was as if a magical bubble of light enveloped their

table, and the person responsible for that bubble was sitting beside her, bringing all of them some much-needed cheer.

By the end of the evening, her face hurt from smiling so much, and she thought that she truly couldn't recall the last time she had felt so happy and content.

Felix remained at the Red Lion, taking up the room he had paid for but not yet used, and the Baxters and Mrs Poole returned home. Estelle flopped onto her bed and fell asleep with a smile on her face.

CHAPTER 12

Felix Esteems Estelle

Felix waited outside St John's Church in Hatfield with his grandfather and great-aunt, eagerly awaiting the arrival of the Baxter sisters. One of them in particular. For a moment he wondered if he'd overfed and overtired them last night and they'd slept through. That would be very poor form on his part.

At last, they came into view, and Felix hurried forward with an eager smile. "Miss Baxter, I'd be honoured if you, your sisters and Mrs Poole would join us in the Ferndale pew. There is plenty of room for everyone."

Mrs Poole shook her head but then smiled, "I have a… ah… another pew."

She darted off in another direction to join a small huddle of friends waiting outside.

"Have I offended her in some way?" He felt terrible that he might have.

Estelle shook her head reassuringly, leaned a little closer and said, "She doesn't get much time to socialise."

"Ah, I see," he said, giving Estelle another smile. Relief flooded him. Then he also wondered, "Would you, ah, rather socialise as well?"

Estelle beamed joy back at him, and his heart soared. "I would very much enjoy sitting in the Ferndale Pew with you and Lord Ferndale and Miss Yates. That will be very pleasant socialising for me, and my sisters!"

For the first time perhaps, she wasn't resisting. Estelle had readily agreed at his first suggestion. He wondered briefly if the sisters had talked about him with Estelle last night, after he'd retired for the night to his room in the Red Lion. They were all looking at him now as they stood about in the church gardens. Louise leaned over to murmur something into Bernadette's ear which made Bernadette laugh, her eyes sparkling as she hastily covered her mouth with her hand.

"Miss Baxter." Lord Ferndale smiled warmly as he stepped closer. Felix beamed at how amicable things were between them now; his grandfather would be pleased, he was sure. "So good to see you. Has my scapegrace grandson been improving your opinion of him?"

"Mr Yates is enthusiastic in his efforts," Estelle said diplomatically.

Felix wanted to groan with frustration at this non-answer.

He'd thought she was warming up to him!

Grandpapa laughed good-naturedly, which only made Felix feel a little queasy.

The bells ceased ringing at that moment, which was the signal for everyone to make their way inside the church. Estelle walked sedately at his side, nodding to friends and acquaintances as they passed, and Felix saw not a few people's eyes widen as he led the Baxter sisters to the Ferndale pew at the very front of the church. Matrons leaned in to each other to whisper, heads wagging sagely, and he felt Estelle's palm stiffen where it rested on his arm.

Her smile remained gracious, but he thought she seemed tense. "We are creating a stir, it seems," he said lightly as they took their seats.

"My sisters and I are the subject of enough gossip in Hatfield, Mr Yates. Our respectability…"

"What could be more respectable than attending church in the invited company of the most respected family in the area?" he asked gently.

She looked as though she might have been about to say something else, but the Reverend Millings's wife sat down at the organ and played the opening bars of the first hymn. It was time to stand up and sing, so he would not be able to keep up a conversation.

Delightful song filled his ears. The Baxter sisters' voices carried the melodies rather beautifully. Of course, he was completely biassed, but he was sure Estelle's tune was the prettiest of all of them. Heaven help him - and he was in the right place for that kind of help - he'd become completely enamoured with Miss Estelle Baxter.

He'd been truthful when he'd told her she was the first woman he'd seriously considered courting. But when had that serious consideration started? Not when they were jesting at dinner, and not when he'd failed to purchase the books.

Perhaps it was while hunting for the cat? He truly couldn't pinpoint the moment when his initial interest had turned to esteem.

He hadn't known Miss Baxter long, but he already admired Estelle as a woman who took things seriously and considerately. She cared deeply for her family and friends and appeared to want the best for everyone. And she was so dashed pretty to gaze upon. He hoped his voice was up to the challenge of matching hers as they reached the second verse. Their fingers came into contact as they both tried to turn the page in the hymn book they shared. A spark ignited at her touch.

He caught a blush in her cheeks and wondered if she'd felt the spark too.

The Reverend Silas Millings's fire and brimstone sermon might have struck fear into many townspeople, but Felix was too full of happiness to let the words settle into his brain and dampen his spirits. Beside him, Miss Baxter tilted her head down like a penitent woman. It wasn't until he angled his eyes further that he saw the edges of her lips canted in a wry smile.

Mirth rippled through his body. He had to look away quickly, lest he laugh in church. He might well be the heir to a barony, but his name would be mud if he committed such a sin as mocking their spiritual leader.

The sermon seemed to go on forever. And did the reverend really believe everything he was saying, about

Woman being put on Earth to tempt Man from holiness? It had been quite a while since Felix had read the Bible, but he was fairly sure there was something in there about Lucifer disguised as a snake being the original tempter. Felix looked at the vicar's wife, sitting on the stool in front of the organ with her hands folded demurely in her lap and her eyes fixed on the floor, and felt sorry for the poor woman. She looked beaten down, as if she never had a reason to smile.

The reverend wasn't even an interesting speaker; he droned on and on and Felix felt his eyelids beginning to drift. The church was quite warm in the middle of summer, packed with people as it was. He pinched himself on the hand, trying to stay awake, and heard a tiny muffled choke beside him. Estelle had spotted the gesture and was smothering a laugh, her eyes sparkling with amusement when he glanced at her. Glancing past Estelle, he was fairly sure at least one of her sisters *was* asleep, though - Marie's head was resting against Louise's shoulder and her eyes were closed, shaded by her bonnet.

Reverend Millings thundered something about women being a temptation to men's eyes, and Felix bit back his own smile and returned his gaze to the front of the church. Yes, Estelle was very tempting to his eyes.

Eventually, the sermon came to its long-winded conclusion and Felix gave Estelle another mirthful glance and a mouthed *"Finally!"* She made a soft shush noise as the sermon started up again. It wasn't over at all - the man of the cloth had merely stopped to sip water before launching into his second act.

This was interminable. He cast a glance at Grandpapa and noticed he had a fixed stare at the wall behind the vicar. For all he knew, his grandfather may have perfected the art of falling asleep with his eyes open.

There were some positive moments, however. Felix was grateful for so many people lowering their heads in prayer, so that he might also catch glimpses of Estelle blushing gently each time he peeked her way.

At long last the vicar concluded his rhetoric and the choir stood again to lead the congregation in a hymn. Felix was glad of it; he'd been seated so long his posterior was growing quite numb. Thankfully, it did not itch at all, and he was once again exceedingly glad to have the assistance of the Baxter sisters in that regard.

He should suggest to his great-aunt that she obtain a few more cushions for the Ferndale pew, he thought, as the service came to its end.Despite his boredom and his sore posterior, Felix found himself almost wishing the Vicar had kept talking, so that he might spend more time next to this delightful woman.

Estelle and her sisters thanked his grandfather and great-aunt, and the group made their way down the aisle into the sunshine outside to chat with friends.

Blinking into the sun streaming through the doors, he couldn't help thinking St John's Church, Hatfield, would be a beautiful place to get married. Perhaps with a different vicar officiating, so that he didn't fall asleep at his own wedding.

Felix was standing in the doorway, about to take the steps down to the front lawn, when his grandfather and

Reverend Millings caught him up in a conversation about raising funds for church roof repairs. Torn between loyalty to his grandfather, who would most likely be pressed most sternly for delivering the funds, and wanting to be with Estelle on this lovely day, Felix remained in position. He may have been standing beside his grandfather and looking at the vicar, but his ears were sternly trained toward the direction of Estelle. He felt rather like a hound straining at the leash, desperate to be released to pursue his quarry, and smiled privately to himself.

A woman's voice he didn't immediately recognise said something about, "a disgrace."

Oh dear! He feigned a cough and looked her way. With a sinking stomach, he realised it was Estelle's cousin, the ghastly Mrs Baxter, who'd made a royal nuisance of herself at the Assembly two nights ago, determined to fling her friends and their daughters at Felix, and obviously just as keen to ensure he stayed well away from Estelle. Mrs Baxter's husband was with her, and from their postures and finger waving, they were thoroughly annoyed with Estelle for some reason.

Perhaps they were simply like that, though, and maybe they didn't need a reason?

"Yes, of course," he said hastily to Reverend Millings. "We shall make this our top priority." He wanted to end this conversation immediately, but Reverend Millings took this as an opportunity to launch a new tirade about the ungodliness spreading through Hatfield.

Blocking out the Reverend's sonorous tones, his ears

picked up the higher register of Estelle's cousin, Mrs Baxter, almost shrieking as she wagged her finger under Estelle's nose.

"You do not belong in the Ferndale pew, you encroaching baggage! You are nothing more than a shop-keeper, you should know your place!"

His pulse thumped in his head and his hands clenched in silent fury.

"Excuse me," he said to both older men and walked away without a backwards glance. Estelle was in turmoil and he needed to intervene. Behind him, he heard the vicar say something in outraged tones, and Lord Ferndale's dry response of; "Since my grandson is not in charge of the disbursement of funds from Ferndale yet, I do not believe he is required in this conversation, Reverend. Shall we continue?"

Bless you, Grandfather, Felix thought silently, and quickened his pace.

Mrs Baxter finished her tirade before he reached Estelle and stalked off with her nose in the air, her hand on her husband's arm. Should he go after them and give him a piece of his mind? No, that would have to wait. Estelle's agonised expression and tear-filled eyes cut him to the quick. He wanted to throw his arms around her, but mindful there must be close to fifty people within clear sight of them, he held his arms by his sides and stood stiffly in front of her.

"I got here as fast as I could, but I am too late. I am so sorry."

"Oh dear," Estelle sniffed, pressing her hand against

her mouth, ducking her head in obvious hopes those around them wouldn't see her tears.

He handed her his freshly-pressed handkerchief.

She dabbed her eyes and asked, "How much did you hear?"

"Enough to know they are not worthy to clean your boots!" He was furious. How dare the Baxters judge her? How dare they judge his right to invite whomever he pleased to join his family at church?

She gave a shaky laugh-sob and dabbed her face again.

"I shall give them a piece of my mind!" he said, moving away to give chase.

She grabbed his sleeve and pulled him back. "Don't, please. It will only make things worse. And anyway, they aren't wrong. I *am* merely a shopkeeper."

"Miss Baxter, you are worth ten of your cousins, any fool can see that."

She sighed and dabbed the last drops from her eyes. Then she gave him a small smile and returned his handkerchief.

"Keep it."

She sniffed and tucked it into her sleeve. "Thank you. You're very kind, Mr Yates - as you always are."

"You do realise," Felix said hopefully, "that if you were Mrs Yates, your rightful place would be in the Ferndale pew."

He bit his lip and held his breath as he watched her expression. She said nothing for a moment, but to his immense pleasure, she appeared to be giving his suggestion deep consideration. Might she actually be about to say yes? She had looked almost as if she might, yesterday morning in the bookshop when she was looking at that document, before he stepped in the mouse entrails.

"Ah, Felix!" Lord Ferndale said as he approached, Miss Yates on his arm.

He glanced up. His grandfather and great-aunt were only a few steps away. And they were also ruining the mood. He loved them both dearly, but at that moment he wished them both far, far away.

CHAPTER 13

More Bugs!

Estelle took a steadying breath to acknowledge Lord Ferndale and Miss Yates. They were lovely friends, but if they had kept their distance for just a little longer, she might have answered Felix in the affirmative.

That's where her mind, and her heart, were headed. Cousin Joshua and Phoebe were ghastly to her and her sisters. They seemed to save their strongest poison for her, perhaps because she was the eldest. But Felix had been right. If she married him, Estelle's position in Hatfield would rise to Felix's level, which was well above that of her cousins.

They would never be able to speak to her like that again.

But did that mean they'd simply shift their choler to Marie? Lovely, clever and gentle Marie who never had a bad word for anyone and who was so sensitive to the world around her. They could try their luck with Louise, but she'd probably laugh them off. Or pour stinking glue on them. That thought nearly made her giggle.

Or would they target Bernadette?

The thought churned her stomach.

If Estelle merely only had to worry for herself, she might have already said yes, but there seemed no easy way to do that without her decision affecting so many others.

Miss Yates sidled up to Estelle and said, "It was lovely seeing you with young Felix." Then she dropped her voice lower and said, "I couldn't find either one of you for the last dance at the assembly. I hope you were not over tired from the dancing?"

Estelle got the message immediately. Their absence was noted, but it most definitely was not for the reason Miss Yates thought. "Miss Yates, there is a delicate matter we must discuss."

The woman's face brightened and she suggested, "Love's first kiss?"

Colour flooded Estelle's face. Yes, but that wasn't the issue. The memory of her kiss with Felix flooded Estelle's system, but she had to brush it away for a far more serious matter. "That's not why we were absent. You see, Felix had," she quickly checked over her shoulder to make sure they would not be overheard, and lowered her voice, "*bedbugs.*"

Miss Yates gasped and said, "From the Red Lion? Surely not!"

"You are correct, it was not from there. Felix tried to book a room but they were full, so he spent the night at

The Swan. That's where he got the bed bugs. I could not let him infest the Red Lion with them, so we slipped away and I found him a change of clothes from my father's wardrobe."

Heat spread over her face at the memories of Felix in his clinging wet shirt in that barrel.

Miss Yates's eyes turned to the side as she counted in her head.

"You are correct again," Estelle said, "After he stayed at The Swan, he returned to Ferndale Hall where he slept in his own bed. I'm afraid that bed will most likely have bedbugs."

Miss Yates patted her chest with anxiety and said, "I cannot even think where to begin resolving such an issue. Do we need to burn the furniture?"

"No, Miss Yates, it is not smallpox, so we don't have to do that. But you will need to instruct the staff to wash all bedding and bedclothes, and as many other regular clothes as possible. Curtains too, just to be on the safe side."

"It's too much!" Miss Yates looked as if someone had asked her to skip all the way to London. Backwards! "It is impossible. You simply must come to Ferndale Hall to help."

Estelle shook her head doubtfully. "Surely your house-keeper, ma'am…"

"What about Mrs Sykes?" Lord Ferndale, who had been speaking momentarily to someone else, joined the conversation. "She has not been well, I'm afraid, Miss Baxter."

Miss Yates jumped in, "Which is why I've begged Miss Baxter to come and stay with us for a spell to help me with the problem, brother," Miss Yates said. When Lord Ferndale looked puzzled, she leaned in and said in a loud whisper; "*Bedbugs.*"

Lord Ferndale's eyes bulged. "Dear Lord, no, not at the Hall! Miss Baxter, you simply must take pity on us!"

She could not say no to their desperate entreaties. "I suppose I could pack a bag and come for a day or two," she said uncertainly.

"Indeed, you absolutely must! Go home now and pack a few things and we shall bring the carriage around and collect you in half-an-hour." Lord Ferndale nodded in satisfaction. "Felix! Walk Miss Baxter back to the book-shop directly, if you please."

"Yes, Grandfather," Mr Yates said, and Estelle cast him a suspicious look, as if they'd somehow planned this.

He did wear a suitably sober expression, so perhaps she was being overly suspicious? As they began walking together back to the bookshop, however, a smile broke out on his lips.

"This is all your fault, don't look so smug about it," she accused crossly. "I really can't just abandon my responsibilities like this!"

"My grandfather's orders are quite hard to resist," Felix said, in a distinct non-apology.

Estelle sighed. "You aren't wrong about that, Mr Yates, and truly I could not say no to Miss Yates, but oh, how I wish you hadn't stayed that night at The Swan!"

They caught up with her sisters who were just

arriving back at the bookshop, and Louise turned to look at Estelle as Marie was unlocking the door.

"Abandon what responsibilities?"

She sighed, aggrieved. She hadn't realised her voice had carried so much. "Miss Yates needs my help at Ferndale Hall. Their housekeeper is unwell. The bedbugs," she explained further.

"Of course you must go," Bernadette said immediately. "Let me make up a big package of herbs for you to take." She hurried up the stairs first, plucking a satchel from a cupboard under the dresser. "Some of that tonic for Lord Ferndale's cough too, Mr Yates!" she said over her shoulder, grabbing up vials and packages.

"I can't just leave the rest of you to manage everything," Estelle said unhappily.

"Of course you can," Marie disagreed firmly. "We have managed perfectly well in your absence before this, when you and Father were off on book-buying expeditions."

"But the bank letter…"

"Will still be here when you return, and I don't know what you think you can do about it anyway." Marie lifted her shoulder in a shrug. "I'll spend some time going over the books. Send another advertisement to The Times, they always do very well."

"And you can take Lord Ferndale's books, they're ready!" Louise said, and though she didn't say it in front of Mr Yates, the unspoken subtext was *and get him to pay for them.* "I'll package them up!"

"You had best put some clothes in a valise," Marie said, "come, I'll help you."

"And you sit down there, Mr Yates, and I'll make some tea," Mrs Poole said in her usual cheerful motherly way, "and you can have some biscuits."

"You are a gem, Mrs Poole," Felix said enthusiastically, taking a seat at the kitchen table.

Estelle allowed Marie to half-drag her away to her bedroom and pull a valise out from under the bed, but drew the line when Marie opened her closet and grabbed every single evening dress off the pegs.

"Marie! I'm only going for a day or two, I certainly don't need three evening dresses!"

"You never know," Marie said, peering owlishly at Estelle through her spectacles as she laid the dresses on the bed. "And they do dress for dinner at Ferndale Hall. You want to look nice, don't you?"

"Well, yes, but…" She didn't even expect to stay for three days. What would be the point of three evening dresses?

"I'll lend you my yellow spotted muslin and my best gloves too, and you had better take your spare bonnet. Come on, get to packing!" Marie flapped her hands at Estelle and left to fetch the yellow dress. Estelle sighed again and opened the valise. It was good-sized, and she supposed she could fit four day dresses as well as the evening gowns and the underthings she would need.

"This is enough clothes to stay for a month," she muttered finally, squeezing the lid down and buckling the straps.

"Silly to take a half-empty case though," Marie said cheerfully. "And since you're going by carriage, you needn't worry about carrying it."

"Good thing too." Estelle tested the handle and groaned at the weight. "Maybe I should take a few things out…"

"Certainly not, when Mr Yates is here to carry it for you!" Marie seized her by the shoulders and looked into Estelle's face. "Listen to me, sister," she said seriously, and Estelle froze. Marie rarely used that tone.

"What?" she asked faintly.

"Use this time as a holiday and enjoy yourself."

Estelle half-laughed, shaking her head. "I wouldn't call dealing with a burgeoning bedbug infestation a holiday!"

"Ferndale Hall has a full complement of maids; even if the housekeeper is indisposed all you'll need to do is give orders. Enjoy yourself. Relax. And take the time to get to know Mr Yates properly, before you make any irrevocable decisions."

Oh, so *this* was the serious point Marie had been working up to. Sobering, Estelle nodded.

The other benefit of Estelle being away for a few days would mean hearty meals at Ferndale Hall and one less mouth to feed at home. That would save a few pennies and help a little. She would return with Lord Ferndale's latest payment and they would work out the best way to approach the bank. That single letter of demand had swept all their small but hard-won gains away so quickly, it was difficult to think how they could proceed.

Perhaps a few days away dealing with something as mundane but frustrating as bedbugs was exactly what she needed?

As Estelle kissed her sisters goodbye, Louise gave her books for Lord Ferndale to Felix, who carried them in one arm. He accepted them without demur. With his free hand, he easily lifted Estelle's valise.

That did not match her first impressions, when he'd barely carried one book into the store from the pile on the street. She'd thought him distracted and unfit. Then the truth hit her. He wasn't weak at all, but he had been distracted by the one book he'd been looking for.

With a sigh, Estelle had to accept that she'd done Felix a great disservice in judging him so quickly. She heard a small grunt as he opened the shop door and saw his neck muscles straining with the weight.

A giggle escaped. He was struggling with the effort, but he was doing his very best not to show it. Somehow, that raised him even further in her opinion, that he was doing his best to help without complaining.

Outside in the sunshine, the Ferndale carriage came into view. The driver slowed the two horses to a stop outside Baxter's Fine Books. Felix's horse was tethered loosely to the back, as it followed behind. He would probably ride it home while Estelle travelled with Miss Yates and Lord Ferndale.

She climbed in and sat beside Miss Yates, while Lord Ferndale sat opposite, and Felix handed her valise to the coachman to put in the boot.

To Estelle's surprise, Felix climbed into the carriage

and sat opposite her as he greeted his grandfather and great-aunt again.

There was little room in the footwell, and his long legs meant his knees were perilously close to touching hers.

Lord Ferndale raised an imperious eyebrow at his grandson. "You're not riding home?"

"I thought I'd give Hannibal a reprieve," Felix answered with his usual irrepressible grin. "He found a patch of red clover outside the church and he will be skittish now."

"Interesting," Lord Ferndale said, but then offered nothing more.

Miss Yates patted her hand to her chest in sign of distress. Then scratched at her sternum. "I am itching already. I dread to think what awaits us at the Hall."

Felix reassured her. "All shall be well, aunt, we have Miss Baxter to save us."

Estelle tried not to smile too much at his praise, but it was rather lovely. And he in turn was smiling so delightfully her way.

He continued, "Why, Miss Baxter knew I had the little biters before I did. She has a sharp eye and knows the signs."

Miss Yates squirmed in her seat, bumping Estelle.

Lord Ferndale rubbed a patch of his thigh and laughed. "The more I think about it, the more I feel like itching as well. Is it possible they are in the carriage seats?"

The carriage went over a bump and Felix's knee

pushed against Estelle's leg, branding her through the layers of fabric.

"It is highly unlikely," Estelle said, feeling the small of her back begin to prickle. "Since Mr Yates only spent one night at the Hall, and didn't use the carriage. They cannot have spread too far in so short a time."

"We should probably change the topic," Felix suggested. "I fear talking about such things makes us think too much and so on and so forth." He too scratched at his arm as the carriage hit another bump and his knees knocked into Estelle again.

Estelle seized upon Felix's good advice. "Lord Ferndale, I hope I'm not speaking out of turn, but Mr Yates mentioned that you are sometimes afflicted with a cough in the evenings. My sister Bernadette is very skilled with herbs and remedies and has provided a bottle of tonic she recommends for such afflictions."

The old gentleman nodded in appreciation. "Well, that is very kind of Miss Bernadette. I shall certainly try it. Goodness knows nothing Doctor Rasley has suggested has helped."

"Perhaps I should also send for Bernadette to come to the Hall, once we deal with the … er … once we're settled, and she may have something for Mrs Sykes?" Estelle suggested.

Felix, drat him, knocked his knee against Estelle even though there was no bump in the road this time to warrant it. All the while he kept smiling his handsome smile and making things flip in her belly. She tried to glare at him, but her heart wasn't in it. The corners of her mouth kept wanting to turn up.

Miss Yates provided a welcome distraction. "I'm sure she'd welcome a chat with Bernadette. Doctor Rasley can be …" she drifted away.

"Off putting?" Estelle suggested.

Felix interrupted. "Old Rasley's not still going, is he? Or has his son stepped up?"

"I forget you've been away," Lord Ferndale said. "Yes, it's the same Doctor Rasley. His son is practising in London and has made it quite clear he has no plans to take over his father's business, at any stage."

"I didn't see Rasley in church," Felix said.

Lord Ferndale coughed discreetly and said, "He's not at his best in the mornings."

"We really should find a way to encourage his retirement," Miss Yates said. "No disrespect to his many, *many* years of service …"

Estelle looked out the window as Ferndale Hall came into view. The doctor's unreliable performance, not to mention his old-fashioned, judgmental attitude, was why so many women came to see Bernadette.

Lord Ferndale sighed in frustration. "If the doctor retires, I'll have to take meetings with the Town Council to agree to appoint a replacement, and I'm afraid I may be in a minority."

A collective grunt of frustration erupted from Estelle and Miss Yates, as they recognised the major problem facing Hatfield's collective health.

"I'm missing something," Felix said, looking around at them all with his brows wrinkled in confusion.

Lord Ferndale chuckled. "You have been away for some time, my boy. The local magistrate is now Miss Baxter's cousin, Joshua Baxter, and with his crony Reverend Millings and several aldermen who like to follow their lead, I'm afraid the mayor and I are often outvoted."

Felix groaned. "Oh God. We're sunk!"

"Not if we can get the new hospital funded," Miss Yates said stoutly. "We shall have the funds to hire two more doctors at least, and you had best believe my ladies on the hospital committee *shall* have a say in who is appointed. The aldermen will listen to their wives!"

"Or they'll be eating pease porridge for weeks?" Lord Ferndale said with amusement.

Miss Yates smirked. "*Cold* pease porridge."

"Perish the thought!" Felix shuddered.

"I hope that tactic works, Florence," Lord Ferndale said, smiling kindly at his sister. "Certainly, it would work on Felix, I believe, but perhaps our aldermen are not so governed by their stomachs."

The carriage slowed in the circular drive and Estelle sighed, looking up at the vast manor house and thinking of the sheer amount of linen and beds to treat. "One chal-lenge at a time. Let's first rid Ferndale Hall of unwanted guests!"

CHAPTER 14

Estelle's New Home

Felix had been fairly sure his great-aunt was merely acting helpless about the bed bug situation in order to get Estelle to Ferndale Hall under false pretences. His suspicions were quite confirmed when Mrs Sykes - who was supposed to be indisposed - greeted them in the front hall, not looking even remotely under the weather.

"I understood you weren't well, Mrs Sykes," Estelle said, her eyes slightly narrowed.

He really shouldn't laugh out loud. He couldn't even look his great-aunt in the eye right now or he'd blow everything. It would be lovely to have a few days to get to know Miss Baxter, away from the town and her heavy responsibilities. Bless Aunt Florence and her machinations!

"Well, I have had a trifling cold, Miss Baxter, but I'm quite recovered now," Mrs Sykes said cheerfully. "Have you come for dinner, miss?"

"Miss Baxter will be staying a few days," Felix said,

gesturing to a footman. "If you'd bring her valise in from the carriage, Matthew? And there's a large parcel of books too, take it straight to the library for Lord Ferndale, if you please."

"Of course, sir." The footman hurried to do his bidding, and Felix turned to Mrs Sykes.

"Would the Yellow Suite be available for Miss Baxter?"

The housekeeper's eyes widened infinitesimally, but aloud all she said was, "Certainly, Mr Yates! Please, Miss Baxter, if you'll come with me, Matthew will bring your things up directly and I'll assign you a maid."

"Oh, a maid won't be necessary," Estelle tried to demur.

"Yes, it is," Felix mouthed at Mrs Sykes over the top of Estelle's head, nodding vigorously.

This would be splendid!

"Oh, we wouldn't dream of not assigning a maid to a guest, Miss Baxter!" Mrs Sykes said, admirably straight-faced. "I think Isabelle will do nicely. I'll send her up with tea shortly."

Estelle looked as though she might be about to argue some more, but after a quick glance at Miss Yates, who was smiling and nodding with approval, she finally murmured a quiet "thank you" and turned to follow Mrs Sykes up the stairs.

"Ah, Mrs Sykes," he heard her say as they went, "I'm not here just for amusement. I'm afraid there's a bit of a problem..."

Mrs Sykes was too well trained to scream out loud,

just as she'd shown no major reaction when Felix asked her to give Estelle the suite reserved for the highest-ranking visitors, one which royalty had stayed in more than once, but she did stop in her tracks for a moment and look back at Felix, tight-lipped.

Felix winced. The bedbugs were all his fault, and he knew it. He wasn't going to leave all the hard work to Ferndale's staff in the next few days, capable though he knew them to be. He would be pitching in and working alongside them to fix the mess he'd made.

"The Yellow Suite?" His grandfather nudged him and chuckled richly. "Now tell me, Felix. Are you making real progress with Miss Baxter?"

"I don't know," Felix said with absolute honesty.

"Well, we have her in the right place now." His great-aunt linked her arm through his and smiled up at him. "Who can resist the combination of your charm and Ferndale Hall's beauties?" She waved around them, and Felix smiled as he looked up at the paintings of his ancestors on the walls. They were a stern-looking lot for the most part, save for his secret favourite, his great-great-grand-mother, Lady Elizabeth. She shared his fair hair and blue eyes, and she had just the slightest smile playing at the corners of her mouth, as though she was about to laugh.

He looked forward to telling Estelle about all the family history. About giving custody of his heritage to her, as stewardess for future generations. He couldn't imagine anyone better than Estelle, with her determina-tion and dedication to duty.

And of course, it didn't hurt that she was one of the

prettiest women he'd ever seen. He cast one more glance up the stairs, already thinking about how soon he'd see her again. About how beautiful she'd look at dinner with her eyes shining in the candlelight from Ferndale Hall's candelabra.

Then he giggled to himself about their last meal here together, where she'd used the candelabra to block his view. He must instruct the footmen to put more candles on the side tables instead. Nothing on the table she could hide behind!

"Are those my books from Miss Louise? How marvellous!"

Felix dragged his attention back to his grandfather. "I believe so. Shall I unwrap them for you?"

"Don't you dare touch my books!" Lord Ferndale clutched the package to his chest possessively.

"Right, right, understood!" Felix held his hands up, laughing. "But I did make a purchase or two at the book-shop you might like to see. I'll just fetch them, shall I?"

***

Estelle took a steadying breath as Mrs Sykes showed her into the Yellow Suite, which Mr Yates had designated for her stay. She and her sisters had sometimes stayed at Ferndale Hall in the past. Just a few days ago she'd stayed the night after the rainstorm prevented her travel back to town. That had been in a comfortable, small room for the sake of convenience. She'd never in her whole life stayed in a room as beautiful and important as this one. It was hard to fight the urge to twirl with delight at the incredible amount of space and beautiful furnishings. As the name suggested, the walls were painted yellow from the high decorative ceilings to the white wainscotting. A series of landscape paintings hung from the picture rail along one wall. Light flooded the room as Mrs Sykes pulled back the thick, golden-hued drapes. A soft gasp escaped as Estelle realised the landscape paintings were of that same view, at different times of year.

A broad oak tree with its green summer leaves provided welcome shade for a hot day. Beyond the oak was a delightful lake that snaked behind another row of trees, giving the illusion it might extend much farther.

The Yellow Suite was several rooms, the first being a beautifully appointed sitting room, the second the largest bedroom Estelle had ever been in. The bed had an enormous, carved oak headboard that spoke of a long history and connection. There were lions and coats of arms carved into it.

Mrs Sykes made a quick bob to Estelle and said, "I hope it is to your liking, Miss Baxter?"

"I am nearly lost for words," Estelle admitted, "It is …"

"Somewhat daunting?" Mrs Sykes said with a smile.

"A little," Estelle admitted, "But it's also inviting and warm." She turned to examine more of the suite, barely believing she would be staying in here, possibly for more than one night. Miss Yates's claims that they needed her to rid them of bed bugs had to be wildly exaggerated. Mrs Sykes appeared in good health. If this was a ruse to bring Estelle and Felix together, it was working. She was falling more in love with this room with every heartbeat.

In the corner under the windows were low shelves of books, keeping them out of direct sunlight. There was a neat chaise longue to entice a reader to stay. How utterly perfect.

"Your bags will be here presently, as will Isabelle to assist you. Please ring the bell if you need any further assistance."

"But Mrs Sykes, I have come here to assist your good self in that other delicate matter. My sister, Bernadette has packed many herbs and posies that will aid us."

Mrs Sykes swallowed. "There really *are* bedbugs?"

"I'm afraid so. You see, Mr Yates stayed at The Swan, and then returned here to his room in the hall, and the next day at the assembly he…"

"…Had those pestilent biters," Felix finished her sentence as he walked in with Matthew carrying her valise and the satchel of Bernadette's herbs. "I thought you'd need these sooner rather than later."

"Mr Yates," Mrs Sykes bobbed a quick curtsey to Felix.

Matthew bowed to Estelle and left the three of them in the room.

Warmth bloomed in Estelle at seeing Felix's beaming smile. He shouldn't be so happy, considering the trouble he was about to put the entire household to, yet here he was, full of his usual joy.

"We have our work cut out for us," Estelle said as she opened the satchel and fetched Bernadette's packages. "Mrs Sykes, these are herbs to add to the wash. This liquid is to sprinkle on the floorboards. These are for putting in the bottom of the drawers or between folded sheets."

The unflappable housekeeper's expression remained steady. "Thank you, Miss Baxter." Then her voice almost appeared to falter as she who helped everyone else asked for the same in return. "I'm not well-educated in herbs and the like. Would you mind instructing Isabelle on which ones to pick from the kitchen garden?"

Felix stepped in. "How about I help as well? After all, I am the cause of this upset. I do feel rather responsible."

Mrs Sykes's eyebrows rose so imperceptibly, Estelle wondered if she had imagined it.

"There's no need, Mr Yates," she said.

Mrs Sykes looked caught between wanting to make a start on treating their infestation, and not wanting to leave Mr Yates alone with their guest.

Isabelle arrived and bobbed a curtsey at the doorway. "We're boiling the coppers this minute, Mrs Sykes."

"Good," Mrs Sykes said, holding aloft one of the packets. "I'll add this mixture to the water."

Oh dear, it was the wrong set of herbs. Estelle had to do something, or Bernadette's work would be wasted. She tilted her head towards the other packet and Mrs Sykes swapped them over. Estelle nodded that she had the right one.

With a little exaggeration, she said, "I would dearly love to see the kitchen garden. I've heard such lovely things about it, and my sister Bernadette asked me for a full report."

"Yes Miss," Isabelle bobbed obediently. "I'll show you where it is."

Felix said, "I should very much like to see the kitchen garden as well. I have only been back a short while and have been remiss in my duties here at the Hall."

Estelle added, "Bernadette gave me a list of plants that will assist. I'm sure most of them will be growing here."

Mrs Sykes nodded deferentially. "The gardeners will cut them for you."

"I'm more than happy to …" Estelle drifted off as understanding dawned. She was not here to work, she was here to give advice only. She could have very well written a list of what was needed. In fact, they might have been better off had Bernadette come instead of herself. But then… she cast a cynical glance at Felix. Somehow, she didn't think Bernadette would have been invited.

Felix offered her his elbow and she placed her hand on the inside of it, letting him lead her to the garden while Mrs Sykes and Isabelle went to the washrooms.

"This is such a glorious garden." Estelle looked around. The high brick walls protected the gardens from wind and weather, and the glass-houses built up against the walls provided a controlled climate for plants that required it. The orderly rows of planted vegetables and herbs grew vigorously in their raised beds. In this garden there were no plants that were purely decorative, everything had some use, and yet it was still beautiful. Two gardeners were working, one of them training peas up against canes, another weeding the strawberry patch.

Both rose to their feet to offer respectful bows as she and Felix walked up.

"'Tis Sunday, Willis, shouldn't you be resting?" Felix said cheerfully to the older man.

"Wife chased me out the 'ouse, sir, and our lad with me. Said she couldn't abide us underfoot all day. Thought we might as well get a few jobs done."

"Good Lord, go fishing or something!" Felix said it with a smile, but Estelle could see he truly meant it. He wanted his people, the workers at the estate, to enjoy their leisure hours, and suddenly her heart warmed towards him. It was a kind gesture that would no-doubt endear him all the more to the staff. Her cousin Phoebe begrudged her maids even a half-day off a week, and gave them Sunday mornings with the stipulation that they must attend church, so the poor girls barely got two hours to themselves. And yet here was Felix telling the gardeners to go fishing!

"Before you go, would you point us in the right direction?" Felix turned to Estelle. "Miss Baxter is in search of several herbs."

"Go and get a basket, lad," Willis said to his son, and the boy scurried off quickly. Willis bowed respectfully to Estelle. "What can I helps you with, miss?"

She recited the list, and Willis nodded before leading her to the herbaceous border and kneeling to begin cutting some fragrant lavender for her and put it in the basket his son soon returned with. Next came rosemary, which she knew was growing well here from the cuttings

Bernadette had supplied to them. Then it was on to the treasure trove of plants in the glass houses, including lemons and their blossoms. In a large earthenware pot grew a small laurel. She'd heard of bay leaves, and although it wasn't on Bernadette's list, Estelle picked a few of the leaves - not too many as the plant was still a small shrub - to dry them. Bernadette would certainly want them.

It occurred to Estelle, as they walked back inside some half an hour later with Felix carrying two baskets filled with herbs and flower blossoms, that the Ferndale Hall servants were being unusually deferential to her. She'd been here quite a few times over the years, after all, and all the servants were Hatfield locals she'd known her whole life. They'd never previously bowed and scraped quite so much as they were doing at the moment. She eyed Felix suspiciously. This had to be his doing.

"Mr Yates," she asked, as they made their way to the stillroom, past footmen and maids busily scurrying hither and thither with pails of hot water and bundles of linen to wash, "what exactly have you said to your staff about me?"

"I beg your pardon?" Felix asked, his brow furrowing in confusion.

Estelle tried not to think how adorable he looked when he wore that expression, because otherwise she'd forget what she needed to ask him. "The servants are being far more deferential to me than I'm used to. What have you told them about me?"

Her heart beat a little faster as she waited for his answer.

"Ah." Light dawned. "You think I've announced that you're Ferndale Hall's future mistress."

She nearly screamed in shock. "Keep your voice down!" Estelle hissed as a passing maid lost her footing and splashed water from her bucket upon overhearing him. The maid quickly regained her composure and scurried off.

"Oh, goodness! Well, if you haven't before, you have now!"

Felix grinned unrepentantly. "I hadn't, I promise. But you are the first lady I've ever brought home to the Hall. I think they might just be, ah, playing it safe perhaps?" His blue eyes were soft as he gazed down at her. Parts of her body thrummed in response. "Perhaps they're hoping that if they impress you, it'll make you more likely to accept me. They couldn't hope for a better mistress than you, and I'm sure they realise that."

She could get lost in those blue eyes. And she didn't want to fault his logic, either. "Well," she wanted to laugh but she also feared how much the staff might talk, "that maid will no doubt be spreading what she's heard among the rest of the staff at the end of the day."

"Excellent. Then I can be absolutely sure you'll be treated with the respect you deserve," Felix answered cheerfully.

He was deliberately misinterpreting her, but she found it impossible to be cross with him. How did he manage to do that? "That wasn't what I meant… you are quite incorrigible, Mr Yates!" She was half-laughing, though, as they reached the stillroom and Felix set down a basket to open the door for her.

It was quiet in the stillroom, fragrant with the scents of drying herbs and curing soap. It was also dim, as there were only small windows that faced north. Felix put the baskets on the long bench at one side of the room and Estelle began to sort the cuttings into bundles, separating those that would need to be used fresh and those that would need to be dried for greater efficacy. Bernadette would be beside herself with joy in this stillroom, but all the same, Estelle was glad nobody else was here.

The door was deliberately left wide open, but she was still very conscious that she and Felix were quite alone in here. Her senses felt heightened, as if she could feel him moving about the room. Without needing to look, she knew he was standing very close beside her, watching with apparent interest as she sorted the various bundles.

Estelle found her cheeks flushing and her breath coming short as their sleeves brushed. Her pulse quickened as he stepped closer. Little by little, he closed the distance between them. Her hands stilled, and she did not move, transfixed in this low light by the closeness of him. The stillroom was designed to be cool, but she felt body heat radiating from him. His eyelids dropped as his gaze lowered to her lips. Throat suddenly dry, she swallowed.

"Estelle," he said, her name a yearning question.

With a shaky breath, she answered, "Felix."

His eyelids lifted again and their gazes locked. Then he said, "I should very much like to…"

"Yes." Estelle closed the infinitesimal distance between them and pressed her lips to his. Warmth flooded her system. Nerves jangled. The softness of his lips, the herbal aromatics and the thrill of the kiss danced together in her blood. She pulled away for a fraction to take in air, and then they were back, luxuriating in the wonder of the moment. Those soft and now warming lips of his were a balm to her soul. There was a growing understanding of what the kiss meant to both of them, but she didn't want to think. She only wanted to feel. To leave her troubles behind and live in joy. Even if only for a little moment.

His arms came around her in a warm and tender embrace. Hers did the same and her hands played with the curls at his neck. They were both breathing a little harder now with so many new sensations.

"Marvellous," he said as he broke away and double-checked they remained undisturbed.

Estelle wanted the kiss to continue; yearned for more. At the same time she appreciated his chivalry. It was one thing for the staff to be talking about her as a potential mistress of Ferndale Hall, but if they were caught like this, the gossip would be far more detrimental in nature.

"We should probably sort the plants," Estelle said, although she was so transfixed by his handsome face she didn't turn back to the sorting bench herself. They simply stood there, looking at each other in wonderment.

Mrs Sykes's voice came into the stillroom from

outside, her steps exaggerated as if she deliberately didn't want to interrupt a tender moment. When she reached the doorway she kept talking and turned her back on them to hang up a gardening hat on a hook. Felix stole a lightning-fast kiss from Estelle then stepped over to the table and announced loudly, "Mrs Sykes, how lovely of you to join us. Miss Baxter was just singing the praises of our gardeners, and your good self of course."

Estelle smothered a laugh with her hand.

Mrs Sykes turned a warmly gratified look on Estelle. "Well, that's very gracious of you, Miss Baxter! My goodness, what a marvellous lot of herbs. Now, Mr Yates." She turned a stern look on Felix. "You're going to be in our way in here, why don't you run along now?"

"I'll get out of your way, Mrs Sykes, but I do feel terribly guilty about bringing bedbugs to the Hall. I can't leave all the work to you and the maids, especially not on a Sunday. What can I do?"

Mrs Sykes considered Felix for a moment before apparently concluding that he was serious. She delivered a nod of approval his way. "That's good of you, Mr Yates. There's a great deal of water to be pumped and hauled. I'm sure you could take a turn at the pump."

"I certainly shall!" Felix squeezed Estelle's hand surreptitiously before heading for the door. "Look after Miss Baxter for me, Mrs Sykes. Show her all about the Hall!"

"You can leave her in my hands, Mr Yates." Mrs Sykes chuckled fondly as he left, shaking her head, before turning a knowing gaze on Estelle. "Yes indeed, Miss

Baxter. Let's get to showing you everything about the Hall. I'm sure it's knowledge which will come in handy in the future."

Estelle blushed.

Furiously.

CHAPTER 15

The Battle of Ferndale Hall

Ferndale Hall smelled very strongly of medicinal herbs by dinnertime that evening, but nobody minded. Given a choice between herbal aromatics and breeding bed bugs, everyone would have gladly chosen the plants any day of the week, Felix was quite sure. His muscles were pleasantly sore from working the water-pump most of the afternoon, but eventually the demands for more buckets for the laundry-maids had ceased and he'd pumped one more bucket to dump over his sweaty head. He'd long since discarded his shirt and jacket by that time and he rather thought he'd seen Estelle peeping at him from a window above the pump-yard.

By the time he blinked the water out of his eyes and looked again, though, she was gone.

He hadn't seen Estelle since leaving her in the still-room, and found he was already missing her presence. When she appeared at the doorway to the salon where the family always gathered before dinner, he jumped to his feet and hurried over to escort her in.

"Good evening. Would you like a glass of sherry? You look absolutely beautiful." She was wearing a lovely gown of yellow-and-white striped silk, her dark hair piled atop her head, a few curls framing her face becomingly. Her cheeks flushed at his compliment.

"A sherry would be lovely, thank you, Mr Yates," Estelle murmured, and he escorted her over to the sofa to sit beside his great-aunt before going to the sideboard to fetch her a glass.

"I have Bernadette's tonic here for you, Lord Ferndale," Estelle said, and he turned back to see her handing his grandfather a stoppered bottle. "Two teaspoons in a glass of wine with dinner."

"Why, thank you, my dear!" Lord Ferndale accepted the bottle. "I do hope it doesn't ruin the taste of the wine."

Estelle laughed. "Bernadette assures me it has little taste. It may make you feel sleepy, though, so I would recommend retiring soon after dinner."

"I shall take my book to my bedchamber to read instead of sitting in the library," Lord Ferndale declared solemnly.

Felix handed Estelle her sherry, and she sipped at it demurely as Miss Yates began recounting a conversation she'd had with another of the Hatfield ladies after church that morning. Felix didn't listen, too busy staring at Estelle, and had to quickly cover his lapse of manners when his great-aunt said "Don't you agree, Felix?"

"But of course, Aunt Florence," he said hastily, and caught Estelle covering up a smirk. She knew he hadn't been listening, drat it all! But it was so hard to focus when she was sitting right in front of him looking so pretty…

"Felix, I'd like you to ride over to the Benbury farm sometime this week," his grandfather said then. "Had a note that they're concerned about the roof. Can't have leaks once the autumn rains start, so go and investigate for me, would you? There's a good chap."

It would be a pretty ride to the Benbury farm, through some charming woodland. Felix determined then and there he'd find a suitable lady's mount with a side-saddle in the stables for Estelle and take her on a ride the following day. A marvellous opportunity to be alone, as well as to take her about the estate.

He got the opportunity to be alone with her rather earlier, however, when after dinner both his great-aunt and grandfather retired rather promptly, leaving him and Estelle staring at each other across the cleared dining-table at only seven o'clock.

"The library?" Felix suggested, and Estelle nodded.

How his heart soared at that simple gesture. They left the library door wide open for propriety's sake, but ended up sitting close together on comfortable reading chairs.

"You know that this is my favourite room in the hall," Estelle said, "But the Yellow Suite is a very close-run second."

"I'm so glad," he said. "The library is almost my favourite room as well."

"Almost?" she said with a smile, tilting her head at him, one delicate eyebrow arching questioningly.

Memories of their glorious kisses earlier today played in his head. "Of late, I've become rather partial to the stillroom."

They both made a soft giggle at that.

"But, the library *could* become my favourite room," he hinted hopefully.

She leaned in at the invitation and he delivered a kiss to her soft lips.

"Now it is," he teased.

He cast a glance toward the doorway and listened for footsteps. Nothing. As if the entire household had allowed them privacy. Turning back to Estelle, her shining eyes and hint of a smile invited another kiss. He gladly obliged.

His heart crashed against his ribs as their lips came together. They matched so perfectly.

As long as he lived, he would never get enough kisses from his darling Estelle.

This.

This was what love truly felt like. Delightful, intoxicating and yet welcoming at the one time. Not itchy at all, that had been the wrong path entirely.

This was love. It had to be.

He, Felix Yates, was in love with Estelle Baxter.

And it was glorious.

Steps sounded in the hall. They were exaggerated for good effect. Estelle pulled away and pretended to read her book. He looked toward the doorway and smiled. It was Mr. Thorne, come to extinguish the candles in the chandelier.

"I did not realise you were still reading," the butler said with a bow. He addressed Estelle as if she was already the mistress of the house and asked, "Do you require further refreshments, Miss Baxter?"

Estelle gave a shy smile and said, "Thank you Thorne, a small sherry perhaps?" Then she looked at Felix and he nodded that he'd like one as well.

The staff were already giving her the respect she was due, and she was handling it magnificently. She would make the most excellent mistress of the hall.

The butler nodded and made another bow. Knowing he'd be back soon, Felix sidled up to Estelle and they shared another quick kiss, then separated before anyone else arrived. When Thorne returned, they were perusing the shelves and the absolute picture of innocence.

As Thorne placed Felix's sherry on a nearby table, he muttered the words, "Very good, sir."

He couldn't help but feel the butler was letting him know that everyone approved of Estelle.

"Thorne, please let the staff know that anyone who had to work extra today, on account of … my indiscretion, is to have tomorrow afternoon off. I'll not deprive them of their rightful rest day."

Thorne smiled and said his usual, "Very good, sir."

As Thorne left, Estelle turned his way and said, "That's very kind of you to do that."

Felix shrugged. "It would have been kinder of me to have never brought the bedbugs home in the first place. I should have known the signs, as I'd had them before, in Greece."

"All the same, I'm sure this is why the staff are so dutiful. They work hard, but they know they are appreciated."

"That they are," Felix agreed. He inhaled with satisfaction at how magnificently Estelle would oversee the staff in the not-too-distant future. "This situation was my fault. I caused the problems, and yet other people had to do the work to fix it. It sits uneasily with me. I should have helped more."

That startled Estelle. "But you carried water all day, and you exhausted yourself."

"Aha, so that *was* you at the window?"

Estelle blushed beautifully, providing the answer.

He chuckled to himself, now that he knew he'd seen her watching him. He truly hadn't been trying to show off, but the work had made him hot and the water was right there. "I'm not afraid of hard work when required," he said.

She nodded and said, "I have witnessed this now, many times. And I am sorry I misjudged you at first."

"Water under the bridge," he waved his hand away. "I am only glad I'm nothing like my father. Now there was a man afraid of hard work."

Estelle reached for his hand and squeezed it in support, encouraging him to go on. Her hand in his felt so perfect. So right.

"I wasn't witness to much, because I was in the nursery most of the time, and after that I was at school.

But he was a terrible wastrel. He made my mother so dreadfully unhappy as well. She hid it as well as she could, but the signs were there."

Estelle nodded with interest, rather than a look of pity. It was exactly the tone he needed to continue.

"She remarried, and she is happy now, living in Ireland with her second husband. I would like to visit her in the near future, but I also don't want to leave my grandfather and Aunt Florence so soon after returning. I admire them both so much. And they need my help here at the Hall. I have a town council meeting tomorrow night to attend with him, and from what I've heard, the numbers are not in his favour."

She nodded and he appreciated that she understood his quandary. "Lord Ferndale and Miss Yates have become good friends to my family in the past few years as well," Estelle agreed. "I can see they are both delighted to have you home."

The sherries were forgotten as they stole some more kisses. Each felt more perfect and more miraculous than the last. For a moment, he was almost grateful for bringing bedbugs to the hall, as it meant he'd had so much more time to get to know Estelle. Felix could have stayed in the library kissing her all night, and he probably would have, but after a while, she stepped back with a shy smile and red-kissed lips and bade him a good night.

At breakfast, Felix's grandfather was full of bright cheer. "My dear Miss Baxter, you must send my best congratulations to Miss Bernadette. I have not slept so well in an age!"

"I am glad to hear that, as I'm sure my sister will be." Estelle beamed at him.

"Good to see Felix up early as well," Lord Ferndale said, turning to him as he delivered the disguised barb.

"Early rising is good for the soul," Felix said by way of greeting. He poured his great-aunt a cup of tea and then delivered the same to Estelle, along with an invitation. "Miss Baxter, would you like to ride with me to Benbury this morning? It's a delightful ride. I'm assured there is a horse in the stable who is a suitable lady's mount, and though it is some years since dear Aunt Florence gave up riding, her side-saddle is still in excellent condition."

He held his breath, waiting for her to accept.

"Thank you, I would love that."

Thank heavens. He was afraid he'd gone too far last night and she might be having second thoughts. Riding together would give him a chance to see the extent of the Ferndale property and show Estelle off to the tenants. He was sure they would love her, just as the staff in the hall did.

Barely an hour later, they were walking their horses along the river under the dappled shade of the beech and elm trees that grew along the boundary.

"You ride very well," Felix noted, "although I think

you said you rented a horse, when you came here last time?"

"Indeed, we don't keep horses of our own, but I have had plenty of opportunities to ride. Father used to take me with him on book-buying trips all over England; I have been to many towns as far away as Wales and Cornwall, and even to Edinburgh on one occasion! We generally travelled horseback with smaller packs as it's much faster. If we bought lots of books, we'd pack them in a trunk and have them sent on ahead."

"So you are well-travelled, then," Felix noted.

Her voice sounded wistful as she answered, "Better than most young ladies, I suppose, but I would not call never leaving this island well-travelled, not when conversing with a gentleman who has been so far as Greece!"

Felix smiled, and shook his head. "I have found that people are much the same everywhere, even if they speak a different language. Their motivations are no different."

"That's rather philosophical of you, Felix."

"Well, I have been in Greece, the home of the ancient philosophers; some of it must have rubbed off!"

She laughed, and joy welled in his chest. A fine day, a good horse, and a beautiful woman who laughed at his jokes; what more could a man ask for, truly? Their conversation flowed easily and happily. Laughter often arose as the warm summer breeze played over them. Felix was starting to believe and hope that Estelle truly was the woman for him, and Ferndale Hall.

They soon emerged from the trees into a field of ripening grain.

"That way, along the hedgerow." Felix pointed. "I would not for the world trample any of the farmer's crop."

They were at the farmhouse a few minutes later, the Benburys hurrying to greet them. Felix swung down off his horse and handed the reins to the farmer while he lifted Estelle down from her mount, savouring the feel of her in his arms for the few brief moments before he set her on her feet.

"Why, it's Miss Baxter, isn't it?" Mrs Benbury said, her smile inquisitive as she looked from Estelle to Felix and back again. She made a bobbed curtsey and said, "Welcome back to Ferndale, Mr Yates."

"I thank you, and I feel most welcome," Felix said as he alighted from his horse and helped Estelle dismount into his arms. He had to let her go quickly, otherwise he might not be able to resist kissing her even with an audience.

Estelle beamed with good cheer at the farmers. "What a lovely farmhouse you have, Mrs Benbury! And hello, young Mary."

Estelle crouched down, and it was then that Felix saw the little girl hiding shyly behind her mother's skirts, thumb in her mouth. "I think I might have something in my pocket you would like... what is this?" She unwrapped a small oilskin packet to reveal a jam tart, and the little girl's eyes lit up.

Estelle already knew the family, Felix realised. She had

known little Mary Benbury was shy, and had gone to the kitchen and begged a treat from Cook to bring for the little girl.

He didn't need to teach her a blessed thing about the Ferndale estates. She knew these people better than he did.

"That's right kind of you, Miss Baxter," Mrs Benbury said warmly.

Little Mary thanked Estelle shyly and stuffed the jam tart in her mouth whole. Felix hid a grin and looked back at the farmer, a sturdy man about his own age.

"My grandfather said there's an issue with your roof. Will you show me?"

"Aye, sir, and thank you for coming out so quickly."

Mrs Benbury invited Estelle to the kitchen for a glass of fresh milk while Felix climbed up into the roof space with Mr Benbury to inspect the damage; he climbed down again ten minutes later and accepted a milk glass of his own.

"I agree, Jacob," he said to the farmer. "No good putting new slates on the roof with the beam rotting like that, and it's not something you can do on your own. I'll look into arranging some men and a new beam, and we'll get it done within the week, if we can. Best to mend it before more rain makes the damage worse."

Estelle was sitting at the table with young Mary in her lap, Mary showing Estelle two corn dollies and earnestly telling her a story. Felix could feel his heart melting as he looked at them; he could envision how wonderful a mother Estelle would be. He wanted to hear children laughing as they slid down the bannisters of the grand staircase at Ferndale Hall, just as Felix himself had once done. The old house needed bringing to life again.

Estelle looked up at Felix and smiled, before gesturing to her top lip. He blinked in confusion before realising he must have a milk moustache. Hastily, he fished a handkerchief out of his pocket to blot it away.

They thanked the Benburys for their kind hospitality and mounted their horses to ride away. As they waved back at the little family, Estelle said;

"Mary should have a proper doll."

"Well, the mistress of Ferndale would be able to put one in her Christmas gift basket," Felix said gently.

"Indeed, she would," Estelle agreed, and she smiled across at him. "You'll see to their roof?"

"Of course! I'll meet with Grandfather's steward this afternoon. It should have been done some time ago; I think I might order inspections of all the estate properties. Make sure everyone's roofs are watertight before winter."

"You're far more responsible than I first thought you," Estelle said. "You'll make a very good master of Ferndale… no matter who the mistress is."

He felt ten feet tall at her praise. Nobody had ever said anything like that to him before, and he found an unexpected lump in his throat. "Thank you," he said thickly.

She smiled across at him, before her smile turned mischievous. "Race you to that tall oak," she said, and she leaned down across her horse's neck and cantered off before he'd even had the chance to gather up his reins.

"Cheat!" he laughed. "Come on, Hannibal, we can't let a lady win; our honour is at stake!"

His horse was perfectly happy to race, but Felix deliberately held him in to let Estelle win for the sole reason that he wanted to see her happy, flushed and laughing with her victory.

Honestly, she seemed to get more beautiful every time he looked at her.

On their return to Ferndale, Aunt Florence and Mrs Sykes greeted Estelle with welcoming smiles and further enquiries about resolving 'the issue at hand' as they modestly called the bedbug disaster.

Seeing the three women collaborating with such harmony warmed Felix's heart even more. Had there ever been a clearer sign that Estelle was not only the woman of his future, but the woman for Ferndale Hall as well?

He may have held fantasies about how easy it would be to run Ferndale Hall - with Estelle by his side - but that afternoon brought Felix back to reality with horrible swiftness. Baron Ferndale presided over town council meetings. Which meant they could not begin until he was there, and he could not leave until all items of business were concluded.

This was going to be part of Felix's unpalatable future.

Joshua Baxter was here, in his esteemed position of town magistrate. Reverend Milings also had a seat, as the town's leader of faith. Doctor Rasley had a seat, and the presence of the old gentleman had Felix realising why the meetings began mid afternoon rather than after dinner - as Rasley himself began to snore after the first hour.

Hadn't someone mentioned that Dr Rasley didn't attend church because early mornings didn't suit him? Early evenings seemed to be pushing his limits as well.

There was also a Mr Wellworth, and Felix didn't quite catch what that man did for the town. It didn't matter, he was aligned with Joshua Baxter as well. Oh, and Mr Burton, the solicitor, who was also in Mr Baxter's cohort.

There were of course three more members people aligned to his grandfather, including Mr Lennox the apothecary, and the mayor, and another alderman who his grandfather had appointed. But they were badly outnumbered.

Felix was unable to vote, as he was granted observer only status. The numbers kept landing five to four, in favour of Joshua Baxter's faction. The minutes felt like hours, draining his last reserves of bonhomie. This was valuable time he could be spending kissing Estelle.

His grandfather raised a discussion about the hospital committee report, which he wanted to read into the meeting's minutes. It was put to a vote but he lost, so he couldn't even raise the issue.

How were they supposed to make any progress in this town if they wouldn't even let a report be read?

The ride home with his grandfather was full of frustration. "What a colossal waste of time," Felix confessed once they were ensconced in the safety of the carriage.

"When you take on the barony, you take the good with the bad," his grandfather said.

"I didn't realise it would be that bad," he groaned.

"It was particularly awful tonight," Grandpapa admitted with a heavy sigh. "Normally they at least vote in favour of reading reports from some of the town committees."

"Why would you not want a hospital?" That was the part that infuriated Felix.

The old man chuckled and said, "Oh, they want a hospital, they were simply sending me a message that it needed to be on their terms, where they want it. And I rather fear they are trying to push for a change of membership of the hospital committee, to include more of their wives."

"A power play?" Felix was all for some good intrigue. "Let me guess, Mrs Baxter wants to be on the hospital committee?"

"Got it in one," Lord Ferndale chuckled.

Felix looked out the carriage window and said, "It probably would have gone better for you if I'd not been there."

"Don't you dare make excuses not to come to the next one," Grandpapa said sternly. "I need witnesses to their obstruction."

They both laughed at that, to cover for the fact that the town council meetings were utterly awful and really needed some restructuring. Fancy blocking a hospital that could help everyone in town because of a personal griev-ance! Felix could not fathom it.

Tuesday morning at breakfast, Felix was looking forward to riding out again with Estelle to explore more of Ferndale's properties. They might inspect some more houses and check for leaky roofs or broken windows. And find some time to enjoy more kisses.

Estelle crushed his spirits with a casual remark that their 'little problem' was well in hand and she needed to return to Hatfield and her sisters.

Chills settled in his stomach. He looked to his grandfather with what he hoped was a subtle but beseeching look. It was too early for her to leave. She couldn't go back to town without a proposal, and he'd been far too busy enjoying her company and her compliments to get around to it. What a pudding-brain he was!

If he hadn't had to attend last night's town council meeting, he might have found a way to ask as well. It truly had been a waste of time.

Grandfather delivered a withering look that Felix had wasted his chance, then he cleared his throat and sounded defeated. "I'm dreadfully sorry, Miss Baxter, er, one of my carriage horses came up a little lame on the way back from Hatfield last night. If you wouldn't mind staying one more night, just to make sure she's fit and steady?"

What a whopping great lie that was, Felix thought, and hid a smile behind his hand.

Grandfather then laid it on thicker than marmalade,

"Unless you're unhappy with the Yellow Suite? Is it not to your liking?"

"Oh goodness, Lord Ferndale. The Yellow Suite is delightful. I am being treated like royalty here."

Grandpapa nodded benignly. "That's good, because we've had the odd Duke stay there on their travels. But I'm delighted to hear it's up to your standards." He delivered the last line with a grin, and Estelle gave a soft laugh and relaxed her shoulders.

"How you do love to jest. The Yellow Suite is delightful and I should dearly love to stay another night. I am only concerned for my sisters, who are having to carry out my many tasks as well as their own."

Then Estelle turned to Felix and she looked suspicious about this new delay, but was nonetheless gracious about her accommodations. She moved to refill her plate with another slice of toast and his grandfather got out of his seat and indicated they should both stand by the window.

Keeping his voice low, Lord Ferndale said, "We can't keep making lame excuses."

"That's a good one, we could say the horse is still lame…"

"Stop it. We can't keep her here indefinitely. Get to courting her, lad."

Felix nodded and knew how serious the situation was. The sun shone brightly in the meadow and the waters on the lake sparkled. An idea came to him, and he could have kicked himself for not acting sooner.

CHAPTER 16

A Picnic with Felix

Estelle could not hear precisely what Lord Ferndale and Felix were talking about, but she had a fair idea she was the topic of their conversation, as both of them kept casting furtive glances in her direction. Certainly, neither of them were experts in subtlety… or lying. She did not for one moment believe any of their horses were lame. Not at Ferndale. They had too many good people caring for their livestock and most likely horses to spare even if one was sore. But she couldn't possibly offend them after they'd gone to such trouble to make sure she was comfortable.

She'd stayed in a room where a Duke had previously slept? No wonder she'd slept so restfully. Thank goodness nobody had been in that room for enough time that the chance of bedbugs was nil.

Felix and Lord Ferndale were standing by the window with their heads together, no doubt plotting a delightful ruse of some kind. She could not be cross with them for seeking a little fun in life. It took a great deal of effort and co-ordination to oversee the estate. If they found ways to create moments of joy along the way, it made life that much more pleasant.

She adored their company, and that of Miss Yates. And she felt completely welcomed by the staff, who were so kind and respectful. Alas, it only served to make her feel more guilty for abandoning her sisters to dealing with the bookshop on their own.

What if more accounts had arrived?

What if Cousin Joshua had?

As if hearing her thoughts, Felix turned his golden head and smiled her way. "Miss Baxter, it appears we'll be in for another beautiful day. Shall we have the staff prepare us a picnic?"

Estelle couldn't remember the last time she'd indulged in such a lovely pastime. And when might she get another chance? She shoved down her feelings of guilt.

Just one more day. She'd allow herself that.

"Thank you, that is so thoughtful of you. I'd be delighted."

Lord Ferndale nudged Felix with his elbow.

What were those men planning?

She found out soon enough when she followed Felix on the delightful walk past garden beds of annuals that extended down to the lake. He carried no picnic basket, which had her wondering if that part had simply been an excuse to walk in this direction?

They arrived at the boathouse and found the staff were setting up an idyll under a willow tree that grew by the lake. Felix directed her to the short jetty, where a rowboat was fitted out with blankets and cushions and a large parasol to keep the sun off her face.

It was superb, and she kept thinking she must be dreaming because it was so perfect.

Felix held out his hand to help her into the boat. Warmth spread through her veins at his kind and gentle touch, and she took her sweet time letting go of it. The boat under them rocked a little, but soon Felix was sitting opposite. He opened the parasol for her as they would soon be moving out into the middle of the lake, where the shade didn't reach.

Estelle rested into the seat and dangled her hand out the side, the water tickling her fingers. If there was a better definition of bliss, she was yet to find it. She spent the next few moments committing everything to memory. The smell of recently cut grass in the air, the warmth of the day, the handsome, golden-haired gentleman gently rowing them about. As they made their way out into the sun, the parasol did its job. However, Felix and his golden curls were in the full sun. To her delight, he removed his jacket, then rolled up his shirt sleeves to display a set of impressively bronzed forearms. She should not be so fixated, but she had the feeling he was putting himself on display for her, and her alone, as he pulled on the oars and his muscles surged.

She could not stop the grin of happiness creasing her cheeks. The urge to look back to the Hall and see if Lord Ferndale or Miss Yates were watching them was strong, but she resisted, preferring to gaze upon Felix.

"This is delightful, I thank you," Estelle said. She'd had so few times in her life to truly relax and wallow in little luxuries. She banished all thoughts of the bookshop from her head. Even Crafty was forgotten for a moment.

Felix rowed them to a secluded spot behind some trees, blocking out any sight of Ferndale Hall or the staff assembling their picnic.

He set the oars and they floated for a while in serenity.

Felix then reached for his jacket and Estelle sighed, realising he might cover his arms again and his beautiful display would be over.

He did not. Instead, he fetched something out of the pocket and moved carefully on the boat, keeping balance to stop it rocking too much. Then he positioned himself before her on his knees.

Estelle sat up straight and dropped the parasol. Luckily it fell into the boat and not the water.

The boat rocked a little at her sudden movement, but they soon steadied themselves. If only her heartbeat would settle as quickly! Her pulse filled her ears and blocked out his words. He was saying something very earnest indeed, as he held out a pearl bracelet that looked very old. Like it might be a Ferndale heirloom.

Time slowed. She swallowed and her ears popped. She could hear his words at last and the most important sentence reached her ears.

"... honour of marrying me?"

Her throat turned dry. Her face warmed with delight and embarrassment. He must have made such a pretty speech and she'd barely heard any of it.

"I am hoping this has not come as a complete surprise?" he said, his expression falling.

Oh dear, he thought she was turning him down? "No."

"Is that 'no' because it's not a surprise or … 'no' to the other very important question?" He looked quite anxious as he awaited her answer.

"Give me a moment to catch my breath," she managed. She wanted this moment to be perfect. The beautiful day, the sparkling light dancing on the lake, the golden man who she'd now seen twice without a shirt on, this incredible estate … and yes, the money and security that came with it. Everything she could possibly want or need in life, now and in the years to come, was being offered to her. Her feelings for Felix were real. They were good feelings, and if not love, she was beginning to think they were getting very close to that destination.

All I need to do is marry this very handsome, lovely, joyful man.

Considering the benefits their marriage would bring to her sisters and how happy it would make everyone - and she included herself in that - it would be selfish and dimwitted if she turned him down.

"Yes," she said. "Yes, Felix Yates, I will marry you."

Felix sagged in relief, rocking the boat.

They both laughed together with relief and happiness once the boat steadied again.

Felix was still holding out the bracelet for her and said, "I honestly thought my heart would stop, and I'd read the situation very poorly."

"Not at all. I simply needed to memorise everything about this moment."

"I certainly won't forget it in a hurry," he said as he looped the bracelet about her wrist and secured the catch. Her skin virtually glowed with it there, the heirloom pearls gleaming. Sunshine filled her. Felix then held her hand in his and kissed her fingers. He looked up at her from under his lashes and her heart flipped.

Carefully, so as not to rock the boat too much, they reached for each other and sealed her acceptance with a kiss.

Warmth bloomed in Estelle at the contact. For as long as she lived, she would never forget this magical moment.

"I do love you so terribly much," he said with a shaky breath as they ended the kiss. "I shall make it my life's work to ensure your continued happiness."

She held his handsome face in her hands and kissed him again for good measure. Their lips fit so perfectly together. Made for each other.

"You have already brought me a great deal of happiness. It will be no hardship at all to be your wife, Felix Yates."

The picnic passed in a blur of happiness, as the staff had set out everything and then made themselves scarce. They did not eat much, being content to simply spend time with each other and enjoy the bliss of the moment.

And so many more kisses.

They ended the meal early and Felix found a couple of staff on the other side of the small boat shed. He said they should enjoy themselves with what remained.

Estelle held Felix's hand and they walked together back to the Hall to give Lord Ferndale and Miss Yates their excellent news.

To Estelle's joy, Lord Ferndale was delighted, and Miss Yates hugged and kissed them both. They even pretended to be surprised at the development, claiming it was "so sudden", though she was quite certain they'd been well aware of Felix's plans. Felix had probably had to get that heirloom bracelet out of Lord Ferndale's safe-chest to present to her.

They celebrated with some wine and sherry from the cellars and Lord Ferndale made a toast to the happy couple.

Lord Ferndale said, "You will make an excellent mistress of Ferndale Hall. And I'm glad Felix saw fit to present you with the bracelet."

"It is beautiful. I shall treasure it always," Estelle said.

"That was my grandmother's bracelet," Miss Yates said to Estelle. "Lady Elizabeth. That's her in the portrait there, the golden-haired woman who looks like Felix. He thought it was very fitting that you should have it."

"I am so honoured, Miss Yates." Estelle wanted to cry at how much the bracelet symbolised her acceptance into the family.

"Oh please, we are as good as family now. Call me Aunt Florence."

Estelle thought she might shed real tears of happiness. Her face was aching from smiling so much.

"Come with me," Aunt Florence said quietly to Estelle

as Felix and Lord Ferndale were busy patting each other on the backs. "I have something else for you, my dear."

Estelle was quite happy to oblige. She followed Miss Yates upstairs to the first floor, and then on up another flight of stairs. Then Miss Yates led her down a narrow corridor and unlocked a door at the end of it which proved to lead to yet more stairs.

It was just as well Estelle had not had too much wine, with so many stairs to climb, and then they'd have to climb back down them.

"Wherever are we going?" Estelle asked curiously as Miss Yates began to ascend.

"The attics. There's something here I'd like you to have."

Estelle doubted any room in Ferndale Hall was allowed to get too dusty, but the attics certainly showed signs of not being much used. The air up here felt still and thick with age, the few pieces of furniture covered in Holland cloths, trunks and boxes stacked against the walls.

"Over here." Miss Yates beckoned Estelle over to a large, leather-bound trunk. "Help me lift the lid, there's a dear."

Together they unbuckled the leather straps and lifted the lid, and Miss Yates pulled away a plain length of white linen lying on top of the contents. "There," the old lady said in a satisfied tone. "Perfectly good."

The trunk was made of cedar, and smelled a little of camphor, obviously used to keep moths at bay. Estelle blinked down at the contents for a moment, before she realised what she was seeing.

"Is that *silk*, Miss Yates?" Folded lengths of silk, in more than a dozen colours and shades, some plain, some figured or embroidered, all very, very expensive in Estelle's estimation.

"Indeed it is. Fifty years old, this year, but never used." Miss Yates lifted out a length of emerald-green silk and unfolded it, showing that there must be at least eight yards of the fine fabric. It rippled and shone in the sunlight pouring in through the attic window and illuminating a path of dust motes.

"Wherever did it come from?" Estelle asked.

"It was meant for my trousseau." Miss Yates smiled a little sadly, before reaching out to wrap the emerald silk around Estelle, draping it in the semblance of a gown.

"Oh." Estelle didn't want to pry, but Miss Yates told her anyway.

"I was engaged once. A lovely young man I met in London. He asked me to marry him on a bright summer's day, very much like this one. We planned to marry at Michaelmas and my mother took me to London; we bought this silk on that day and brought it home, planning to make up new gowns for my life as a married woman. But before we even had the chance to begin cutting it up, the news came; my Henry fell from his horse at the first hunt of the season and… passed."

"I'm so sorry," Estelle said softly. Life could be so cruel, no matter how much comfort a person was born into.

Miss Yates picked up another length of silk, this one a golden yellow, and held it against her. Her faded blue eyes were far away, lost in memories of another time.

"I could have married another," she said, and her tone was one of reassurance rather than bragging. "I had opportunities and proposals, but none of the gentlemen made my heart beat fast the way my Henry did." Miss Yates draped the golden silk around her shoulders and smiled, and in the curve of her lips and the high arch of her cheekbones Estelle could see the great beauty Florence Yates must have been, fifty years ago.

"My brother never pressed me, and he and dear Emily, God rest her soul, never made me feel as though I should have to leave Ferndale. I have had a good life, Miss Baxter, don't feel sorry for me. But this silk has been lying unused long enough. I want you to have it, else it will only moulder away in here for another fifty years!"

There was no possible way Estelle could decline, not after that poignant story. Instead, she stepped forward, opening her arms, and Miss Yates accepted the embrace, resting her head on Estelle's shoulder. They stood there, hugging tightly in their wrapped yards of silk, until a cleared throat at the stairwell made Estelle smile.

"Did you really follow us up here, Felix?" she asked.

"I can barely stand to have you out of my sight for more than a few minutes," he admitted cheerfully. His words had her grinning so much she would ache for a week.

Felix stepped closer, gazing at them wide-eyed, and asked, "Whatever is all this?"

"My wedding gift to your bride," Miss Yates said briskly, letting go of Estelle. Estelle pretended she didn't see the older woman wiping at her eyes. "Doesn't she look absolutely marvellous in that green, Felix? Brings out the green in her eyes."

"I adore Estelle in green," he agreed, "though I admit I have never seen her look less than beautiful in any colour. I do believe she could even successfully pull off wearing a burlap sack."

"Burlap, indeed!" Miss Yates huffed, smiling fondly at him. "Nothing but the finest for the future Lady Ferndale, you cheeky wretch!"

"It certainly looks like it," Felix agreed, taking a look inside the trunk. His eyebrows flew up, and his gaze slid sideways to Estelle. She could see him mentally calculating the value of what was in that trunk.

It was tempting - oh so tempting - to think about selling the silk, or at least some of it. She could pay the eighty pounds to the bank straight away if she did, but Estelle would not insult Miss Yates so. The gift wasn't meant for that.

"There must be enough silk for twenty gowns here," she said thoughtfully. "Would it be all right with you, Miss Yates, if I had a gown or two made for each of my sisters as well?"

Miss Yates made a funny tisking sound, as if the question was silly. "Of course you may, my dear; what a delightful thought! And you will need cotton and muslin enough for petticoats and linings too; purchase it at the drapery and I will send them a note that the account is to be given to me."

Estelle tried to demur, but every thing she said only seemed to inspire Aunt Florence and Felix to further generosity. The more she tried to steady them into being sensible, the more the two of them became more determined to heap largesse on her.She had to keep pinching herself to avoid becoming caught up in this new world of pretty things, when her reality in Hatfield was anything but.

By the time they had descended the attic stairs again and Felix had sent two footmen up to bring down the trunk, Miss Yates had somehow also declared that she was purchasing as many new shoes, gloves and hats as Estelle might possibly need to go with her new gowns, and enough for her sisters too.

CHAPTER 17

The Second Crate

E stelle could have floated home in a bubble of happiness. The Ferndale carriage was a very close second best. Felix, his grandfather and great-aunt remained at Ferndale Hall to prepare for the wedding, while she travelled alone to Hatfield.

She stepped into the bookshop and the door tinkled. Louise looked up from the counter and squealed with delight. In seconds they were in each others' arms, embracing as if they'd been apart for months, not a few days.

"Did he propose?" Louise asked.

Heat stole over Estelle's face.

Marie walked in bemoaning, "Must you be so loud, Lou?" Then she saw that Estelle had returned and threw her arms around them both. "Oh, very well, you're allowed to squeal when it's good news like this. I thought you'd stepped in Crafty's leftovers."

The commotion brought Bernadette and Mrs Poole

into the bookshop and all four of them tried to hug Estelle at once.

"Girls, girls," Mrs Poole said, "Let Estelle breathe." Even though Mrs Poole had contributed plenty to the crush herself.

The love of her sisters filled her with joy. Estelle beamed and was about to tell them everything in the right order when Bernadette blurted, "He *has* proposed, hasn't he?"

"Yes," Estelle nodded, realising it was impossible for them to speak sensibly. Caught up in happiness, she hugged her sisters again. Individually this time.

Louise held Estelle by the shoulders and said, "You *have* accepted? Yes?"

For the briefest moment, she wondered about trying to make a jest, but she didn't have it in her. In any case, her smiling face gave her away. "Yes," she confirmed.

They smothered her with love and congratulations. Then Bernadette spotted the bracelet on her wrist and shrieked, making her hold it up so they could all admire it.

"Wait until you see Miss Yates' gift," Estelle said with a grin. "That gift, I can share with all of you."

"Where would you like it, Miss Baxter?" The two footmen who'd ridden on the back of the coach hauled the trunk packed with silks in through the bookshop's narrow doorway.

"We'll never get it up the stairs. Put it here behind the counter and we'll empty it out, and get Mr Thomas next door to store it until you can take the empty trunk back to Ferndale," Estelle decided.

Everyone was giddy with curiosity to see what lay inside it. Estelle was equally impatient to share it with them. There was an awed silence when she lifted the lid of the trunk. Marie reached out a wondering hand to stroke a pale pink silk stitched with tiny white flowers.

"That is the most beautiful thing I've ever seen." Marie almost whispered it. "Where did Miss Yates get these?"

"They were for her trousseau. They're fifty years old, can you believe it?" Estelle was telling her sisters Miss Yates' rather poignant story when the doorbell jingled and the last voice she wanted to hear said;

"What are you girls looking at?"

Estelle slammed the lid of the trunk down, almost catching Louise's fingers, and turned, forcing a smile to her lips. "Why, Cousin Joshua. And Cousin Phoebe. What a pleasant surprise." She kept her wrist with the pearl bracelet below the level of the counter. She wasn't quite ready for her cousins to know about her betrothal just yet.

"We received some more books from Father," Marie said blandly. "Proof that he's still very much alive."

What a whopper fib, and most unlike Marie to tell! Marie had always been scrupulously honest. Estelle sneaked a sideways glance at her sister, but Marie's expression was smooth and untroubled.

Cousin Joshua, on the other hand, looked as though a black cloud had descended on his head. He huffed and puffed, and then turned right around and walked back out the door again, Phoebe twittering in his wake.

They all breathed quiet sighs of relief. Thank heavens this hadn't been a drawn-out confrontation like previous times. Estelle was too filled with happiness at her upcoming marriage to Felix to let anyone ruin it. Especially Joshua.

"Well, that got rid of him without him finding out about the silk, but what a lie, Marie!" Estelle looked at her sister in astonishment. "I didn't think you had it in you."

"It wasn't a lie. Another crate of books from Father did arrive, yesterday." Marie grinned at her. "But we unpacked them and took them all upstairs already. I didn't actually say to Cousin Joshua that's what we were looking at."

"Was there a letter? Where is he now?" Estelle asked eagerly.

"No letter." Marie grimaced. "At least, not that we've found yet. I thought there might be one tucked into one of the books and we didn't find it yet, that's why we took them all upstairs. Didn't want to accidentally sell the book with a letter in it."

Bernadette and Louise had re-opened the trunk and were staring at the silks again. Estelle smiled at them. "I want you to choose two each. I told Miss Yates and she thought it was a lovely idea for you to have some of it as well for new gowns, and there's enough here for twenty dresses."

"At least," Louise agreed, picking up a gorgeous sage-green silk. "Are you really sure, Estelle?"

Out of nowhere, Crafty appeared and jumped into the box of fabrics.

Everybody yelled at the cat to get out, as she rolled around and made a nuisance of herself.

Mrs Poole grabbed the cat while Marie gently pulled the silk away from her claws and managed not to rip the threads.

"Of course I'm sure." Estelle put an arm around Louise's waist. "You'll look lovely in that green. You can wear it at my wedding."

"Well, let's get them all upstairs," Mrs Poole said practically, shooing Crafty away. "We can lay them out in your father's room for now to keep that cat off them, while you decide what patterns you want made. I know a few girls who sew a nice straight stitch who'll be glad of the work to make your trousseau, Estelle."

"Oh, but we can't afford…" Estelle fell silent, thinking. They still had the bank loan payment to worry about, but - should she ask Felix for the money? Now that they were engaged, it didn't feel quite so awful. He had practically begged her to let him help, after all, and the real help she needed was monetary.

Bernadette said, "We shall miss you once you marry, but you'll only be at Ferndale Hall and that is but an hour's ride. I was also wondering," she smiled and paused a little, "would Lord Ferndale mind so much if I grew some herbs in his garden? The glass houses would be suitable for ginger."

Lousie and Marie pretended to measure up fabrics,

but they'd gone quiet so they had to be listening for the answer.

Estelle blinked, a little confused. "Well, I… can't imagine Felix and I will be moving to Ferndale Hall so soon…"

"Why ever not?" Bernadette shot back.

"I really hadn't considered that. Lord Ferndale runs the Hall and Miss Yates is the mistress. I couldn't possibly assume Felix and I would be required until Lord Ferndale passes, and I hope that is not for a long while yet. Oh, by the way, he thanked you most graciously for the tonic."

Bernadette beamed at the compliment, but then her expression became stern. "Miss Yates can't be expected to carry the load for much longer. She is nearly seventy."

Meanwhile, Louise pressed one of the cream-coloured silks against a more vibrant blue and gasped at how beautiful they looked together with a satisfied, "Oh yes."

Marie said, "She's right. Miss Yates has more than done her duty at Ferndale, she should have more leisure."

"Let's not get ahead of ourselves. They have Mrs Sykes, who is very capable," Estelle said, her mind whirring with the expectations of her new duties. How would she oversee Ferndale Hall and the bookshop at the same time?

"So, the books that arrived," she said, changing the subject, "Marie, may I see them?"

"Of course," Marie neatly folded the silk she'd been holding and put it back in the trunk. "And keep Crafty away!" She closed the lid firmly.

"I'll pop next door and get Mr Thomas." Mrs Poole

flushed a little, but they forebore to tease her. "Ask him to carry that upstairs and put it in Mr Baxter's room."

Upstairs, Estelle and Marie looked over the pile of books, picking up each in turn and gently giving them a shake before adding them to a specific stack. Marie had already begun sorting some.

"This pile is for listing in our next advertisement in The Times. There are valuable titles here that I know collectors will want. This pile is for books we can shelve here in the shop, and this pile is for Louise to rebind."

Bless Marie's organisational skills. She really knew her titles. A great many of these were in French, and as they gently turned the books upside down to see if letters would shake out, Estelle caught sight of illustrated pages.

"Oh good heavens!" It wasn't her fault that the book fell open on a specific colour plate that had her blushing from her forehead to her toes.

Marie glanced over and giggled. "We may need a separate pile for books to keep under the counter."

More nervous laughter broke free, as they continued. As Marie shook out the final book, she signed with resignation. "No letter."

Estelle joined her in disappointment. "So frustrating."

"At least there are books, and we can sell many of these by order, so father did well."

"But without a letter, how do we know when he sent them?" Estelle asked.

Marie sat back and said thoughtfully, "You were looking forward to him walking you down the aisle."

Estelle nodded, heat prickling her eyes. "And we have no idea when he'll be back."

Marie patted her hand and said, "Oh well, you'll just have to let the next in line do that duty."

Estelle shook her head and said, "The next in line is…"

"Cousin Joshua!" they both said at once.

Estelle shuddered.

Marie, blast her, cackled with merriment. "Can you imagine how much he'll hate that? The moment he hands you over, you outrank him! And he'd have to be on his best behaviour because all of Hatfield would see him misbehaving."

"Oh dear!" Estelle took a steadying breath. "We should delay the wedding until father comes home." It sounded loyal to say that, even though she was growing fonder of Felix by the hour and rather wondering how soon they could wed.

"Don't you dare. I'm going to enjoy watching Joshua and Phoebe squirm as they are forced to congratulate you through gritted teeth."

"Maybe they'll be out of town?"

Marie sombered. "You don't think they'll object to the banns, do you?"

There was no knowing how mean Cousin Joshua could get. "Felix is speaking with Reverend Millings this afternoon, to read the first one out this Sunday."

"Will Old Brimstone be doing the service?"

Estelle grimaced, recognising the private name many had for the local vicar. "Probably."

Marie sat down beside Estelle and gave her a friendly nudge. "The wedding ceremony itself might be something to endure, but afterwards, you'll be Mrs Felix Yates and in-effect-if-not-in-fact, mistress of Ferndale Hall. We shall book extra carriages and horses to take invited guests from St John's to Ferndale. We shall place Joshua and Phoebe on a far table so you will barely notice they're there."

"There is a lot to organise," Estelle said, rubbing her head.

"And we will be here for you every step of the way," Marie said.

For the next two weeks, wedding preparations consumed Estelle's waking moments. She was incredibly grateful for Mrs Poole, who took everything in her stride. The bookshop buzzed with the regular amount of visitors shopping for books, but also an irregular number of seamstresses and tradesmen who came to measure them for dresses and provide quotes for services.

Another daily visitor was Felix, who often appeared with thoughtful small gifts for everyone, and always bought some extra books to take home. He claimed they were for Lord Ferndale, and they accepted this mild falsehood without demur.

Because they were so busy, Estelle asked Louise if she could hold off on repairs that required the stinky glue.

"I cannot," Louise objected. "The new delivery of

Minerva books have arrived. They won't last a week in the lending section if I don't replace their cardboard covers with heavy boards and cloth binding."

Estelle pleaded, "How about we hold off replenishing the lending section until after the wedding?"

Louise tilted her head, "I suppose I could always read them carefully first. Can't have anything unsuitable on our shelves, just in case somebody reports us to Brimstone."

"Bless your heart," Estelle said, giving her sister a squeeze.

She nailed a new piece of hessian to Crafty's scratching post, then checked behind the counter for entrails. Urgh. Another one. At least she didn't step in it this time.

After cleaning it up, she unlocked the front door and set about checking their correspondence.

The front door bell tinkled as a customer came in.

Not a customer, alas. It was Joshua and Phoebe, with Little Sticky in Phoebe's arms and the other two Baxter boys following. The eldest, Benjamin, stood beside his father, arms folded in an imitation of Joshua's aggressive stance. He'd grown taller of late and had developed a menacing sneer he'd obviously learned at his father's knee.

Brutus slipped behind a tall shelf to look at books. Phoebe put Little Sticky down. He ran for Crafty, who was sleeping on a lower shelf. He picked the cat up by the middle and squished her into his face. The cat made a soft uncomfortable yowl and turned her eyes to Estelle as if to say, "Are you seeing this?"

"Put that animal down, Barnaby!" Phoebe called out.

Little Sticky did. His sticky hands and face were now covered in dark cat hair.

At least he won't get as much jam on the books, Estelle thought.

"You are getting married," Joshua announced portentously.

"Thank you, I am," Estelle said, noting his complete lack of congratulations.

Joshua huffed a little and said, "Will your father return before the event?"

He would not spoil her joy. She would not let him. "I dearly hope so. But in his absence…"

"… The obligation falls to me," he completed for her.

So that was why he was here, trying his best to ruin her day. He could have said *honour* instead of *obligation*, but he was at least acknowledging the fact. Estelle managed a polite, "That appears to be the case."

The bell tinkled again and relief spread through Estelle that they might have a customer for distraction and Joshua would not make a scene in front of them.

It was Felix, appearing before her like a guardian angel. He must have spent the night at the Red Lion to be here so early.

"Mr Yates," Joshua said, with the most imperceptible nod.

"Mr Baxter," Felix replied, with so little emphasis on the "Mr" he may as well not have said it.

Felix grinned cheerfully at Joshua, and Estelle had to smother a laugh. She'd never seen her cousin alter from superiority to extreme discomfort so quickly.

"I heard the banns yesterday," Joshua said, addressing Felix. "You are to marry my cousin, Miss Baxter."

Felix replied, "That I am. And I thank you for your congratulations."

He'd made none, of course.

"You did not seek my permission, Mr Yates." Joshua's tone was chilly, and for a moment Felix froze, glancing at Estelle.

"We do not need your permission, Cousin Joshua," Estelle said quickly. "Since I am five-and-twenty, you are no longer legally my guardian in my father's absence. I am able to consent to my own marriage."

It was Joshua's turn to freeze, and he frowned, looking away as though mentally counting years in his head.

"My birthday was last April," Estelle added, "as you might know, if you had bothered to acknowledge any of our birthdays in the last two decades or so."

"The disrespect!" Phoebe began, and she huffed loudly to show how upset they were making her. Good.

Joshua waved her to silence, looking back at Felix.

"Her father has not returned," Joshua said in an imperious tone. "There is nobody to give her away."

Felix's smile barely dimmed, but a flicker of doubt was there, because Estelle had become so familiar with his expressions and noticed the subtle change. Her favourite expression of his was when he smiled at her and looked down at her lips, because it meant they were about to share another beautiful kiss again.

"I would assume," Felix said, "that as you are her closest available male relative, that honour would transfer to you?"

Joshua puffed himself up. Phoebe looked incredibly pleased with herself too. They weren't going to refuse, were they?

Joshua said, "As it so happens, I *might* not be available."

He what? she thought.

"Oh?" Felix said at the same time.

Phoebe was gloating. They'd clearly cooked up obstacles to throw in the way of Estelle marrying Felix, and were smug that one of their plans might work.

Over my dead body, Estelle thought.

Joshua continued. "You shall have to delay the wedding until I am."

"I see," Felix said. From his expression he appeared crestfallen. "When might you be available?"

Joshua made himself tall and gripped the lapels of his coat. "Well, you see, that's the rub of it. I do not know. If Matthew Baxter is alive, he should walk his daughter down the aisle when he returns. I'd be usurping his position to do it in his place. If, on the other hand, we knew for certain that he was never returning, then I could step in. But that would also signify Matthew Baxter was no longer in this world."

He'd rehearsed that pretty speech, Estelle was sure of it. It was too convenient. She would not let him get away with this. "I'm sure when my father returns, he will be delighted to know you stepped up to the occasion because he was otherwise engaged on the continent."

"Yes, yes," Joshua batted her argument away. "On the other hand, if we knew he was no longer with us…"

Felix cut in, "Not to worry, I'm sure my grandfather would be delighted to perform the task."

"What?" Joshua and Phoebe said at the same time.

Felix beamed as if he'd found a sixpence in the Christmas pudding. "Lord Ferndale is more than happy to step in and represent any family in the parish when requested." He turned to Estelle and her whole body felt lighter at how quickly he'd undercut them. "I'm sure he'd stand up for Estelle in her moment of need. So if you aren't available, then not to worry, we have another avenue."

Joshua blustered and blinked several times, then said, "I never said I *wasn't* available, only that I might not be. I shall clear it with my man of business and… get back to you."

Felix beamed. "Thank you, Mr Baxter. I look forward to hearing in the affirmative. And soon." There was iron in the last word.

"Come along," Joshua said hastily, rounding up his family and not meeting either Estelle or Felix's eyes. Phoebe scooped up Little Sticky and then stalked out.

"Can I stay for a while?" Brutus asked from behind the shelves.

"Suit yourself, you know the way home," Joshua said, and left without him.

Felix took the last few steps to Estelle and they embraced with relief.

"Thank you, so much," Estelle said. "I don't know how I would have dealt with him on my own."

Felix kissed her and softly said, "You don't have to deal with anything on your own any more, my darling."

She took a deep breath, looking up at him. "You asked me to let you help, and you've done so much already, but…"

"Tell me."

She fished in her pocket and pulled out the letter from the bank. "When Father left for France to go looking for books, he took out a bank loan. A rather large one. We understood, because he needed funds for travel and book buying, and we've been keeping up with the payments on the loan… until now."

Felix took the letter and read it, his brow furrowed. "But didn't you say your father's definitely alive?" he asked, obviously puzzled.

"Yes, but since the last crate of books arrived without a dated letter in it, we can't prove it to the bank. I personally think Cousin Joshua supplied the rumour about Father's death to the bank in the first place." She shrugged miserably. "There's nothing I can do about that; the bank won't even talk to me because I'm a woman."

"They'll talk to me. Let me take care of this payment for you, Estelle, and next week I'll go into London and ask to meet with them. The simple fact that more books keep arriving from your father should be evidence enough that he's still alive. I'll get them to reduce the repayments back to their normal rates."

"Thank you so much." Relief sagged her shoulders. He'd told her she could ask him for help, and he'd followed through. He would end up helping a great deal.

"I'd have to speak to Grandfather to get access to more funds, but I could pay off the whole loan… call it my wedding gift to you…"

"Absolutely not!" Estelle shook her head. "Thank you for offering, Felix, but I feel bad enough asking you for this much. When we sell the books which Father has sent, we'll have plenty for the next loan payment, even if you can't get the amount reduced to what the original instalments were. And then Father will be back, soon, I hope," she added stoutly.

"I hope so too." Felix folded the letter and put it in his pocket. "Well, I will do what you let me, my love, and I'm honoured you allowed me." He kissed her again, and took himself off.

A sound behind her made Estelle whirl, hand to her throat, and she gasped as she saw Brutus emerging from among the bookshelves. She'd forgotten the boy was there. How much had he heard? She wracked her brain in a momentary panic, trying to think if she'd said anything Cousin Joshua could use against them if Brutus relayed what he'd heard to his father.

"Mr Yates seems like a very nice man," Brutus said, and Estelle smiled despite herself.

"He is."

"I'm glad you're marrying him. You deserve someone

nice." Brutus hesitated, and then gave her a shy smile. "And if you're married to someone rich, Pa won't be able to force you out of the bookshop."

Estelle relaxed. Brutus was on their side! How Joshua and Phoebe had raised such a kind-hearted child was beyond her. She beckoned him closer. "Would you like to help me for a little while, Brutus? I have some books to shelve. I could show you how we organise them by subject and author…"

Brutus' eyes absolutely lit up, and he nodded eagerly. "Oh, yes please! I would love to help. I love books," he added.

"I know you do," Estelle said, making a mental note to order in some more books which would be suitable for a boy of Brutus' age. Even though Cousin Joshua would never pay, Brutus could read them in the shop and Estelle was sure she could find other buyers. "Here. Can you carry these? They're quite heavy."

"I'm strong," Brutus said determinedly, allowing her to pile books on his spindly arms. "You can rely on me, Cousin Estelle."

Perhaps she could, at that. He was young, but old enough to learn. And with Ruth to help as well, perhaps it would be enough extra help for Estelle to leave her sisters to manage the bookshop for a part of each week, at least.

CHAPTER 18

Cross Purposes

F elix whistled merrily to himself as he swung down from Hannibal's back and gave the horse a pat before handing him over to a groom. "Make sure he gets a good rub down and plenty of oats. I took it easy on the way back from London, but it's been a warm day," he instructed.

"Right you are, Mr Yates!" The groom touched his cap respectfully, leading Hannibal away, and Felix took the steps up to Ferndale Hall's front doors two at a time.

"Welcome home, sir," Thorne intoned as he took Felix's coat and hat.

"I was only gone one night, Thorne!"

"Yes, but to London, sir, and we all know what a den of iniquity that is." One eyelid fluttered in the ghost of a wink, and Felix laughed.

"You aren't wrong, Thorne. I can't bear the place. Too many people and not enough air, especially on a hot summer's day. A cool tankard of ale would be just the thing while I wash off this road dust..."

"I'll have one sent up directly, sir."

A large ale, a cool bath and some clean clothes later, Felix felt duly refreshed. Making his way back downstairs he popped his head around the library door, smiling as he saw his grandfather seated in a comfortable chair with a book on his lap.

"What a surprise to find you here, Grandfather! May I join you?"

Lord Ferndale looked up, smiled, and removed his glasses. "Cheeky pup, where else would you find me? Of course, come in, come in. How was your trip to London? Productive, I hope?"

"It certainly was!" Felix took the seat opposite his grandfather. "Thank you for your note of introduction to Lord Ellesmere; I'm sure the bank would have kept me kicking my heels quite a lot longer without intervention from one of their trustees."

Lord Ferndale nodded a little smugly. "Pays to keep up correspondence with one's old friends, Felix, let that be a lesson to you."

Felix thought guiltily that there were several friends he owed letters to, not least to inform them that he was getting married, and nodded penitently. "Your point is taken, Grandfather."

"And was your business with the bank concluded successfully?"

He beamed with success. "Indeed it was, I settled the

loan payment as I promised Estelle I would, and when I showed the bankers the last letter the Misses Baxters received from their father, which they were kind enough to entrust to me, it turned out to be dated on the exact same day the bankers had received intelligence of Mr Baxter's passing. Proving, of course, that their intelligence was so much codswallop." Felix smiled in satisfaction. "They wouldn't tell me who had provided the information, but in my opinion it could only have been Joshua Baxter."

"That one's trouble," Lord Ferndale grumbled. "Should have done more to keep him from being appointed magistrate." He shook his head in disgust. "But it was the year after your grandmother died…"

"You were in mourning, Grandfather, don't blame yourself. I shall keep a close eye on Joshua Baxter, I promise; he means no good to Estelle and her sisters and I won't have him tormenting them." Felix had kept to himself the matter of Joshua Baxter's attempted interference in his and Estelle's wedding; no good would come of his grandfather becoming angry over the matter, and if Joshua Baxter failed to do the right thing and walk Estelle down the aisle, well, Felix knew Lord Ferndale would be happy to do the honour.

"Anyway, the bank agreed to revert the loan payments to the original schedule, allowing the Misses Baxters to skip the September payment due to the large payment I made." Felix smiled in satisfaction. "I also got them to promise they won't take any further actions without more positive proof of Mr Matthew Baxter's demise. *And* to agree to come to me first, so that Estelle isn't worried by any sudden demands."

"Indeed!" Lord Ferndale gave an approving nod. "That was very well done, Felix; well handled throughout. A solid negotiation; you walked in with your paperwork in order and left with the outcome exactly as you desired."

A warm feeling spread through Felix's chest at his grandfather's praise. He ducked his head, feeling a little bashful, but Lord Ferndale wasn't finished.

"I've been thinking it's time I handed more of the financial matters of Ferndale over to you, after your marriage, of course. Once you and Estelle are settled here, you and I can spend some time going over the books."

"Of course, sir! Anything I can do to ease the burden from your shoulders."

Lord Ferndale smiled warmly at him. "You've grown up into a fine young man, Felix. I'm very proud of you. I want you to know that."

Felix's cheeks were burning and his eyes felt oddly hot. He managed to mumble a thank-you, and then, blessedly, his grandfather changed the subject, leaning over to a side table and picking up a letter, which he held out towards Felix.

"This came for you today."

"Oh!" The letter was still sealed, Felix saw as he took it, and then he turned it over and saw the direction written in his mother's firm hand. There would have been just enough time for his letter informing his mother of his betrothal to reach Ireland and a response to come back, he calculated as he broke the seal and unfolded the letter. He smiled as he read.

"She's inviting me to take Estelle to Ireland for a visit. A honeymoon."

"That sounds like a grand idea," Lord Ferndale said approvingly. "Leave soon after the wedding and go in the autumn, before the weather gets nasty and you have a rough sea crossing. Spend Christmas with your mother and come home in the spring."

"Estelle wants to travel," Felix said happily. "What a marvellous plan! As long as you can do without me for so long?" he checked.

"Of course we can. And it's been, what, six or seven years since you last saw your mother? You should take your bride to meet her. In fact, I insist upon it!"

"I shall talk to Estelle about it tomorrow. It's Saturday; I plan to take a maid or two and a couple of footmen and go and have them clean their residence. Give the Baxters and Mrs Poole a break."

"That's very kind and thoughtful of you, Felix. I'm sure Miss Baxter will appreciate that, just as much as she'll appreciate you dealing with the bank for her." Lord Ferndale put his glasses back on and opened his book again. "Now push off, there's a good chap, and leave me to read. I want to finish this chapter before dinner."

Laughing, Felix left his grandfather in peace. He had plenty to do, anyway, not least of which to begin planning travel arrangements to take Estelle to Ireland!

The following morning Felix arrived at the bookshop bright and early with a couple of footmen who entered the shop with a travelling case. Estelle was sitting behind the counter, writing in a ledger, and she looked up and gave the most beautiful smile when she saw him, making his heart leap with joy and his step quicken as he hurried towards her. Before taking the last step, though, he quickly looked down to check for anything dangerous and squelchy on the floor.

"That is a good habit to have," Estelle said with a laugh, "but I did already collect Crafty's morning offering today."

He adored this woman so much. Felix delivered her a broad smile followed by a quick kiss. "I know Saturday is usually your clean up day, but I have brought some help and plan to give you, your sisters and Mrs Poole a reprieve."

"Oh, you are too thoughtful, thank you!" she said, with another of those heart-melting smiles, which disappeared from her face far too quickly for Felix's peace of mind.

"But you seem sad. What is the matter?"

"We still haven't heard from my father. It is vexing."

Felix took her hands in his and kissed her knuckles. "I am sorry. But in lighter news..." he let go of her hands and reached into his pocket, where he produced his mother's letter. "I heard from my mother. She sends her heartiest congratulations and best wishes."

"That's lovely!" Estelle said, her eyes brightening.

"She says she cannot wait to meet my new bride, and

that we must visit her in Ireland soon. I was thinking we could leave no later than autumn, and perhaps spend some time with them and then visit the countryside, remain for Christmas and winter, and then return in the spring."

Estelle pulled her hand away, her expression turning doubtful. "That is … a lot."

"But she has invited us, and I have not seen her in a great many years. You will love her, I know it. And I'm sure she will adore you."

Estelle's voice pitched to a higher register. "We'd be away for six months!"

"It would need to be," Felix frowned, uncertain why this seemed to be distressing her. Estelle wanted to travel, didn't she? And here was a golden opportunity! "It would be dangerous to sail home in winter."

She cried, "It's impossible. I can't be away from the bookshop for that long!"

Felix truly didn't understand what she meant. "You won't be running the bookshop. You'll be my wife."

Estelle swallowed, looking stricken. "I have to give this up?"

Everything tumbled inside Felix's head. How was this good news landing so poorly?

"I thought you'd accepted that?" How could she possibly be the new mistress at Ferndale Hall, and still manage Baxter's Fine Books? It was logistically impossible.

"Dear God, Felix, No. I can't!"

His brain shut down so fast he could only blink for a

moment until he caught his breath again. "What… what are you saying?" Felix thought his heart might give out. He could not for the life of him work out where this blissful road to happiness had taken such a terrible turn.

Estelle wanted to remain working in the bookshop even after they married? What madness was this?

"I thought I was taking you away from this drudgery?" he said.

"Drudgery? This is my life. I love it!"

His world came crashing down. He'd told Estelle how much he loved her, and she had not said those exact words back. He was hoping they would come soon. But she loved the bookshop?

"Do you love it more than me?" Heat prickled his eyes and he might very well fall to pieces if she said she did.

"What?"

"You heard me. I think it's important we know this as we are about to become married and that's a rather large step." He waited with bated breath for her answer.

Every second more that he waited was a knife in his gut. The silence hung thickly between them. How had they come this far and not discussed what their marriage truly entailed?

He couldn't cope waiting any more. "When we marry, we will live at Ferndale Hall. I have responsibilities to my grandfather and the estate. This is why you needed to meet the staff, as you'd be mistress of the hall."

"But not straight away, surely?" she shot back.

He had nothing to counter that.

"It is too much," she said as tears fell from her eyes,

ripping at his heart. "You do too much and ... I think you *ask* too much."

It took all his strength not to wipe those tears away for her. He wanted to do everything for her to help, but he'd obviously overdone it. "It's how I help," he said with a croaky plea.

A heavy sigh sagged her shoulders as she said, "This is my life, and you are asking me to give it up."

"You also wish to travel. You've said as much. I can facilitate that, but logically that would always mean months away from Hatfield, no matter whether it's Ireland or the continent. I don't understand your reticence. I sincerely hope this is merely a case of last-minute nerves because otherwise you make no sense. Did you honestly think I would come and live here after we -"

"Be quiet!" She slapped her hand over her mouth at the shock of her own words.

He clamped his jaw shut as well, and waited. The silence ate away at him like rust.

"This is my fault," Estelle said finally, shaking her head slowly. "This has happened too fast. I hadn't given it enough thought and it's all a rather large shock. But I had, in a strange way, thought we could split our time between here and Ferndale. Just, not so soon."

He opened his mouth to speak and she held her palm up to stop him.

"It's not just about us, Felix. There are so many other people involved. My sisters and Mrs Poole, and young R- Miss Millings needs us and Cousin Brutus needs refuge and..."

He could no longer hold it in. "I have responsibilities too. To my grandfather and great-aunt and Mrs Sykes and the entire staff at Ferndale, and, in time, the people of Hatfield."

"But this is my *home*!"

"Which will still be here. I don't understand. When people marry, they live together."

"And what do I do? Become a lady of leisure and spend your money?"

"You've had no problem so far!" The moment the words were out of his mouth, he knew he'd done badly. So horribly badly. He wished with all his might he could take them back, but they hung over them like a sword of Damocles.

CHAPTER 19

Poorly Chosen Words

Estelle thought she might cast up her breakfast. Why was she fighting with Felix when they were about to marry?

"Perhaps you should leave … until we both have clear heads," she said, hoping to have a moment to herself to think. Really think about the direction her life was taking, which was away from the bookshop and everything she'd ever known, or imagined for herself.

"I think I should stay." Felix stood firm before her. "We need to work this out, because in a few days we shall be married and it will be too late to work it out then."

A headache pulsed behind her eyes and she snapped. "If you're having regrets, by all means call it off."

He pulled back and gasped. "No!"

She'd gone too far, but could not seem to make herself think clearly in the heat of the moment. "Delay it for a few weeks until … I don't know."

"I have already set things in motion for our journey to Ireland."

Estelle slumped against the counter. "You just go and do these things thinking you're helping, but can't you see how you're making it worse? Expecting me to live at Ferndale is one thing, but at least that's a lot closer than Ireland!"

"You said you wanted to travel!" he pleaded, his stricken expression tearing at her heart.

She clenched her hands into frustrated fists. "I did. I do! But… I can't!"

"I don't think you know what you want!"

"I don't think *you* do either!"

Felix drew back and stared at her.

"Do you?" Estelle pressed on, hardly knowing what she said but desperate to somehow get him to stop asking her these questions, stop pushing her to make a decision she was in no way ready to make. "Do you even know what you want, Felix? Apart from, apparently, me to come and make your life easier by taking the running of Ferndale Hall off your hands? Oh, it was pretty obvious that Miss Yates and Mrs Sykes were showing me the ropes. And what will you do while I do all the work? Carry on your merry lighthearted way?"

She wasn't being entirely fair, and she knew it, but she couldn't seem to stop herself. "You want to take me away from my work here just so I can work for you. Pretty dresses and money won't buy me, Felix!"

"I never thought I could buy you," he said quietly.

"You just thought I'd fall into your lap like everything

else in your life always has, is that it? You've never done a real day's work in your life. You've never had to work for anything, I don't think you even know what work is!"

Felix took a deep breath. "You're angry. We need to take a breath, cool our tempers. Take some time to calm down."

"We don't have time to work this out, Felix," Estelle said, and suddenly everything was very clear to her. "I should never have agreed to marry you at all, and certainly not with my father not even here."

"Estelle, don't do this." He paled. "I don't want this…"

"Because this has all been about what you want, hasn't it? Not about what I want. You saw a vulnerability because of my situation and you took advantage."

"You're not being fair!" He was beginning to look angry. "You don't even know me!"

"Exactly!" she almost yelled at him. "I don't! For all I know you're as useless as your father was, and you just saw a competent woman and thought I'd make your life easier - exactly what your father did to your mother! This is just history repeating itself, and I won't be a part of it!"

For all the angry words that had come out of Estelle's mouth, those were the ones that broke Felix. He took a step back, feeling almost as though she'd slapped him. It would have hurt less.

"You think I'm like my father." The words were almost a whisper.

Estelle shrugged, looking down and not meeting his eyes. "I didn't know your father," was all the answer she gave.

"Why ever would you agree to marry me, if this is your opinion of me?" She still wouldn't meet his eyes, and the reason dawned on Felix. "Because of the money. You're marrying me for my money."

"Everyone marries for money," she said, still not looking at him.

Felix felt as though she'd twisted a knife in his heart. He pressed a hand to his chest, suddenly struggling to breathe.

There was a long silence. Estelle fiddled with some papers on the desk and didn't speak.

"The final banns are to be read tomorrow, and then we're to be married next Friday," Felix said, trying desperately to keep his voice even. "Do you want to marry me or not, Estelle?"

Her hands stopped moving, but she still didn't look at him. The silence dragged on.

"I suppose that's that, then," Felix said, barely believing the words falling from his lips. He turned away, his shoulders sagging, and headed for the door. As he got there, he looked back at Estelle. "I'm sure you don't want to see me hanging around. I'll make that trip to Ireland to see my mother - it's been years, and I would like to see her - but I'll go alone."

As he reached for the door, Crafty darted up to his feet. "Oh no. Not this time, cat." He reached down and turned the cat around, giving her a push to send her back into the bookshop. "You stay here."

Crafty walked away, waving her tail nonchalantly, as though she hadn't even considered trying to escape. Felix shook his head. If he hadn't let that damn cat out, would Estelle have formed a better opinion of him from the beginning? Too late now. Perhaps her opinion of him had been fixed from that day. Shoulders sagging, he pulled open the bookshop door and walked out.

He blinked in the bright sunshine; after the dimness of the bookshop, it hurt his eyes. That must be the reason why they were stinging, though he couldn't quite explain why his cheeks were wet. Striding towards the carriage, he paused as he remembered the footmen and the maids, even at that moment upstairs helping to clean.

Well, they might as well stay and complete the job. He'd go back to Ferndale Hall and send the carriage back for them. He couldn't stay here, not for another moment.

He should go into the church and tell the vicar not to call the banns tomorrow, and to cancel the wedding, Felix realised as the carriage rattled past St. John's, but he really didn't want to deal with Reverend Millings at that moment; no doubt the fire-and-brimstone vicar would have some choice things to say about women being the cause of all sin, and Felix just didn't want to hear it.

Right now, he couldn't face anyone.

Of course, the very first person he saw was the last

one he wanted to see as he walked back inside the Hall; his grandfather happened to be walking from the foot of the stairs to his study at that precise moment and turned to look at him with a puzzled frown.

"Whatever are you doing back here, boy? I thought you were spending the day with Miss Baxter?"

Felix's throat closed. He shook his head.

Lord Ferndale's face darkened. "What have you done?" he said, and his voice was very cold.

"I need to pack," Felix managed to get out. "I'm going to Ireland."

"Not until I've got to the bottom of this nonsense, you're not going anywhere!" Lord Ferndale pointed towards his study. "In here! Now!"

This is about to be the worst interview of my life, Felix thought. Somehow, he made his shaking legs carry him forward, until he could sink into a chair in the study and put his head in his hands.

Everything was turning to dust in his hands. "I made a mess of it, Grandfather," he said hollowly.

"Obviously," Lord Ferndale bit out, stomping around his desk and sitting down in his chair. "Now what happened?"

"I... made assumptions," Felix admitted bleakly. "I didn't ask Estelle what she wanted, or make it clear what I wanted. I just assumed she'd fall in with my plans without taking what she needs into account."

"Hm." Lord Ferndale sniffed audibly. "Sounds exactly like your fribble of a father. He never did give the slightest thought for anyone else, in the whole of his useless life."

Felix groaned aloud. He'd spent his entire life trying to be the opposite of his father, who had been the black sheep of the Yates family and a huge disappointment to Lord Ferndale. It hurt that both Estelle and his grandfather seemed to think Felix was too much like him; just another let down.

"But you're not your father, and I'm not just saying that, it's the truth," Lord Ferndale said firmly, and Felix looked up to see his grandfather staring a hole in him. "You're much smarter and more sensible than he was, for a start. So tell me, what are you going to do to fix the mess you've made? Because running away to Ireland isn't the answer."

"I don't know what else to do!" Felix cried out. "She doesn't want to marry me."

"And if she doesn't, it's because you haven't tried hard enough."

"I've done everything I could," Felix wracked his brains for answers, but all he could admit was, "She doesn't love me. She loves the bookshop."

"I saw the way she looked at you, boy. She could love you if you just gave her half a chance!"

"*She* won't give *me* a chance!" Angry, Felix jumped to his feet and walked out of the study, ignoring his grandfather's irritated demand for him to return. Striding briskly through the hallway, he spied his great-aunt coming down the stairs and turned away, quite unable to face another person reproaching him.

He ended up outside again, in the kitchen garden where memories of Estelle assailed him. The gardeners took one glance at his black-as-thunder expression and made themselves scarce.

Felix kicked a rosemary bush. "Why?" he shouted at the bush. "Why won't she give me a chance?"

The bush didn't answer, and Felix slumped down onto a bench and glared at it.

"Why didn't I give her a chance?" he said quietly after a few minutes. "Why didn't I ask her what she wanted, instead of making assumptions and grand gestures to try and impress her?"

He knew Estelle had a responsibility to her sisters, in her father's absence, and he hadn't really taken account of that at all. He'd been too busy worrying about his own future responsibilities to think about the ones Estelle had to manage right now, today. The bookshop and her sisters; they had been Estelle's priorities long before Felix came on the scene, and it wasn't fair for him to expect her to just drop them because he had money to throw at the problem.

"I can't just expect her to walk away for six months," he said aloud. "Not with her father still away. It's not fair on her." Honestly, it wasn't fair to demand she marry him right now, either; of course Estelle wanted her father to be at her wedding!

"I can wait. She's worth waiting for. However long it takes!" Felix sprang to his feet, wondering if the carriage had turned around to go back to Hatfield yet. Well, if it had, he'd saddle Hannibal and ride there.

And this time, he wasn't going to walk out on Estelle because of some silly disagreement. He could make compromises, whatever compromises she needed.

Because Estelle was worth it.

She was worth everything.

CHAPTER 20

Much Better Words

Misery engulfed Estelle at how badly her world had turned. And how quickly. The Ferndale Hall staff were at that very moment happily making her life, and the lives of her sisters, so much easier, and she'd interpreted Felix's assistance as interference.

"I've gone mad," she said as she reached for Crafty and gave the cat a cuddle. Her fur was soft and warm, and with a sinking heart, she realised the cat was heavier than usual. Stroking the cat's sides, she felt the outward curve of her belly and sighed again.

Crafty biffed her head against Estelle's chin and then flopped onto the counter. "I am an idiot," Estelle told herself, as tears splashed into Crafty's fur. The cat let out a mew of protest at having water dripped on her, sprang up and scarpered away.

Estelle wiped her face and sniffed loudly. There was nothing for it; she buried her head in her hands and sobbed. Guilt added to her sorrows. Their debts were under control, thanks to Felix, and they had beautiful fabric for new dresses thanks to Miss Yates. She should be the happiest bride in all of England, but instead she was a miserable wreck who'd thrown it all back in Felix's face.

And oh, the fabrics! She should give them all back, but they'd cut most of them up already and Mrs Poole had half a dozen local girls stitching away frantically to get them made up by the time of the wedding… and oh no, she was going to have to face Reverend Millings and probably have to listen to one of his awful lectures and…

"Estelle?" Marie's voice said softly, an interminable amount of time later. "What ever is the matter?"

"Everything," she wailed into her hands. "I've ruined it all."

"I'll get Louise. She'll know what to do."

A minute later, Estelle was surrounded by her sisters and their worried faces. She burst into a fresh bout of tears. "I've been awful to Felix and I called him useless and now there won't be a wedding and it's all my fault," she said in a rush of emotion.

Louise pulled Estelle away from the counter and wrapped her in her arms. "There there, I'm sure it's not that bad."

"It's worse," Estelle sniffed loudly and Bernadette pressed a handkerchief her way. "We had a fight and he's going to call the wedding off."

Marie asked, "Why would you fight? You are perfect for each other."

"That's the problem. I thought he was so perfect as well, but he was doing too much and he was taking over.

And even worse than that, he thought I'd simply up and leave you all to manage the bookshop without me!"

Bernadette laughed.

Estelle stopped crying immediately and stared at her youngest sister.

Bernadette shrugged, "What's the problem with that?"

That was not the response Estelle was expecting. "I'm needed here. Running the bookshop is a lot of responsibility."

Louise, Marie and Bernadette exchanged glances. Louise said, "We're not infants. We are perfectly capable."

"But father…"

"… Will come back. At some point," Marie reminded her. "Just because he left you in charge doesn't mean you have to *always* be in charge. He told us to use our initiative, and we have. We will continue to use our initiative. We will manage very well. We started discussing it even before you accepted Mr Yates. I even talked to Reverend Millings, and though he won't let us pay Ruth wages, he's said she can come to work for us properly as long as we put two shillings in the collection plate for her every Sunday. She'll do very well behind the counter with a little training, so we won't even be short-handed."

"And Brutus has asked if I'll teach him book-binding," Louise put in, looking rather pleased with herself. "I said yes, of course, and I'm going to use your room as the drying-room, so we'll be able to expand my binding operations."

Estelle looked for reasons to argue and all she could come up with was, "So, you're saying I'm not needed?"

They'd already arranged to replace her, even made plans for her room, without saying a single thing about it!

Bernadette put her hands on her hips in frustration and raised her voice. "We never said that! Stop twisting things! No wonder you had a fight if you turn people's words around like that!"

A fresh wail erupted from Estelle but Bernadette cut her off. "Mr Yates is the best thing that ever happened to you. It's one thing to be nervous, but another entirely to throw away your chance of happiness."

"He wanted to take me to Ireland. We'd be away for up to six months!"

"Ireland!" Louise looked amazed. "My goodness, what an adventure! You lucky thing!"

"No, but… but…" she couldn't say that she didn't want to go to Ireland. The lie burned her tongue.

"You got scared," Bernadette said when Estelle couldn't get a coherent word out. "You're supposed to be the sensible eldest daughter, but you're acting like a baby!"

"I am not!" Estelle raised her voice in denial, though she sounded querulous and petulant even to her own ears. Slowly, she turned to Louise and Marie, who shrugged and shook their heads.

Louise said, "I think you are. Mr Yates is lovely. He's handsome, thoughtful and he'll take excellent care of you. Actually, not just you, he's also making sure the rest of us are looked after. He told me yesterday he ordered me *four* brand-new book presses from London!" Her face shone with happiness. "I said he was too generous, and do you know what he said? He said that he'd never had a sister, and now he has three, so he fully intends to spoil us!"

Estelle looked around at them, seeing the sincerity on their faces, as well as their concern for her. They meant every word they were saying, she realised. And not only that, but they were all grown women, even Bernadette; they weren't her baby sisters any more. They'd sat down together - while she was deliriously distracted by Felix - and worked out a plan for exactly how they were going to cope without Estelle. A good plan, too, Estelle doubted she could have come up with a better one.

Marie adjusted her glasses and said, "We'll still be here for you, when you get back from Ireland. And the bookshop will be here too. I'm sure Father will be home by then as well. You really won't have anything to worry about."

"We will be fine," Bernadette said, handing Estelle another handkerchief when Estelle sniffed loudly. "But if you stay here moping about and not marrying Mr Yates, you will drive us all mad with how you drove the loveliest man away for the silliest of reasons."

"But I want to look after you," Estelle said, realising the truth of her feelings. "I'm worried what will happen to you when I'm gone."

"For goodness' sake!" Louise shouted. "Let go of this weight of duty or expectation or whatever else it is that's making you act so addle-headed and get out there and marry that man!"

Goodness, her sisters could really cut her down to size when they were like this. Estelle wasn't sure they'd ever all ganged up on her this way before; it was quite lowering.

But she had a sickening feeling that every word they'd spoken was the truth.

"Am I really being so stupid?" she asked timorously.

"YES!" the three of them yelled at her.

Lightheaded dizziness took hold and Estelle thought she might faint. "What have I done?"

Louise clapped her hands together, shaking her head and half-laughing. "She gets it! Finally!"

Clarity dawned through her misery. "I don't want to lose Felix."

Marie shook her head and said to nobody in particular, "I don't understand people in love. They act so silly."

"I *am* in love!" Estelle said, suddenly realising the truth. "I love Felix Yates, and I've... I've sent him away! Oh dear. How can I fix this?"

Bernadette put her hand on Estelle's shoulder and said, "Go and get him, silly."

"But he's gone to Ireland! He said he was going to go on his own because he was sure I wouldn't want to see him..."

"I'm fairly sure he won't have ridden directly to Bristol to get on a boat," Marie said dryly. "Trips like that do take time to arrange. He'll be at Ferndale Hall, packing. I'm sure you could catch up to him."

"And if I don't catch up to him, I shall find out where in Ireland his mother lives and follow him there." Estelle set her jaw determinedly.

"There's my big sister who doesn't let anything stop

her when she wants something," Bernadette said proudly. "What are you waiting for?"

"You're right!" Estelle rushed out the door. A moment later she rushed back in and ran for the stairs, shouting "I need my riding habit!"

"I'll come and help you change," Louise said, laughing as she followed Estelle up the stairs. "Calm down, Estelle. You'll catch up to him."

Mere moments later, Estelle was in the livery yard behind the Red Lion, becoming reacquainted with Somerset Valley Four.

Just as she was leaving, Cousin Joshua displayed his impeccably awful timing and caught her in the archway.

"Where are you off to?" he asked. It sounded more like an imperious demand.

She had no patience left for him and shouted, "Leave us alone!" then clicked her tongue to the horse to trot away.

"Come back here immediately!" Joshua shouted, but he was behind her and Estelle pretended she hadn't heard.

Paying back only a little of Joshua's rudeness did not feel good, because it immediately made her fret about how he might take his temper out on her sisters. Surely he'd go straight into the bookshop and give them a piece of his mind.

As much as she wanted to turn back and help them, they had assured her they were capable of looking after themselves. Joshua would surely test them, but she had to let them handle the annoying man on their own.

At this moment, she had a drumbeat in her heat: *Get to Felix. Get to Felix.*

Had he already called off the wedding? He might have gone straight to the church after leaving the bookshop, to tell Reverend Millings not to call the last banns tomorrow. It would be all her fault if he had; after all, she'd told him to.

I'm such a fool, I only hope I'm not too late to tell Felix I love him. I will never stop telling him I love him.

Her heart nearly cracked at the thought of never seeing him again. Never seeing that wide, joyous smile of his or hearing him crack a joke in an obvious attempt to amuse her. Kissing him. Suddenly, she remembered Miss Yates' words about her long-lost fiancé; "None of the gentlemen made my heart beat fast the way my Henry did."

Felix makes my heart beat like that, Estelle thought, urging Somerset Valley Four to trot faster.

I really do love him, she realised. She could not imagine the rest of her life without Felix in it.

Beside her. Wherever they lived.

But first, she had to get to him.

If he'd already departed for Ireland, she really would beg Lord Ferndale for his mother's address and go there to find him. And she'd apologise profusely to Lord Ferndale and Miss Yates for making such a mess of things; she shuddered to think of how disappointed they must be!

So many mixed thoughts swirled through her head as Somerset Valley Four took her through the streets of Hatfield. St John's church was just ahead. She'd put up with Brimstone marrying them if she could only right her stupid mistakes.

The sight of Felix approaching the church from the other direction made her shudder in fear. There he was, the man of her future, but he was on his way to cancel their wedding.

She pulled Somerset Valley Four to a stop and slid out of the saddle onto the road. Tears turned the world blurry as she ran towards Felix. "I'm sorry, I'm sorry!" she called out.

Felix pulled up his horse and climbed off, holding on to the reins. His face looked stricken, his eyes red. She'd done this to him.

She had to fix this terrible wrong. "Please, Felix, I'm so very sorry. I'll understand if you want to call it off, but please don't just yet. I love you. I really do love you and it feels so good to say that at last. I've been such a fool and I…"

Felix tethered Hannibal to a water trough in the street, then reached for her and held her tightly.

"My darling Estelle, tell me this is not some feverish dream and that you're really here?"

"I am here, and I'm so sorry."

"Is everything all right?" He held her face in his hands. "How - no, I won't say that."

Estelle sniffed and smiled through the tears. "You were about to ask how you could help, weren't you?"

"Guilty," he said with a shy smile.

"Please don't cancel the wedding. I do want to marry you, Felix, if you still want to marry me. Because I love you, and I realise that now. My sisters ganged up on me and helped show me how foolish I was. And how awful I was in accusing you of taking over. You weren't, not at all. You really were helping. *Are* helping. I think I was angry with myself that you'd helped so much. Maybe I thought I could do everything but I was also not letting my sisters step up and help either. They're not children any more, they're grown women and I need to stop making decisions for them..."

Felix's lips descended on hers in an emotional kiss that was a little less delicate than their earlier ones on account of their heightened emotions and their free-flowing tears.

"My darling Estelle," he said.

Hearing those words made her heart sing. "I love you, Felix."

He said nothing more as they kissed again, openly and quite scandalously outside St John's.

When they eventually stopped kissing, Estelle said, "I'm so relieved I reached you before you reached the church."

His brow creased. "I wasn't going to church. I thought you were."

"I was coming to you."

He laughed and kissed her again, "I was on my way to *you*, to beg forgiveness and ask you to give us another chance. To tell you that I don't care where we live; all I care about is that I live with you."

They laughed and kissed again and held each other.

"I want to live with you in Ferndale Hall," Estelle said,

realising that the words were true even as she spoke them. "We're perfectly able to help from there if my sisters need us, but you're right. You really did make it clear to me from the beginning that you needed me to be mistress of the Hall - so did your grandfather! - and I wasn't being fair. I do want that, and I think I could be good at it."

Felix half-laughed, shaking his head. "You will be incredible at it, something everyone but you already fully understands."

"And I want to go to Ireland to meet your mother. I want to sail on a ship, and maybe even go and see Greece one day - though I really do think I want to wait until after Father gets home for a trip that far."

"Quite understandable!" Felix looked overjoyed. "Would you like to delay the wedding?" he asked quite seriously. "Of course you want your father there on your wedding day. I am happy to wait for you as long as need be."

The dear, darling man. Estelle shook her head. "No. Father might be months, or even a year. I don't want to wait that long to marry you. Besides, Louise has plans to take over my room with the four new book presses you ordered for her." She pinched his arm lightly, smiling up at him. "You are too generous."

He shook his head, still grinning foolishly, and kissed her again.

Estelle looked around and realised something. "Somerset Valley Four is missing."

"What?"

"The horse I hired. I was so distracted I forgot to tether him."

Felix puffed himself up and held out the crook of his arm to take. "Well then, my darling, I believe it is incumbent on us to find that wandering animal and return him home."

They retrieved Hannibal and walked back toward the Red Lion, assuming the hired horse would make his way back to the yard.

"I need to apologise to you as well," Felix said. "I was overdoing it. I was trying too hard to impress you and overstepped. I should have helped *with* you, rather than making decisions without consulting you. I should have listened more rather than making assumptions."

It felt so good to hear those words, although she felt far too guilty that she'd messed this up so much. "We've made rather a muddle of things, haven't we?"

"We can begin to un-muddle them in our sweet time. I was excited about Ireland and leapt into action instead of asking you first. I do have to work on that side of myself. Please keep me sensible when the insensible occasion arises."

Estelle wiped away another tear, this one of happiness. "You bring joy when it's most needed. Please don't change."

They kissed again and Estelle felt so loved and adored. When they came up for air, she said, "I love you so much, Felix Yates. I know that whenever life brings us low, you will find a way to bring some joy."

Felix joked, "I have a feeling we might spend a good deal of our time hunting for stray animals."

"At least this one won't get pregnant. It is a he, and a gelding at that."

They giggled and held hands as they continued to search for the hired horse. They turned the corner to see it heading through the arch into his home behind the Red Lion.

"Ahh, clever horse." Estelle said. "I have heard they have an excellent sense of direction and always find their way home."

"Just as I will always find my way home to you, my dearest, wherever that might be."

Her heart could not be more full, and yet Felix had found a way to do just that.

"I do love you so much," she said, holding his hands in hers and leaning in for yet another kiss. "Let us never argue again."

He kissed her with such gentle passion she quite lost her head. When he pulled back, he said, "I shall do my best to make sure we never have a reason to do so."

An angry male voice behind her said, "Stop this disgusting display immediately!"

Estelle sighed deeply.

Felix looked to Joshua, then to Estelle, his eyebrow raised in question.

That's when she realised what he was doing; asking her permission before he stepped in to help.

The beautiful man. She smiled at him and whispered, "Be my guest."

"Ahh, Cousin Joshua," Felix exclaimed loudly. "Your timing is impeccable. I shall be a moment. Wait for us inside the bookshop."

Joshua's jaw dropped open but he quickly shut it. Estelle had never seen him so lost for words.

Felix handed Hannibal to the livery stable hand and gave him a coin, then he extended his elbow to Estelle and they made their way into the shop for yet another completely unnecessary confrontation.

"We are a team," Estelle said determinedly. "We can manage this."

CHAPTER 21

Wedding Bells

No sooner had they closed the shop door behind them than Joshua started marching up and down in front of them, shaking a solid finger in their faces. Phoebe stood to the side, leaning against one of the bookshelves looking rather as though she might faint.

Estelle's sisters remained behind the counter with weary expressions. Joshua had clearly been giving them a hard time and they'd had to deal with him alone. Well, not alone, as there were three of them, but they'd dealt with him without her. They were still standing, the bookshop was still standing.

And then she realised, they really had dealt with him. Together. And all three of them were standing tall, a united front. Confident, mature women who could stand tall against this bully.

Joshua shouted at Estelle, "You have scandalised us too many times. This will not do!"

Felix looked to Estelle first, to make sure she was happy with him stepping in and assisting.

She beamed at him and nodded, 'Yes please."

"I was not aware of any public laws that forbid a soon-to-be married couple from showing affection," Felix said, his tone cool.

"Not you," Joshua shouted, then waggled his finger into Estelle's face. "Her!"

He was so close she could see something stuck between his teeth from his last meal.

Felix cleared his throat, stepped between Joshua and Estelle and kept his voice dangerously low. "You will not speak to the future Mrs Yates and Baroness Ferndale in such a way. If I had my way, you would never have permission to speak to any of us again, no matter the tone. You are a prig who took advantage of my grandfather's grief to inveigle yourself into a position you are ill-equipped and lack-tempered to handle, that a... a blind donkey could perform more competently."

Shocked, but obviously recognising the foolishness of shouting at Felix, Joshua clenched his jaw and muttered something under his breath.

Felix added, "You will treat my future wife with respect, or you'll have to answer to my grandfather... and to me, and you'll find my fist in your face if you *ever* dare shout at her again."

Estelle touched her hand to Felix's bicep and appreciated the strength underneath his shirt. He turned to her and said penitently, "I probably went too far again, didn't I?"

Estelle tilted her head in thought, then said, "I think you were just right." Then she squared her own shoulders and borrowed some of Felix's strength to bolster her own as she faced Joshua, making her tone honey-sweet. The stick and the carrot, she thought; Felix had made threats and now she could offer a gracious way out for Joshua. In a cool tone, she delivered a not-very-veiled threat. "It would be such a shame, and deeply embarrassing to you and Mrs Baxter, to be turned away from the wedding celebrations at Ferndale Hall."

She'd never spoken to her cousin like that before. Her heart raced with the nerves rushing through her body. Having Felix beside her gave her the courage to achieve almost anything. But there was another important thing she needed to say to Joshua.

"You *will* walk me down the aisle, as the head of the Baxter family in my father's absence. You *will* be on time and you will be *exceptionally* well behaved. Is that clear?"

He screwed up his mouth as if he wanted to verbally attack her again, but Felix stepped forward, fists clenching at his side, and Joshua hastily spluttered out a simple, "Fine."

Felix moved back, reaching for Estelle's hand.

"But I won't enjoy it," Joshua said, obviously wanting to get the last words in.

A laugh escaped Estelle. She had plenty of responses she could give to her cousin, but it wasn't worth it. There seemed to be so little Joshua did enjoy - other than shouting at Estelle and her sisters - that she almost felt sorry for him. She glanced at Phoebe, who hadn't said a word throughout the exchange.

"And do you have anything to add, madam?" Estelle asked. "I thought not," when Phoebe quickly shook her head. "Miss Yates is very keen for me to join her committees, and I understand you keep trying to get invited onto them. I have no idea why nobody has thought to invite you, truly. You would be so good at hosting the meetings. I do so look forward to working with you, Phoebe."

Louise snorted with laughter.

Phoebe looked as though she was sucking on a lemon, but she forced a semblance of a smile and nodded. "Of course, Estelle," she said.

"You may leave now," Estelle said, opening the door to the street to show them out.

Estelle watched them go, as she and Felix together closed the door on their cousins.

Felix smiled warmly down at her and said, "We make an excellent team."

"That we do," Estelle agreed, and wrapped her arms around him for a glorious kiss.

Her sisters cheered them on from behind the counter. When they pulled apart, the three younger women ran forward and smothered the pair of them with a hearty embrace.

"Is the wedding back on?" Louise asked.

"Yes," Estelle said. "And thank you for helping me see sense."

Her ears filled with cheers and cries of, "Thank goodness!"

At the end of that very long and emotional Saturday, Felix helped his staff into the carriage. Louise gave the maids some Minerva books from their lending shelf as a token of appreciation.

Bernadette gave Felix another bottle of tonic for Lord Ferndale. "I will visit him when you're in Ireland, to make sure of his health."

"That is so good of you, Bernadette, you put my mind at ease." He bent to kiss her cheek fondly. "You shall see us in church tomorrow, please all join us in the Ferndale pew. Mrs Poole, too, if you're not otherwise busy."

Mrs Poole blushed at being singled out.

Estelle had already kissed Felix farewell inside the bookshop, so that she would not become carried away and create another spectacle in public. Nevertheless, she felt the pull toward him as he was about to climb onto Hannibal. "You have my thanks," she said, then dropped her voice low so that only the two of them would hear. "And my heart."

"I shall always treasure you," he said, giving her a soft kiss before he mounted the horse.

The sisters waved Felix off and turned to go back into the bookstore, Estelle catching Crafty as the cat tried to sneak out between their ankles.

"Oh, no you don't, madam! Far too late for all that nonsense anyway, unless I miss my guess. Have you all noticed how plump she's getting?"

"Kittens around the end of August, I believe," Bernadette said wisely. "You'll be in Ireland!"

"And we shall deal with the kittens as well as we'll deal with everything else that comes up in your absence," Louise said, putting her arm around Estelle.

She sighed with happiness and said, "Felix did promise to help find them homes…"

"Crafty is such a good mouser her kittens are always in demand," Marie said. "Although perhaps Lord Ferndale and Miss Yates would like one, for the Hall? Did you see a cat there, Estelle?"

"I didn't. I shall be sure to ask if they would like a kitten," Estelle promised, thinking that she would rather miss having Crafty around, once she removed to Ferndale Hall. A kitten would be nice, though she hoped it would not inherit its mother's habits of leaving half-disembowelled offerings in inconvenient places!

Friday, the day of Estelle's wedding to Felix, dawned with bright sun and a few thin clouds in the sky.

Joshua walked her down the aisle stamping his feet and muttering all the way, his face a thundercloud. Under his breath he said, "You won't be here to protect your sisters while you're in Ireland."

Estelle smiled and acknowledged the many parishioners seated in the church. Friends from across Hatfield and distant relations they had not seen since the last big family gathering. Many dabbed their eyes with emotion, overcome with joy for her. "My sisters are more than a match for you," she told Joshua as she kept smiling.

Nothing he said could dampen her mood. Try as he might, nothing could upset Estelle on this most glorious day.

At the altar stood Felix and Lord Ferndale. She had thought her future husband was handsome, but the look of admiration on his face gave him the most beatific glow; he could have descended from the heavens. Lord Ferndale raised one eyebrow toward Joshua and the man stopped muttering.

Soon, Joshua gave her over into Felix's hands and her spirits soared.

Not even the droning from Old Brimstone could dampen their joy. Felix had shown her how to find joy in small things. The more they did that, the more joy they found.

At one point Felix tried to dampen a laugh, when Reverend Millings started thundering on about how it was a wife's duty to submit to her husband in all things and agree with him in all matters. Estelle thought she'd burst into giggles herself, so she had to look away. Searching for a distraction, her eyes alighted upon her sisters sitting at the front of the church in the Ferndale pew with Miss Yates and Mrs Poole, all of them smiling and wiping tears off their cheeks. Pride filled her at how much her sisters had matured since her father had set off on his travels. Their father might not be here, but he was in their hearts and constant thoughts.

When the vicar asked if Felix accepted the oaths of

marriage, Felix's voice was thick with emotion when he said, "I do."

No hesitation from Estelle when it was her turn, but her voice wavered a little as she bubbled with happiness and repeated her, "I do."

They both might cry with joy at this rate. They would start their married life as they intended to go on, perfectly in harmony and utterly, completely happy.

The wedding guests cheered as they took their first kiss as husband and wife. Outside the church, they were swamped with well-wishes and congratulations from everyone except Phoebe and Joshua, who remained well back.

Soon they were in the carriage to take them to Ferndale Hall for their wedding breakfast, and a few days after that they would be on their way to Ireland.

"You can return to the bookshop as often as you need," Felix said to her as the carriage rolled away and Estelle waved back at the cheering crowd assembled.

"Thank you." She squeezed his hand, knowing he meant it. She was grateful for his understanding. "But I have a feeling I shall enjoy my new home."

Felix nudged her. "Our home?"

"Yes," Estelle said, beaming with joy and kissing him again. "*Our* home."

One week later, Miss Marie Baxter and her two sisters, Louise and Bernadette, along with Mrs Poole, waved off their eldest and insensibly happy sister Estelle and her new husband as they departed on their trip to Ireland.

As their carriage disappeared from view, Marie sighed, looking forward to the quiet of the bookshop.

A little peace and quiet after so much chaos held tremendous appeal. She would need the time to herself to resettle. Too many people and too much excitement had the effect of discombobulating her. A recombobulation was exactly what she needed.

Tomorrow would be their clean-up day, so there would be no customers to worry about; no extra people to deal with.

If fortune smiled upon them, trade in the shop might be quiet today as well.

A girl could dream, couldn't she?

Correspondence was now a task she completed at the front counter, along with her usual accounts and book-keeping requirements. Estelle had nothing to worry about, as Marie was excellent at managing her paperwork in between customers, and Ruth was learning fast how to assist customers when they came into the shop, often only interrupting Marie when a sale needed to be completed.

Louise maintained Crafty's scratching post and checked behind the counter for entrails each morning, bless her. That was a task none of them had wanted to take on. Mrs Poole had eventually made them draw straws to keep things fair.

Marie flicked off the seal of a letter and stepped over to the window to read the spidery scrawl. She pushed her glasses higher on her nose, squinting at the paper and turning it this way and that to try and decipher the words. Goodness, it looked as if it was written whilst travelling in a badly-sprung carriage.

"The entitlement!" she cried out to nobody in particular.

Bernadette poked her head into the shop. "Everything all right?"

Marie looked at Bernadette over her glasses and shook the letter at her. "Have a read of this. The entitlement of some customers! It's unbelievable."

"What's wrong?" Bernadette said, quickly scanning the page before she said, "Oh!"

"Yes, Oh! I'm not going all the way to Cumbria to personally deliver this man's books, even if he is an Earl!" Marie shook her head, taking the letter back and dropping it on the desk. "What an absolutely ridiculous idea!"

We hope you've had a wonderful time enjoying Estelle's romance with Felix. Turn the page to read the prologue of book 2 in *The Bookshop Belles, Marie's Merry Gentleman.*

Marie's Merry Gentleman
PROLOGUE

August 1814
Baxter's Fine Books, Hatfield, England

"Cumbria. What an absolutely ridiculous idea!"

Marie Baxter, the second eldest and definitely the most sensitive of the four Baxter daughters of Baxter's Bookshop in Hatfield, Hertfordshire, looked at the correspondence in her hand and sighed with frustration.

The composer of the correspondence may well be an Earl, but there was simply no way she was about to travel all the way to Cumbria and deliver two books. No matter how valuable they were. She lifted her pen and wrote a note of response, the nib digging into the paper with her frustration.

"I have neither the time, nor the inclination to subject myself to the interior of a mail coach with all and sundry for the best part of a fortnight to deliver two books. There are people I trust in Hatfield who could easily do this task, whilst I remain at the bookshop and keep an eye out for more of the titles on your list.

Yours etc, M. Baxter."

Why would this man not entrust a messenger to carry the books? His entitlement knew no bounds! She sanded the letter, then folded it and headed straight to the Red Lion next door to get it on the next postal carriage taking the Great North Road. The late afternoon had turned cool and she wrapped her shawl around her shoulders and ears to keep warm.

The door bell tinkled as she re-entered the shop. Crafty the cat did not bolt for the door as she expected. Now that she thought about it, she hadn't seen the rotund black cat for a little while now. She'd either escaped when nobody was paying attention, or she'd found somewhere to make a nest for her soon-to-be-born kittens.

SEPTEMBER 1814

The next letter from the earl was no better.

"I trust nobody to deliver these titles other than your good self. Third parties are worse than useless, they are careless. The books may arrive, but in what condition? Only someone with your breadth of knowledge and experience would understand not merely their monetary value, but their symbolic and deeply intrinsic value to the world of literature. That is why you and you alone must deliver the books to me. You will be compensated accordingly for your time and trouble. They would be here already and you would be well on your return journey if you'd done as I originally requested."

Marie rolled her eyes. They weren't requests, they were demands, and they were growing more demanding.

"We would have successfully concluded our business by now. No more delays. Bring me my books.

Renwick."

She showed the letter to her sister Louise, who was stretching out her back after stirring a fresh vat of stinky glue. The cooler autumn wind howled through the windows and nipped at their necks, but open windows were the only way to draw the stink out.

Crafty's little kittens scarpered through the bookshop like fluffy black voids. When two of them rolled about and played together, it was impossible to see where one kitten began and another ended.

"They are so adorable," Louise said, laughing as one of the kittens pounced on a trailing boot lace.

"That they are, and we shall need to find homes for them very soon."

"Why can't we just keep one of them, to give Crafty company?"

"Because if we kept a boy, he'd grow up and spray his scent on the books. And if we kept a girl, she'd probably be just as bad as her mother. Then we'd no doubt have two batches of kittens to find homes for at some point," Marie said practically. Someone had to be practical.

"Then I shall enjoy them while they are small and adorable," Louise said, scooping up a passing kitten and smushing its soft little body against her face. "You'd better write back to the Earl of Demanding and tell him where to shove his demands."

"I need to be nicer than that! He sends another letter every time we put an advertisement in *The Times*, requesting we add more books to the order. It's almost a hundred pounds' worth by now."

Louise whistled between her teeth in an unladylike manner. "Perhaps you should go. Estelle definitely would have."

That truthful observation caused Marie a pang. She had faithfully promised their eldest sister that they were perfectly capable of running the bookshop in Estelle's absence.

The four Baxter sisters had already been running the bookshop in their father's absence. Then Estelle had married her dear Mr Yates and was currently in Ireland visiting his mother.

Louise was right: Estelle would have long since set off for Cumbria, viewing the trip as an adventure. Marie, however, considered it a nightmare. She had never been further away from Hatfield than London, and on that trip had despised both the journey and the city. The noise of the city drilled into her head, giving her the worst megrims. The very last thing she wanted to do was spend a week or more each way in a crowded, stuffy coach being jolted through every rut from here to very nearly Scotland!

Marie came up with an excellent rebuttal: "Estelle would have taken the books, come back, and then been immediately confronted with an order for more books," she pointed out.

Louise nodded. "Fair point. Well, you'll have to find some way to convince him, Marie. A hundred pounds is not to be sneezed at!" She kissed the kitten one more time, making it squeak in protest, before setting it down and making her way back upstairs again.

Marie penned her reply and was as polite as possible, which included the final paragraph;

"We are short staffed at the moment and I cannot leave the

responsibility of the bookshop. Please reconsider your preferred delivery method.

Yours, M Baxter."

OCTOBER 1814

"Where are you, and where are my books? I need them here by Christmas!"

This last missive from The Earl of Demanding really irked Marie. They were coping well enough without their father and Estelle, but their workload had increased of late. They were lucky to have some extra help with young Ruth Millings and their cousin Brutus Baxter assisting in the store. Brutus also didn't mind the glue stink and seemed genuinely excited to be learning the craft of repairing and binding books, proving a competent and enthusiastic apprentice to Louise. They were able to increase the number of titles they could repair and bind in any given week, which was a welcome boost to the bookstore's income.

To their delight, two crates of books had arrived in quick succession, and the titles had proved incredibly popular. Selling them was easy, and helped them build funds towards paying off their father's enormous bank loan.

Even more delightful than the books was finding a short note from Papa, which was an incredible relief. It was undated, however, which proved an irritation. Louise cleverly spotted the clue about the date in Papa's hastily scribbled note.

Am in Tours again. Heavy autumn rains roads north miserable at best

"Aha! The last note said he'd arrived in Tours," Lousie said. "That one did have a date on it. So this one says he's in Tours *again*, therefore, this note was written after the previous one." It almost had to be, since that note had arrived almost three months previously, but it was good to have confirmation.

"You're a genius!" Bernadette said.

"I have my moments." Louise grinned at solving the puzzle.

Marie chuckled and said, "He's obviously having far too much fun." It was a relief that Louise had worked it out so quickly. They were a good team.

But if Marie left Hatfield to travel, the previous work of four sisters would land on only two sets of shoulders while she was away. She was the eldest sister left at home

She couldn't go. She absolutely couldn't.

Not even with two additional books the Earl had requested, bringing his total order to a hundred and ten pounds.

It was entirely out of the question.

About The Authors

Catherine Bilson and Ebony Oaten are long-time collaborators, creating bestselling multi-author Regency romance anthologies over many years.

At the 2024 Romance Writers of Australia conference in Adelaide, they were busy running the Indie Book Store when they came up with the idea for this series. A bookshop would feature strongly - they were living their fantasy of selling books to readers anyway.

Why not set an historical series in a bookshop itself? With sisters who each find love in a bustling town. Instantly they brainstormed complications and issues - what if their father raced off to France after Napoleon was exiled away on Elba, to gather rare books? The characters weren't to know Napoleon would escape only a few months later and wreak havoc on France!

Also, at this conference, Catherine won the RUBY - the Romantic Book of the Year award - for her novella *The Bride Said No*. This novella had started life in one of their collaborative anthologies, of course.

Ebony had also won the Ruby several years earlier, for one of her sweet romance novels, *The Girl and The Ghost*.

With their powers of romance combined, surely they could come up with something wonderful.

You can follow the authors by heading to their respective websites and joining their newsletters.

Catherine is here:

https://www.catherinebilson.com/

Ebony is here:

https://ebonyoaten.link/

ABOUT CATHERINE:

"I grew up in a 14th century manor house in North Wales and spent most of my youth making up stories about the people who might once have lived in it. I ran off and married a handsome Australian a few years later and now live with him and our two sons in the permanent sunshine of Queensland.

I write original Regency romance, Austen-inspired variations, and Pioneer American romance. I also write contemporary romance and romantic suspense under the pen name Caitlyn Lynch."

ABOUT EBONY:

Ebony is from Melbourne, Australia and used to be a journalist at several suburban newspapers across the city. Then she turned her hand to writing romance and hasn't looked back. She married a Welsh 'boyo' and they are raising their son in Melbourne, where it can be stinking hot one day, pouring with rain the next.

The Bookshop Belles

NOVELS:

Estelle's Ardent Admirer

Marie's Merry Gentleman

Louise's Christmas Champion

Bernadette's Dashing Doctor

EXCLUSIVE BONUS NOVELLA FOR SUBSCRIBERS:

Matthew's Willing Widow

www.ingramcontent.com/pod-product-compliance
Lightning Source LLC
Chambersburg PA
CBHW062008190726
48283CB00002BA/546